HIDDEN GIFTS

THE WITCHES OF CANYON ROAD:
BOOK ONE

CHRISTINE POPE

DARK VALENTINE PRESS

HIDDEN GIFTS

Copyright © 2018 by Christine Pope

ISBN: 978-1-946435-11-8

Published by Dark Valentine Press

Cover design by Lou Harper

PROLOGUE

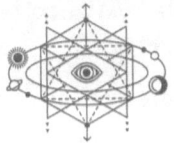

Santa Fe, New Mexico, twenty-one years from now....

GENOVEVA CASTILLO SET HER PHONE DOWN on the bulky carved desk that dominated the study, a small smile touching her mouth. "She is on her way."

Like the cat that swallowed the canary. In that moment, watching the quiet triumph on Genoveva's face, Rafael Castillo thought he'd never hated his mother as much as he did right then. However, he knew better than to betray anything of what he felt; Genoveva was the *prima,* or head witch of their clan, and her magical gifts only enhanced an already powerful gift of observation. The two of them had shared an uneasy détente for more than fifteen years now, ever since he was old enough to truly begun to understand what this horrible bargain entailed for him. No chance to choose the woman of his heart, no opportunity to make his life his own, and all because his grandmother had made a deal with the *prima* of the McAllister clan in Arizona to provide some desperately needed magical help when they needed it most. Rafe couldn't even blame Angela McAllister all that much; she'd been caught in what must have felt like a trap she couldn't escape, fighting a dark warlock whose powers had seemed invincible. This terrible arrangement hadn't even been her idea, but had sprung from some fancy of his grandmother's.

Voice as level as he could make it, he said, "I can't believe you're actually going through with this."

Genoveva's smile faded. Perfectly coiffed head held high, she turned away from him and went to the window of her study, twitching the heavy tapestry drapes aside so she could gaze out at the grounds of the property. This late in October, most of the leaves had fallen from the sycamores, but the cottonwoods were gamely hanging on, bright gold against the sullen sky. "Why shouldn't you believe it? We've been planning this for the past twenty-one years. You've had plenty of time to get used to the reality of Miranda coming here."

That was a load of crap. Rafe knew he would never get used to the idea of an arranged marriage, of having someone he'd never met foisted upon him. And Genoveva actually thought he was supposed to be happy about all this? "Keep telling yourself what you want to believe, Mother."

Her lips thinned. Back in happier times, he'd called her "Mom." But as the distance between them grew, he'd slipped into using the much more formal epithet. Rafe could tell that Genoveva didn't like it, because she wanted to pretend that everything was fine between them, that they were a model family and an example for the rest of the clan.

There was a joke. His older sisters Louisa and Malena had managed to make their escape already, had lives and families of their own, and could safely distance themselves from their mother. Cat, his little sister, hadn't been so lucky, even though more than once Rafe had encouraged her to date on the down-low, to maybe try seeing civilians in her quest for the man of her dreams. But as free-spirited as his younger sister could be in some ways, she didn't have quite the strength to break away from their domineering mother. He couldn't really blame her; he knew the only reason he had as much independence as he'd been able to enjoy in his adult life was that his future had already been sewn up neatly—at least, in Genoveva's eyes.

"There is no need to sulk," she said, her voice cold. "You would think we were marrying you to a gargoyle."

Miranda McAllister was anything but a gargoyle. Rafe knew that for a fact, because he'd seen the pictures Angela McAllister, her mother, had sent Genoveva. And that wasn't the point. What difference did it make how beautiful Miranda was if he didn't get any say in the matter? As his jaw clenched and he tried to think of the best way to reply, his mother continued.

"It is not as if I had any say, either," she said. "The *prima*-in-waiting must go with the consort that God decrees for her."

"False equivalencies," he shot back. "No one arranged that bond. It just happened. And at least you knew Dad."

"Not well," she replied, although her tone wasn't quite as forthright as it had been a moment earlier, as if she knew she was on shaky ground here. True, Rafe's father Eduardo had grown up in Belen, south of Albuquerque, and so hadn't spent a lot of time with the Santa Fe branch of their witch clan, but at least he had met Genoveva a handful of times before they shared the fateful kiss that bound them together forever.

"But he wasn't a goddamn stranger."

"Language, Rafael." Genoveva turned her back on the window and faced him, arms crossed. "You have had plenty of time to reconcile yourself to this marriage. Stop acting like a child and accept your responsibility to your clan."

"Responsibility" and "clan" were two words Rafe would be happy never to hear again. "And what if I don't?"

This time true anger, rather than mere irritation, flashed in his mother's dark eyes. Her elegant, patrician features hard with displeasure, she said, "You will go against the will of your grandmother, her vision that this was the match fate had decreed for you?"

"Her words to you," Rafe shot back. "It would have been nice if she could have specifically mentioned why it was so important that I marry Miranda McAllister. Vague mentions of possible futures don't really do it for me."

"Things happened quickly. I did not have much time to speak to her before she went with the McAllister *prima* and her Wilcox consort to confront the dark warlock in California." Genoveva drew herself up; she was not a short woman, but she still had to work to look directly into her son's eyes. "But your grandmother's sight was never wrong, Rafael. She might not have had enough time to tell me the particulars, but she knew that Miranda McAllister must come here to

Santa Fe, and I would never question her judgment. "

"Well, that's convenient," Rafe remarked. He was tired of this, tired of the whole thing. The clock on the wall told him he had only a few hours of freedom left. No, the wedding wouldn't take place the second Miranda McAllister stepped off the train, but as soon as she set foot in Santa Fe, he would be as bound to her as if he'd already put a ring on her finger. He ran a hand through his hair, then said, "Text me when she gets to the house."

"Rafael—"

He had no desire to stay and have his mother browbeat him any further. Without responding, he turned and left the study, and slammed the door behind him. A childish gesture, he knew, but the only thing he could think of to show how angry he was without actually becoming violent.

In a few hours, his life would be taken away forever.

And there wasn't a damn thing he could do about it.

1

SPIRIT WALK

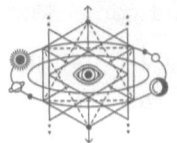

Miranda McAllister

THE COLD MORNING AIR STUNG MY CHEEKS. I suppose I should have been used to it—I'd spent half my life in Flagstaff, was all too accustomed to the extremes of weather there. But, standing on a train platform at a little past four-thirty in the morning on a bitter October morning, I thought my surroundings were even colder than they should have been, the chill of the pre-dawn air penetrating even the warm packable down coat I wore.

Two bags sat on the ground beside me. That was all I'd been allowed—two weekender bags to carry everything I might need in my new life.

My mother had cried on the drive over here, although she'd done her best to hide her tears from me, had tried to blame her sniffles on her allergies acting up. I'd known better, as I was sure my father had as well, but neither of us called her out on her little white lie.

I'd cried, too, but not on the drive. No, the last of my tears had come hours earlier, when I'd lain on my bed and stared at the ceiling of my bedroom and realized I'd never see this room again, or this house, or any of my friends or family, whether they were Wilcox witches and warlocks in Flagstaff or McAllisters in Jerome. Even though I might not have been the daughter my parents expected, they'd never shown me anything but continuing love and support, and the thought of being separated from them was terrifying.

Jessica Rowe, one of my best friends in Flagstaff, had wanted to throw a going-away party for me, but I'd shot down that idea, mostly because I wasn't sure how well I'd hold it together if I was forced to see all the important people in my life gathered together in one place. Such a gathering would only reinforce the realization that I probably wouldn't see any of them ever again. Close as I was to Jessica, I didn't want to confess such weakness to her. Instead, I told her that I didn't want to make a big deal out of this, and, thank the Goddess, she hadn't pushed the issue. Really, all I wanted was to slink away in the night.

Well, four-thirty in the morning was close enough.

My mother looked past me to the approaching conductor in rather the same way a dying person might gaze at the Grim Reaper as he came to claim their soul. "I can't—" she began, then stopped as my father laid a comforting hand on her harm.

"We can, because we have to." He glanced over at me, saw that I had my ticket confirmation open on my phone so the conductor could easily scan it. "Genoveva said she would call to let us know you've gotten there safely, but remember—"

"No calls or texts unless it's an emergency. Yeah, I know." I reached down with my free hand and slung the heavier of the two bags over my shoulder, then slipped the other one on my arm so it hung in the crook of my elbow. So many strange commandments from the woman who was going to be my mother-in-law. My parents had done their best to negotiate all of them, but Genoveva Castillo, the *prima* of the Castillo clan, wouldn't hear of any objections.

"I ask that she do these things because it is for the best," she'd said coldly to my mother during one of those conversations. I'd been eavesdropping, since this was my future they'd been discussing, and luckily the volume on my mother's phone had been turned up enough that I could catch most of what Genoveva was saying. Although my mother—a *prima* in her own right —had clearly hated having to cave to any of the Castillo witch's commands, she'd done so because the last thing any of us wanted was to be at odds with a powerful clan like the Castillos. No, the debt had to be paid.

And I was the payment.

The conductor came up to me. He was a stocky man probably in his late forties or early fifties, dark, a thick plaid muffler wrapped around his neck. Part Navajo? Maybe; there were a lot of Native Americans who lived and worked in the Flagstaff area. "Ticket?" he asked.

I held out my phone, and he scanned the screen.

"Train leaves in less than five minutes," he said. His tone was so neutral, he could have merely been providing me with necessary infor-mation…or warning me that, like time and tide, trains waited for no man…or woman.

"I guess I'd better go," I said. At least my voice hadn't wavered. I wanted my parents to believe I was strong, even though inside I felt as though I was being torn apart.

Tears once again glittered in my mother's eyes, making them look like watery emeralds in the light from the overhead CFC bulbs in the debarkation area. "Oh, Miranda—" she began, then stopped, as though she knew that if she attempted to say anything else, she'd break down into sobs right then and there. The platform wasn't all that busy, but there were still enough people around that she would have made something of a scene.

My father's expression was stoic. I knew this whole mess was hurting him as well, but he seemed to realize that there was nothing he could do about it, and so losing control would only give me a distorted memory of him.

My last memory of him.

He took me in his arms and gave me a fierce hug, bags, phone, and all, and then my mother pulled me to her and pressed a quick kiss against my hair.

"I don't care what Genoveva says," she whispered in my ear. "If you run into any trouble, you call us."

I nodded, although I knew the train would have to be raided by a bunch of bandits before I made that phone call. A promise was a promise. And although I didn't think I had a whole hell of a lot to offer the Castillos, or the man who was supposed to be my husband, I wanted them to know that we McAllisters kept our word...no matter how much it hurt.

The train whistle sounded, and I said, "I have to go."

"Miri—"

I didn't know what my mother had intended to say. Deep down, I wasn't sure I really wanted to know. Better to go now and go quickly, the same principle as quickly tearing a bandage off a wound rather than removing it slowly.

Without meeting either of my parents' eyes, I turned and hurried up the steps into the train.

Even as I made my way down the aisle, searching for the perfect seat, I felt the floor beneath my feet jerk slightly, a faint shudder telling me that the train had begun to leave the station. I turned and caught a glimpse of my parents out the window, my mother's long dark hair gleaming in the lights that illuminated the boarding area, my father's face set and pale.

And then they were gone.

Because the trip to Albuquerque only took about seven hours, I hadn't booked a spot in a sleeping car. The car where I stood now was almost empty, so I had my pick of the seats. I chose a spot near the window around the middle of the car, then shoved my bags in the overhead compartment before settling in. I hadn't expected there to be anyone of witch-kind on board the train, and there wasn't. Only a group of regular nonmagical people making their own journeys...and me. I should have been relieved, I suppose, and yet knowing I was the only witch among civilians only made me feel more alone.

A gibbous moon hung overhead, bathing the landscape in its cold light. Such a crazy hour to be setting out, but train schedules didn't care about my life, my petty problems. The train left Los Angeles at a decent time of day, but by the time it chugged into Flagstaff's historic station, it was around four in the morning.

Why the train? I still didn't know for sure. It would have been a lot easier to drive down to Phoenix and have me catch a plane there, but no, Genoveva insisted that I had to take the train. The suggestion to have my Uncle Lucas fly me himself —he owned a small plane, which he kept at Flagstaff's small airport—had been summarily shot down as well. I got the feeling that Genoveva didn't want any of my family members crossing over with me into New Mexico. Which, in an abstract way, I could almost understand.

It didn't stop me from resenting her more than ever, though.

I probably should have tried to sleep, since I'd gone to bed at almost eleven and then had gotten up at three in order to catch the train. Tired as I was, though, I somehow knew I wouldn't be able to sleep through this journey. Instead, I sat and watched the dark landscape pass by outside the window, watched with listless interest as we pulled up to the station in Winslow and took on a few more passengers at a little before six, the sun just beginning to peek above the horizon.

No one took a seat near me, which was fine. I'd read that on the coasts, where high-speed rail connected all the major cities, people often preferred to take the train rather than fly. Here in the center of the country, though, where Amtrak still operated trains that were older than I was, no one traveled this way unless they didn't have any other choice, despite the alluring offer of free wi-fi in all Amtrak trains. So even as people boarded in Gallup just on the other side of the Arizona/New Mexico border, the car where I sat was never more than a quarter full.

I wondered what had brought those other travelers to sit here now—the man who looked only a few years older than I, a large backpack much bigger than Amtrak's specified luggage dimensions sitting on the empty seat next to him; the tired-faced Navajo woman with her worn brown purse sitting on her lap; the older man who kept his head down and focused on his laptop the entire trip. Since I didn't possess the energy or the will to strike up a conversation with any of them, I'd never know their reasons for making this journey.

However, as I watched the desert landscape pass by, growing brighter and brighter as the sun rose overhead, I began to get some idea of why Genoveva Castillo might have forced this journey on me. I'd read of how shamans and others seeking enlightenment would head into the deep desert to be cleansed, to leave behind everything from their former lives that had been weighing them down. As the miles between myself and Flagstaff stretched and stretched, I began to experience an odd sensation of lightness, as if the Miranda McAllister I'd been back in Flagstaff and Jerome had been left behind on the station platform with my parents. I didn't know who this new Miranda would be, but I began to think maybe I could look forward to meeting her with anticipation, rather than doubt and worry.

If only I thought those who waited for me in Santa Fe might be feeling the same way.

My mother had explained the situation to me so many times that by now, just as I turned twenty-one, her explanations had no real meaning anymore, were only strings of words describing a fate I couldn't escape. Before I was even born, a dark warlock had risen, threatening not only the McAllisters and the Wilcoxes, my parents' clans, but also the de la Paz family, who lived in the southern part of Arizona. The threat had been so great that my parents had turned to the Castillos for help, since they knew the Arizona clans could not defeat the warlock and the clans he was connected with—the Santiagos and the Ludlows in California—without help from outside.

That help had come…at a price. The *prima* of the Castillos, Genoveva's mother, lost her life fighting the dark warlock. And my mother, who was pregnant with me at the time, had to make a terrible bargain to secure the Castillos' help—she had to swear that she would send the child she carried to Santa Fe when the time came, so her daughter could marry the Castillo *prima's* grandson.

I was that daughter. And now I traveled across the desert to marry a man I'd never met, or even seen.

Oh, yes. I still didn't know whether it was Genoveva's capriciousness, or whether she was trying to hide something, but I wasn't allowed to see a single picture of the man who was going to be my husband. My mother had pled my case on more than one instance, saying that I had a right to see the person I was supposed to marry, but Genoveva had remained firm. I would see Rafael—that was her son's name—when I arrived in Santa Fe, and not a moment sooner. And whenever I'd tried to search for images of him online, or on social media, I couldn't find a damn thing. Maybe someone in the Castillo clan had a way of blocking that stuff. The blackout didn't even have to be supernatural in nature; for all I knew, their clan had a few hackers in their midst.

All of Genoveva's strictures seemed positively medieval to me, but there wasn't a lot I could do about any of it. I told myself there must be something very wrong with this Rafael, and tried to do my best to steel myself for marriage to some kind of a monster. While I was in high school, I had quite a fetish for Beauty and the Beast types of stories—*The Phantom of the Opera, The Hunchback of Notre Dame,* all the million and one incarnations of the original fairy tale—in the hope that I might reconcile myself to my fate, convince myself that it would be all right, that behind even a beastly exterior might beat a kind and loving heart.

Problem was, those stories were all fiction. This was my life.

Still, with resignation comes a kind of freedom. I was here now, on the train taking me to Santa Fe. Well, slight correction. The Amtrak only went as far as Albuquerque; from there, I'd get on the area's local light rail, the Railrunner, to travel the final leg of my journey, to the station in Santa Fe's Railyard area. I still didn't know for sure whether Rafael—or Genoveva, or someone else from the Castillo clan—would be there to meet me. It was entirely possible that the Castillo *prima* would send a self-driving car to pick me up. After all, if Rafael really was so deformed that she didn't even want him going out in public, then I doubted he'd be there in the Railyard to greet his future bride.

At least I was traveling light. If I had to complete the last leg of the trip on my own, I didn't have to worry too much about wrangling my luggage.

As we pulled out of Gallup and continued east, I wondered what my parents were doing now. Had they gone to console themselves over the loss of their youngest child by visiting their other children? My brother Ian was married and living in Flagstaff with his wife Mia, although I didn't know whether he would have appreciated having my parents show up on his doorstep at five in the morning. Emily, my sister, had stayed in Jerome, as was proper for the McAllister *prima*-in-waiting. It would be a slightly more acceptable hour by the time my parents showed up there, but since Emily's son Jeremy was only four months old, I doubted whether they'd impinge on her hospitality, either.

Thinking of Emily made me frown. Oh, I loved my sister, but it seemed as if everything had always gone right for her. Whereas I....

The de la Paz clan—and other Spanish-speaking witch clans—had a word for my condition. *Nunca*. In Spanish, it simply means "never," but in the witch world, the phrase was used to refer to someone who was born to witch parents and yet never developed any true magical talents. I hated the word, hated how I couldn't help over-hearing it in people's conversations from time to time, although no one was callous enough to say it to my face.

The way it generally worked for us—the way it was *supposed* to work—was that everyone with witch blood could perform very simple tricks like opening locked doors or bringing flame to a candle or logs laid in a hearth, but a witch or warlock generally manifested their unique talents around ten or eleven, talents that could range from seeing the future to healing the sick. As those talents grew, they would be used to help the clan, depending on the particular gifts of the user and how strong they turned out to be.

In my case, though, I never developed my "true" talent. I'd never progressed beyond unlocking doors with a touch, or putting a fingertip to a candle wick and calling flame from the air to light it. Quite the failure, when you considered that my parents were both almost unbelievably skilled, the leaders of their clans. Ian and Emily were also blessed with gifts far beyond what most ordinary witches and warlocks possessed, probably because of having such talented parents. However, it seemed the well had run dry when it came to me. I couldn't do much of anything. To compensate, I'd attempted to be a model daughter in other ways—getting straight As in school, trying to be a helpful member of the both the McAllister and Wilcox clans, whether that meant taking on last-minute babysitting requests or helping with the setup for the big clan Christmas party in Jerome.

And yet, it had never felt like enough.

My parents were always supportive. They did their best to let me know they were proud of my other accomplishments, the ones that had nothing to do with magic, but some part of me couldn't help but think that I'd let them down at a fundamental level. They'd also tried to use my lack of magical gifts as a way of getting out of this terrible arrangement with the Castillos, which should have proved to me how much they wanted me to stay in Arizona. I knew they'd done everything they could to let Genoveva Castillo know that if her mother had been expecting to have a powerful witch marry into their family when she made her bargain with my mother, she would have been extremely disappointed. However, all their arguments were in vain. Genoveva had been adamant, had said she didn't care about my lack of gifts, and that I would come to them on my twenty-first birthday, as had been agreed upon so many years before.

Yes, I was spending my birthday on the train, but really, compared to all the other things I had to worry about, the lack of any sort of festivities to celebrate the occasion was fairly far down on my list of priorities. It was also Halloween, but again, not that big a deal. In a few days, they'd be having the Day of the Dead celebration in Tlaquepaque Village in Sedona, an event my family had attended ever since I was old enough to remember. Whether my parents would have the heart to do so now that I was gone, I had no idea. We really hadn't talked much about what they planned to do after they'd fulfilled their side of this unholy bargain. In a way, I didn't want to know. I didn't want to think of them going on with their lives without me there.

Maybe there would be some sort of Day of the Dead event in Santa Fe. I supposed I could have tried to look it up online, tried to find a local a calendar of events so I'd know what was happening in the place that would soon be my new home, but I realized I really didn't care one way or another. If I couldn't see the face of the man I was supposed to marry, then I might as well let everything else about my future existence be a mystery as well.

The train pulled into the station in Albuquerque at a little past one—almost an hour and a half behind schedule, but I'd been warned that

Amtrak would probably be running late. Luckily, the Railrunner train that would take me to Santa Fe wouldn't be leaving for another half hour, giving me time to use the restroom and then get a latte at the Starbucks in the station. I'd barely eaten anything and found I didn't have much appetite, but I needed the caffeine to take me through the home stretch.

The Railrunner was a lot more crowded than the Amtrak. I had to thread my way along the narrow aisle to find an empty seat in one of the rear cars, and had barely stowed my bags in the overhead compartment and sat down in my seat before I heard a male voice say, "Do you mind if I sit here?"

I looked up from my purse, and the tube of lip gloss I'd just shoved in an inner pocket, to see a Hispanic guy around my age standing in the aisle and pointing at the empty seat next to me. He had thick black hair and angular features, with high cheekbones and eyes as black as his hair. A backpack hung off one shoulder.

"No, that's fine," I replied, trying to sound cool and casual. He was pretty good-looking... which shouldn't have mattered at all. I was promised to someone else, and so every man in the world except Rafael Castillo was off-limits to me. Still, looking didn't hurt anyone. I figured I might as well spend the last part of my journey sitting next to someone who was easy on the eyes, considering I had absolutely no idea what my future husband looked like.

The stranger eased his backpack off, then sat down next to me and shoved it as best he could under the seat. "I'm Simon," he offered.

Not giving him my name would be rude. Anyway, a first name shouldn't get me into too much trouble. "Miranda," I said.

He nodded. "Going all the way to Santa Fe?"

I recalled that the Railrunner stopped a number of times before it reached its final destination, mostly at the pueblo communities that ranged between Albuquerque and the state capital. "Yes. You?"

"Yeah. Your first time going to Santa Fe?"

Despite myself, I couldn't help smiling at the question. "Is it that obvious?"

His shoulders lifted. He was wearing a long-sleeved black T-shirt and faded jeans, a completely unremarkable outfit, but their very simplicity served to enhance the sharp beauty of his features. "I don't know about 'obvious,' but you did have kind of a lost look about you. Are you here to sightsee, or...?" The words trailed off, almost as if he had just realized he might be prying a bit and so didn't quite know how to end his sentence.

"Family stuff," I said, hoping I could leave it

at that. There was no way I could tell him the truth.

"Ah," he replied. He went silent then, probably realizing that it wasn't exactly kosher to start prying about family matters with someone you'd just met. After that pause, he asked, "Where are you traveling from?"

That question was still sort of personal, but I didn't mind answering, albeit with a half-truth. "Flagstaff." I decided it was better not to mention Jerome; after all, I had spent almost as much time in Flagstaff as I had in the little mountain town, and since Flag was one of Arizona's larger cities, it was the sort of place that it seemed logical to be from.

"Cool. Well, at least you're used to cold weather. It's kind of funny how many people come to Santa Fe and expect it to be really warm, just because it's in New Mexico."

I knew better than that because the climate in Santa Fe was one thing I actually had researched. At the time, I'd told myself it was only that I wanted to know what kinds of clothes I should bring with me, but that excuse wasn't the whole truth. Actually, I'd needed to know how alien my new home would be, how different it was from northern Arizona. As it turned out, Santa Fe could be nearly as cold as Flagstaff, which meant I'd brought sweaters and long-sleeved shirts with me, as well as the down coat I'd worn on the train platform earlier in the day. Already it felt as though my goodbyes to my parents had taken place a hundred years ago.

"No, I checked on that," I replied. To tell the truth, I was hoping it would be chilly in Santa Fe when we got there, because Albuquerque had been almost mild when I'd disembarked from the Amtrak car, and I'd wondered whether my cardigan and boots would turn out to be overkill. Then I cocked my head slightly and gave Simon a sideways glance. "Do you live in Santa Fe?"

"Oh, yeah. My whole life. My parents, too, and my grandparents, and—" He stopped there and grinned. The expression lit up his dark eyes, and I had to do my best not to stare. He really was kind of gorgeous. "Well, we've been there a long time, but that's not so strange. Lots of families in Santa Fe go back hundreds of years."

That was the impression I'd gotten, hearing my parents talk about the Castillos, but of course I couldn't exactly bring up that particular fact. I nodded. "I'd heard that," I said vaguely.

He didn't seem to notice my lackluster response. "I go to school at UNM," he said. "But my car died a week ago and I'm still trying to scrape together the money to get it fixed, so it's mass transit for now."

Wow. How far was it from Santa Fe to Albuquerque? Around fifty miles, if memory served, but that probably didn't take into account whatever distance Simon had to travel to get to the Railrunner station in Santa Fe, or the distance from the station in Albuquerque to the University of New Mexico campus. There was some dedication to higher learning.

I supposed you could say something similar about me. Not that I had to take the train to go to school or anything—Northern Pines University in Flagstaff was only about ten minutes from the family house there—but because I'd been determined to get my degree before I turned twenty-one and doom descended. That meant some extra summer school classes in addition to the AP credits I'd earned in high school, but I still managed to get a bachelor's in European history despite my constrained circumstances. If nothing else, I could say that was something I'd accomplished on my own, something that was still mine, even when the rest of my life felt completely out of control.

"That must be a pain," I said, my tone sympathetic. Because yes, while my future apparently had been decided for me, I'd had a very nice life up until this point. Both of the houses my parents owned were large and comfortable, I'd gone to good schools, and I'd never had to worry about money in my life. The McAllisters weren't quite as prosperous as the Wilcoxes, but even so, I didn't know a single person from either clan who couldn't afford to repair a car, or pay for groceries, or any of the hundreds of niggling financial problems that could worry at you when you didn't receive a stipend every month which guaranteed you'd never have to want for any essentials.

Or nonessentials, I thought with a mental grin, remembering my Uncle Lucas and his plane. All right, it was just a four-seat Cessna, and not some private jet with leather upholstery and walnut cabinets, but still. I didn't know too many other people with their own planes.

Simon didn't appear to notice my abstraction. Pushing up the sleeves of his long-sleeved T-shirt, probably because it was slightly stuffy in the Railrunner car, he said, "It's not so bad. I can study on the way down in the morning. And I don't have any Friday classes, so I'm done now until next Monday."

How was I supposed to respond to that? Was he sending out a subtle feeler, trying to see if I'd be interested in spending any time with him over the weekend? I honestly didn't know, since I'd spent most of my life trying to avoid male company unless it was someone I happened to be related to. At college, that sort of contact had been unavoidable, but I'd still done whatever I could to seem detached, casual, not someone you'd want to approach. The tactic had worked fairly well, but it had also left me lacking much in the way of useful skills when it came to deciphering male attitudes and responses.

"Oh, that's good," I said, my tone noncommittal, then turned my head so I could look out the window. There really wasn't all that much to see; at this time of year, the open land that surrounded us was yellow and dry, so leached and sere that I wondered if it was ever truly green. Off in the distance were some high, jagged mountains, but I couldn't remember their name.

If Simon was put off by my less than enthusiastic response to his comment about being free for the weekend, he didn't show it. He said, "This probably isn't the best time of year to come here. There are still some trees in Santa Fe that have some color, but earlier in October is better for that kind of thing."

"I suppose I'll see it next year," I remarked as I settled back in my seat and turned away from the window, and he lifted an eyebrow.

"You're staying that long?"

Damn. I probably should have paid more attention to what I was saying. Well, too late now to take the words back. "Um, probably," I hedged. "It's not all completely settled yet."

That comment earned me a sideways glance, but he seemed to realize that maybe he was getting a little more personal than our brief acquaintance should have allowed. He shrugged again and reached into the pocket of his jeans to pull out his phone. "Well, if that's the case," he said, retrieving some wireless earbuds as well, "then you'll get to see all of Santa Fe's seasons. Winter can be hard sometimes, but if you're from Flagstaff, you should be used to that."

I nodded, then was relieved to see him put in the earbuds, thus saving us from further conversation. It wasn't that I didn't like talking to him—it was that I liked it too much. And I knew I shouldn't be doing that, not when I had Rafael waiting for me at the end of this journey.

To make things a little less awkward, I pulled out my phone as well. It was brand-new, purchased for me only a few days before I left on this trip. The contacts list was conspicuously bare, and only contained my parents' cell phone numbers and email addresses, and Genoveva's phone number as well, just in case I needed to get in touch with her sometime during my travels. Yet another of the Castillo *prima*'s quirks—she'd insisted that I have a new phone, so my friends wouldn't be able to reach me. That stricture also applied to not having any of their information in my contacts; I wasn't supposed to reach out to them, either.

The whole thing was very strange. In a way,

though, as much as it hurt to leave behind the people I'd known in high school and college, it would have hurt more to still talk to them after I'd reached Santa Fe, to hear how normal their lives were in comparison with mine. Better to make a clean break, to continue with this odd ritual of purification.

When a shaman went on his spirit walk, he went alone.

I didn't try to reach my parents. I only muted the sound on the phone, then played a game until the train got to the outskirts of Santa Fe. Then I was much more interested in watching the sights outside than I was messing around with my phone. Simon also put his earbuds away, and, seeming to decide it was okay to start talking again, said, "This is the first stop here, by the National Guard armory. We'll stop again near the 25 Freeway and Zia Road. The next stop after that is the Railyard."

"Thanks," I told him, although my heart began to beat a little faster at his mention of the Railyard, my final destination. I still didn't know who would be meeting me there, only that someone from the Castillo clan would be on hand to pick me up and take me to the *prima's* house off Canyon Road.

Simon gave me another of those piercing glances, as if he could somehow tell that I was hiding something. "Do you have someone picking you up there? Because if you don't, you should use the Ryde app to call a car for you."

"No, I'm fine," I said hastily as we pulled away from the first station and began chugging our way along to the next. "My um—my cousin is going to be there to get me."

The words must not have sounded too convincing to Simon, because his brows were still pulled together in a faint frown. To my relief, though, he didn't argue, didn't try to push it any further. "Oh, that's good."

He got his backpack out from under the seat and stowed his phone inside rather than returning it to his pocket. I likewise busied myself, putting my phone in my purse and then getting my sunglasses out of the side pocket where they'd been resting ever since I got on the Railrunner in Albuquerque. By the time I was done fussing around, we'd gotten to the next station, which looked like it was across the street from a fairly large shopping center. A good number of people got off here, leaving the car half empty.

And then it was on to the final stop, passing through a part of town that seemed to be a weird mix of modern commercial buildings and shops and warehouses, and older ramshackle adobe structures. The tracks cut across a busy intersection with at least four lanes going in either direction, and then we were moving through more warehouses, the train slowing down as we finally pulled into the Railyard, which was busier than I'd thought it would be, with restaurants and shops and what looked to be a movie theater.

The train stopped, and once again I could feel the way my heart pounded in my chest. I didn't know what was waiting for me. All I knew right then was that I wanted to stay on the train, wanted to keep talking to Simon and postpone for as long as possible what was coming next.

He seemed to detect my unease, because he asked, "You're sure you're okay, Miranda?"

"I'm fine," I said quickly. Knowing that I didn't dare have him anywhere near when I met my first Castillo, I added, "Oh, I see my cousin waiting for me. It was—it was really nice meeting you, Simon."

A smile touched his lips, even as he stood up and waited for his chance to move out into the aisle. "It was nice meeting you, too. And who knows? Santa Fe isn't that big a town. Maybe we'll bump into each other again."

"Maybe," I repeated, even though I knew that wasn't going to happen. "Good luck with your car!"

His smile didn't fade. He just tilted his head toward me, as if acknowledging my words, then began to make his way toward the front of the car.

After I saw him go down the steps and exit the train, I figured it was safe to reach up and pull my luggage out of the overhead compartment. My fingers shook, but I managed to wrestle the bags down and slide them on my shoulders, my purse dangling from the crook of my elbow.

Then there was nothing left to do but take a deep breath and move forward as well.

Toward my future.

2

HIGH WALLS

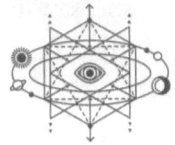

I SCANNED THE PLATFORM, BUT I DIDN'T SEE any sign of Simon. Good. Apparently, he wasn't so invested that he'd hung around to see who was coming to meet me. That could have been awkward, to say the least.

There weren't a lot of people in my immediate vicinity; it seemed like most of the Railrunner's passengers must have headed directly for the parking lot. Of the ones who lingered on the platform, none seemed likely to be part of my Castillo welcoming party—I saw a casually dressed couple, probably a few years older than I, walking away toward what appeared to be a brewery and restaurant, and there was a gray-haired Native American woman with two young children in tow. Probably her grandchildren, since she looked too old to be a mother to kids who couldn't be much more than five or six.

Then I saw a black-haired girl around my age, in jeans and a puffy dark green jacket, walking toward the platform. A smile spread over her pretty features when she saw me, and she quickened her pace. As she approached, she said, "Miranda McAllister?"

"Yes," I replied, figuring she must one of the Castillos if she knew my name and knew what I looked like.

Her smile widened. "Hi. I'm Cat. Rafe's my older brother."

Rafe. That sounded infinitely friendlier than "Rafael," a name that conjured images in my mind of some stuffy upper-class Spanish don or something. I smiled at her in response, although something about the expression felt stiff, as if I had to fight to move those muscles after my long and uncertain journey. "Hi, Cat."

"Let me take one of those," she offered, reaching toward one of the bags I had slung over my shoulder.

I handed her the lighter one, grateful for the offer. "Thanks."

"My car's over here," she said, and gestured with her free hand toward the parking lot.

Since I really had no choice but to follow, I went with her as she walked away from the train platform, toward a well-tended lot with planters separating the various sections. At this time of year, most of the trees were completely bare, but it still looked nice. My spirits lifted, if only slightly.

Cat led me to a shiny black Mercedes SUV. If it wasn't brand new, it still couldn't be much more than a year old. She pulled out her phone, and used the car's app to open the rear hatch, then slid my weekender bag inside. I put the one I was carrying inside as well, and she shut the hatch once my meager luggage was safely secured.

Although I wanted to know why she was the one who'd come to get me, and not Rafael or her mother, I figured it was probably better to remain quiet until I got inside. I opened the passenger door and climbed in, and she took her place in the driver's seat. However, she didn't touch the steering wheel, but instead pushed the button on the steering column to initiate the self-driving function.

"It's a city ordinance," she said in answer to my unspoken question as the Mercedes maneuvered us out of the parking lot and then headed down a narrow street lined with a bewildering array of shops and restaurants. "No manual driving within a mile of the Plaza. It cuts down on accidents, but the tourists still like to complain."

"You'd think they'd feel better, not having to worry about navigating around here," I remarked, glad that she'd opened the conversation with a neutral topic. I didn't know much about Santa Fe, but even the first impressions I was getting as I looked out the SUV's window told me it didn't seem to be a very driver-friendly town. Was it a people-friendly town? I supposed only time would tell.

"You'd think that." Another smile, although a slightly rueful one. Then she sent me a sideways glance through her thick lashes. "And you're also probably trying to figure out why the heck I came to pick you up, instead of my brother."

"Not really," I lied quickly, but she only chuckled.

"Oh, come on. You can tell me the truth. I mean, I know I would have been thinking the same thing if I'd been in your situation."

Her expression was mischievous, and although I knew I should still remain on my guard, something within me relaxed slightly. I thought I could like Cat. For some reason, in all my tortured imaginings about whatever fate awaited me here in Santa Fe, I hadn't expected that Rafael might have a sister close to my age, someone who in time might turn out to be a friend.

A friend. I had a feeling I could use one of those right about now.

"Well, maybe," I admitted.

She tapped her fingers on the steering wheel,

although I noticed she was careful not to interfere with the SUV's self-driving mechanisms. "I figured I was probably the least frightening option," she said. "At first my mother was going to be the one to meet you, and I told her no way, she'd scare the living daylights out of you. And since she was adamant about you meeting Rafe at the house, and not on some train platform, that didn't leave us a lot of options. I suppose one of my sisters could have done it, but they both have little kids they would've had to bring along, and that might have been kind of overwhelming."

There was a lot to unpack in her comment, so I tried to narrow in on the one that had the most immediate impact on my life. "Is your mother really that scary?"

Cat's lips pursed. "Well, I've had my whole life to get used to her, so she doesn't bother me most of the time, but she can come on a little strong for the uninitiated. But don't worry—she doesn't bite. Much."

I didn't know whether I should be reassured by Cat's words or not. Anyway, I figured I'd better reserve judgment until I'd met Genoveva Castillo for myself. So far I had no reason to think particularly well of her, just because my family and I had been forced to put up with her capricious demands, long-distance though they might have been. It seemed safer to move on to a different topic. "Do you have a lot of sisters?" I asked. All I knew was that Rafael was Genoveva's only son. I had no idea how big the family was otherwise.

"Two," Cat replied. "Louisa is the oldest, and then there's Malena. Rafe comes after her, and I'm the youngest. But," she went on, as if noticing that I didn't appear entirely thrilled by the idea of Rafael having two older sisters, "they're married and live elsewhere in the area. It's just my parents and me at the house now."

"Rafe doesn't live with you?" I asked, trying the nickname on my tongue, just to see how it felt. After thinking of him as Rafael for so many years, it did seem a little strange, but I hoped I would get used to it.

The SUV abruptly lurched to a stop to avoid hitting a couple of pedestrians who'd decided to jaywalk right in front of us. I put up a hand to grab the dashboard, while Cat did the same—and muttered a curse under her breath. Something about tourists, and I had to repress a grin. The Goddess only knew I'd done more or less the same thing a few thousand times myself. Spending part of my life in tiny, picturesque Jerome, which could see more than a million tourists pass through in a year, I'd had my own run-ins with people who couldn't figure out how to negotiate the town's twisty, narrow streets.

"No," Cat said as the Mercedes began to move

forward again, only to have to pause again before taking us down a side street. This had to be the part of town close to the Plaza, with all these shops and all the people crowding the sidewalks. It looked old, but not really older than the historic downtown section of Flagstaff, and a lot of the architecture wasn't all that different, either. "Rafe has a house not too far away. He moved out a few years ago."

In a way, I was obscurely reassured by her reply. If he'd moved out, that meant I wouldn't have to live with the terrifying Genoveva. From the way my parents had described the Castillo *prima's* house, it certainly sounded large enough to house her whole family and their respective spouses, but that wasn't the point. At least Rafe and I would be able to set up our own household.

"Oh," I said, which I knew sounded silly. Unfortunately, I really didn't know how to respond. The last thing I wanted was to tell this girl I'd just met—as friendly as she seemed to be —was that I'd been less than thrilled at the prospect of having to live with her mother.

Cat opened her mouth, as if she intended to reply, then appeared to stop herself. What she'd meant to say, I didn't know, because she gave a little self-deprecating chuckle and went on, "I suppose I should have moved out, too, but my mother wouldn't hear of it. No daughter of hers was going to leave the house, unless it was to get married."

"She's old-fashioned?"

"Positively hidebound. Part of it's this place." Cat waved a hand toward the world outside the SUV's windows. Now we'd gotten out of the densest part of downtown and were driving down a road that appeared to curve eastward, toward hills and mountains. Here I could see houses and buildings that looked positively ancient, the adobe that formed them making them appear more as if they'd grown on the spot, like mushrooms, rather than been built by human hands. "The Castillos have been here for three hundred and fifty years. People can get positively fossilized in that amount of time."

I hadn't thought about it that way, but Cat was probably right. The McAllisters and the Wilcoxes had occupied northern Arizona for almost a hundred and fifty years, and that seemed like an insanely long amount of time, considering how young our country was in the grand scheme of things. But three hundred and fifty? No wonder Genoveva Castillo insisted on following traditions. How could she not?

As to the rest of Cat's comment...I wasn't really sure what I should say. I hadn't known her long enough that it seemed appropriate to comment on the fact that she wasn't married, even though, now I'd been around her for a little while, I guessed she was probably a couple of years older than I. Witch-kind generally married early, just because most witches and warlocks had an innate sense of who would make a good life partner. That special sixth sense wasn't infallible, but they tended to get divorced at a far lower rate than the general population.

Maybe it would be that way for Rafe and me, crazy as it sounded. Maybe what Isabel Castillo had seen all those years before, the thing that had made her cook up this insane bargain in the first place, was that her grandson and I were meant to be together, and she feared it would never happen if matters were allowed to run their course naturally. I wanted this to be true, because despite the help they'd offered all those years ago, our clans hadn't mingled at all. They kept to themselves, just as tradition decreed they must.

As Cat had said, hidebound.

She must have guessed at my thoughts, though, because she said, "It's crossed my mind that the best way to get away from my mother is to get married. But, despite looking high and low throughout New Mexico, I still haven't found the right one."

"That's too bad," I replied. "And too bad that you can't go looking outside your clan. I've got lots of cousins who would love to meet someone new."

"It is too bad," she agreed, a light dancing in her eyes that told me she wasn't as upset about the situation as some people—namely her mother—thought she should be. "I've heard about those Wilcox men."

I couldn't help smiling a little, although I also wondered if I should be offended on behalf of the McAllisters. Still, if I was trying to be completely impartial, I would have to admit that my Wilcox cousins did tend to be better-looking than my McAllister ones. "I didn't know they were that famous."

"Oh, word gets around."

The Mercedes took a hard right onto Canyon Road. I was able to tell that was where we were because a large sign at the intersection called out its name on a big bright blue sign with white lettering. Here were more shops, but also many, many art galleries, some with wind sculptures outside, their fanciful shapes turning lazily in the wind. I'd seen some of the same types of sculptures in Sedona, but here they seemed more impressive, just because so many of them had been clustered together in one spot.

"World-famous Canyon Road," Cat said, her tone so dry that I knew she was being slightly mocking.

"Your house is on this street?" I asked. I couldn't exactly call it commercial, not with all the differently shaped buildings, some of which looked like houses that had been converted to gallery space. Still, it didn't seem like the kind of place to find a witch clan, not when we had to try so hard to keep our true natures from civilians.

Then again, I supposed you could say the same thing about Jerome.

"One street over. It's a little more residential there."

This proved to be the case, because after we'd driven a few more blocks, the SUV turned left onto a side street. Immediately we were away from the galleries and the shops and the foot traffic, and headed toward a huge property that sat at the intersection of the road we were on and what I thought was Palace Avenue, if the glimpse I caught of a street sign we passed was correct.

The entire block seemed to be hidden behind a high adobe wall. Beyond it, I was able to catch sight of a large house, one that would be mostly concealed during the months when the trees that surrounded it were leafed out. Now, though, the cottonwoods were beginning to lose their golden leaves, and the sycamores were nearly bare, definitely not thick enough to block my view of the two-story hacienda-style house, something that looked solid and heavy enough to have been here for the entire 350-year reign of the Castillo family.

Cat disengaged the self-driving mechanism and took the steering wheel in her hands, then circumnavigated almost the entire block before pulling up to an electronic gate at the rear of the property. She pushed a remote clipped to the sun visor overhead and waited as the gate slowly opened.

"Are we more than a mile outside the Plaza?" I asked. It didn't seem as if we'd driven that far.

"Close enough," she replied. "And there's some wiggle room when you're within a hundred feet of your property. I don't like letting the car park itself, because it always seems to get too close to the wall of the garage, and then I have to squeeze out."

It wasn't a problem I'd had to deal with. My family's vehicles had the self-driving mechanisms as well, but in Arizona the only real rule was that you couldn't manually drive on the highways. Around town, you could drive yourself if you wanted to. I almost always did, just because it was one of the few parts of my life where I felt like I had some control.

The garage was huge and detached from the house, with five bays. Cat maneuvered the big Mercedes SUV into the bay in the center, then turned off the engine. "Well, we're here."

A sour, sick feeling began to form in the pit of my stomach. As we were driving over to the Castillo property, I'd almost been able to pretend that I was just out with a friend, but now my future had come up to slap me in the face. "Great," I said, trying to summon a smile.

Cat's expression was all sympathy. "I know this may sound weird, but I'm sure it's all going to be fine. You'll like Rafe. I mean, he and my mother don't get along—like, at *all*—but I can't really blame him for that. Otherwise, he's pretty mellow."

Her comment should have encouraged me. If nothing else, hearing that he and his mother weren't exactly chummy was something of a relief, because I was already predisposed to dislike her. Still, I hated not even knowing what he looked like.

The words blurted from my lips before I could stop them. "He's—he's not disfigured or anything, is he?"

Cat had been reaching over to push the button to open the driver-side door, but she stopped then and gave me a shocked look. "What?"

"I'm—I'm sorry," I said, regretting that I'd opened my damn mouth. "It's just…your mother never sent me any photos of him. I know my mother sent your mother images of me, but…I guess I just had to wonder if she was hiding something." I stopped there. I'd already said too much; no point in making matters worse.

To my surprise, Cat grinned, even as she shook her head. "No, Miranda, Rafe is *not* deformed. He's very good-looking—although don't you *dare* tell him I said that. I'm sure my mother didn't send photos because she wanted it to be a surprise. Or it could have just been to torture you, since she can be loads of fun that way."

Damn. I already had a low opinion of Genoveva Castillo, but now it sounded as if I was going to have Cruella de Vil for my mother-in-law. "Well, that's a relief," I managed, even though I wondered how I was going to be able to act civilly toward the Castillo *prima*. She really was a piece of work, if Cat's words were to be believed, and my stomach knotted at the thought of having to face her in the next few minutes.

"You'll be fine. Come on."

Cat got out of the SUV then, so I didn't have any excuse to linger. Jaw clenched, I pushed the button to open the passenger-side door and climbed out as well, then went around to the back to get my things. Once again Cat took one of my bags, and I slipped the one remaining over my left shoulder while I let my purse dangle from my right hand.

"This way."

I followed her out of the garage and down a path that led through the property's extensive gardens. Although the trees were in the process of shedding their leaves, there were hardly any on the ground, a sign of some highly obsessive-compulsive gardeners. Or maybe it wasn't the gardeners themselves, but Genoveva cracking the whip.

Since the lot was so big and surrounded by trees, the sounds from the street were muffled, far away. It was hard to remember that the bustle of the Plaza was only a mile from here, since this place felt like it was part of another world, another time.

More adobe architecture here, in the high, rounded privacy wall and the looming structure of the main house. I'd always thought the Victorian mansion in Jerome and our sturdy, modern house in Flagstaff were large, but this place was easily twice the size of the Jerome house. I found something foreboding about the heavy dark beams that jutted out from the walls, the shadowy front porch, even though I knew that was probably my own imagination more than anything else.

Cat went up the porch stairs, and all I could do was follow her. With each step, my heart seemed to pound a little harder, and the hand that held my purse strap got a little more damp. And the cramping in my gut made me very happy that

I hadn't eaten anything, had only drunk some coffee. Although maybe that hadn't been such a good idea, what with the way all my limbs wanted to shiver and shake. Deep down I knew it was nerves and not caffeine, but it was nice to have something else to blame.

We moved through the house, which felt cavernous and dark, and colder than the day outside warranted. Yes, Santa Fe had turned out to be quite chilly, the sky overlaid with high, thin clouds that turned the light milky, but it wasn't so cold that I should be able to feel it in my bones like this, my limbs icy, a shiver slipping down my spine.

After passing through a living room decorated with furniture as dark and heavy as the house, we came to a hallway. Cat paused at the second door on the left, murmured, "My mother's study," and led me inside.

It wasn't quite as dark in here, possibly because the room wasn't built on such a grand scale, or possibly because the heavy draperies had been pulled fully back from the window, granting a view of a rose garden and a fountain beyond. As far as I could tell, the fountain was dry, probably because they'd already shut it down for the winter.

A woman stood by the window, her elegant profile sent into clear relief by the pale sunlight slanting in past the drapes. She wore a dark, slim skirt and a gray blouse, the open neckline of the shirt revealing an oversized cross of silver and coral. As soon as she heard Cat and me enter, she turned, a smile on her lips that I didn't believe for one second. I could see an echo of her features in her daughter's face, the slim nose and large dark eyes, but Cat's expression had a liveliness I was pretty sure this woman had never possessed.

"Ah, Miranda," she said, coming toward us. Before I could react, she had folded me into her arms and given me a brief hug. I stiffened, but then she let go and stepped away again, putting a safe distance between us. "It seems you've managed to survive your journey without incident."

No thanks to you, I wanted to say, but I held my tongue. It was probably the same capriciousness that had made her put me on the train that had also prevented her from sending me any photos of her son, and what would be the point in calling that out? Somehow, I would have to learn how to live with this woman, no matter how much she rubbed me the wrong way.

"It all was fine," I replied. "The train was a great idea—I had a chance to see a lot more of the country than I normally would."

The faintest hint of a frown line between her brows told me she was analyzing that remark and trying to see whether it contained a veiled criticism. Which of course it did, but I only stood there, wearing a faint smile and—I hoped—looking completely innocent.

Cat frowned as well, but for an entirely different reason. "Where's Rafe? I sent him a text to let him know we would be here in a few minutes."

Now Genoveva Castillo's expression was studiously neutral. "I'm sure he will be here shortly."

Clearly, Rafe wasn't any more eager to meet me than I was to meet him. Or rather, I actually did want to meet him, just to confirm that what Cat had said about his appearance was the truth. Not that I suspected her of outright lying, but she might have been exaggerating just a bit in order to make her brother look good.

"So typical." Cat turned toward me, openly apologetic. "He can be like that. Gets wrapped up in things, forgets about the time."

If we'd been alone, I would have asked what sorts of things he got "wrapped up in," but with Genoveva standing there, I couldn't do much more than lift my shoulders and try to look appropriately understanding. Still, I wondered what Rafe's hobbies might be, what his interests were. Most of the time, witches and warlocks didn't really have to work for a living, and that financial freedom allowed them to pursue avocations they might otherwise not have had time for. Did Rafe paint? Write? Build giant bronze sculptures? Hike? Shoot? Obsessively play virtual reality games?

I had absolutely no idea. I knew his name was Rafael Castillo, and I knew he was twenty-six years old, and that was about all I knew.

Except for the part about not getting along with his mother, which I could completely understand.

Then there was a rustle at the door, and we all turned. Standing there was a man who surveyed all of us with an expression of grim amusement on his face. He had to be at least six foot two, and was broad-shouldered and well built without being overly muscular. His hair and eyes were dark, one brow was lifted at an ironic angle, and he was absolutely the best-looking man I'd ever seen.

"Hey," he said. "I'm Rafe."

3

CATS AND CASITAS

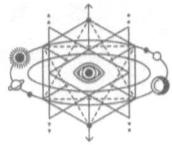

"Um, hi," I managed, trying my best not to look as gobsmacked as I felt. No, Cat hadn't been lying. If anything, she'd downplayed her brother's good looks. I still couldn't figure out why in the world Genoveva had felt the need to keep her son's appearance from me, but right then I thought I might be able to forgive her, considering the gorgeous specimen who stood before me right now.

Genoveva stepped forward, clearly doing her best to take control of the situation. "Rafael, better late than never, I suppose. Still, it was not very kind to keep Miranda waiting after the long journey she's had."

At once his dark, arched brows pulled together and his eyes glinted with irritation, but I thought it better to say something conciliatory before they could really get into it. "Oh, that's fine, Genoveva. I don't mind."

"You are too kind." From her inflection on the word "kind," I got the impression that kindness wasn't a virtue the Castillo *prima* valued all that highly. "But now you are here, Rafael, you and Miranda should take a walk around the grounds, get to know one another a little better."

Oh, dear God. Actually, I wasn't sure what would be more awkward—to have to stand here and try to talk normally in front of Cat and Genoveva, or to go off and wander around the gardens together with someone I barely knew. Then again, we'd have to talk alone at some point. Might as well get it over with.

Judging by the way Rafe's jaw set, I got the feeling he was as thrilled by his mother's suggestion as I was. However, he only nodded and said, "Sure. Miranda?"

I gave him a smile that was probably as saccharine as it felt and replied, "Sure." Realizing I still had one of my bags slung over my shoulder, I touched the strap and added, "Should I leave my bag here, or…?"

"You can show her the casita, Rafael," Genoveva commanded. "Cat, give your brother Miranda's other bag."

Looking a little dubious, Cat went over to Rafe and handed the bag to him, murmuring something as she did so. I couldn't quite catch the words, but it almost sounded as if she'd said, *Play nice.*

He didn't respond, except to shrug slightly as he took the bag from her. Then he looked over at me and said, "I can take that one, too."

"Oh, it's all right," I said hastily, even as I wondered what Genoveva had meant by mentioning the casita. Did she want me to stay in the guest house, rather than here with her and Cat?

Rafe said, "We can go out through the French doors at the end of the hall. It's a shorter walk that way."

I didn't have time to reply, because he headed out into the corridor after that comment, and I didn't have much choice except to follow him. As I exited the study, I thought I saw Cat give me an encouraging smile, but since my back was mostly to her, I couldn't be absolutely sure.

Hurrying after Rafael's retreating form, I caught up with him just as he was opening the French doors. Immediately beyond them was a covered patio, with steps that led down to ground level. A path wound away from those steps, heading toward the little house I'd noticed when I first passed through the garden.

Neither of us spoke as we headed toward the low, square structure. I didn't know what in the world I was supposed to say, and it was pretty clear that Rafe wasn't going to start a conversation without prompting. Had he hated me on sight? Or was he just naturally quiet?

As we approached the casita, I finally summoned the nerve to say, "I'm kind of surprised I'm not staying in the main house."

A lift of his shoulders as he paused at the door, which was painted a cheery cyan blue. "I guess my mother thought you might like to have some space. Or rather, Cat probably convinced her that it would be easier for you to stay here." After making that clarification, he put his hand on the doorknob and pushed the door inward, leading me inside.

Although my shoulders had been tense with nervous anxiety, I couldn't help but relax as I walked into the casita. Here was everything the main house wasn't—cheerfully hand-painted local furniture, bright pottery, houseplants taking advantage of the half-hearted October sun coming in through the windows. From what I could tell, the casita had one large living area, with an alcove for a round table and two chairs, a small efficiency kitchen, and a short hallway with three doors that opened off it. Plenty of room for just me.

That is, I assumed I was the only one who'd be staying here. Rafe had his own house somewhere else in Santa Fe, and so far no one had said anything about exactly when we were supposed to get married. I damn well wasn't going to ask, either. This was all Genoveva's doing. If she wanted me to marry Rafe to fulfill some decades-old vision or prophecy or whatever, then she could handle the details.

"It's really cute," I said as I set my purse on the table and my weekender bag on the floor next to it.

Rafe came over and put the bag he was carrying next to the one I'd just set on the red-tiled floor. He didn't look particularly impressed by the compliment. "Cat did most of the decorating. That was her project over the summer."

Getting it ready for me? Maybe, but I didn't want to ask. However, Rafe's comment explained why everything in the casita looked so new and shiny, didn't have that patina of age which seemed to lie over the main house. On closer inspection, I could tell that the Saltillo tile floor beneath my feet wasn't new, and certainly the structure itself must be fairly old, but the furniture and the appliances in the kitchen might as well have sparkled with their newness. Normally, I liked old houses, liked the sense of history that clung to them, but something about the Castillo home was oppressive, heavy. I was glad I hadn't been given a room there.

"It's very cozy." I paused then, all too aware of

the tension between us, the way Rafe was radiating an "I don't want to be here" vibe so strongly, he might as well have been shouting in my ear. "So um…we were going to walk in the garden?"

"Sure."

He headed back to the door and outside, and I followed, pausing only to close up the casita behind me. The air was cool and crisp, but really not any colder than it would have been in Flagstaff, and enough for my long-sleeved shirt and suede jacket to handle.

A gravel path wound away from the casita, heading toward the fountain and the rosebushes that surrounded it. Rafe went in that direction, saying, "My mother is very proud of her roses. It's too bad you came at this time of year. A month ago, they were pretty spectacular."

There was almost a note of accusation in his tone, as if it was my fault that my birthday fell at the end of October rather than at some other more convenient time of year. I could only blame that on the universe, since I'd come early, hadn't really been expected until the beginning of December. Not that having a December birthday was much fun, either, according to friends who'd bemoaned having their birthday presents mixed in with their Christmas ones.

"It's still pretty," I said. "But I suppose with

everything in bloom and the fountain going, it would be spectacular."

Rafe stopped and looked at the fountain, hands jammed in his pockets, dark eyes opaque. Really, he was about the most closed-off person I'd ever met, but that shouldn't have surprised me. This had all been forced on him, and I could tell he didn't intend to give up anything more of himself than he absolutely had to.

"We shut it down for the winter a week ago. Our first hard freeze came early this year, and that's always the warning to winterize anything that hasn't already been protected."

I knew about winterizing because we had a water feature at the Flagstaff house, a carefully "natural" small pond with a little waterfall and artfully arranged rocks. My parents had put it in when I was eight, probably figuring that by that point, they didn't have to worry too much about me drowning myself in it. But I remembered how it always made me sad when they had the spa guy come out in the fall and drain it and cap off the pipes so they wouldn't burst in cold weather.

And I also knew we were making small talk about the fountain because neither one of us wanted to confront the real reason why we were here together. I understood why, but I also hated that I couldn't quite find the courage to talk about something real.

From nowhere, I thought of Simon on the train, and how we'd been able to talk so easily. I hadn't felt tongue-tied or awkward around him, even though he was a complete stranger.

Then again, no one expected me to marry him, either.

It also didn't help that there was something physically overwhelming about Rafe. Maybe it was only that I knew I'd be expected to marry him at some point, and so my mind couldn't quite help imagining what it would be like if he bent down and kissed me, if those strong hands with their long, sensitive fingers cupped my face as he touched his mouth to mine.

Heat flooded my face, and I turned abruptly away from him, pretending to look toward the walled-off street. "Do you go over to Canyon Road very often?"

"No," he said. "Too touristy."

I wanted to ask him if there was a part of Santa Fe that wasn't touristy, but I thought that would sound too rude. "Oh, that's too bad. Some of the shops and galleries looked interesting."

To anyone else, that might have been an opening to offer to take me there so I might look around. Clearly Rafe had no such intention of being a tour guide, unless his mother insisted. And his next words just proved that to be the case.

"My mother wants me to show you around

Santa Fe tomorrow. Down by the Plaza, places like that. Then back up here to Canyon Road."

The words left my mouth before I had a chance to stop them. "And what do *you* want to do?"

He paused on the path, dark eyes boring down into mine. One corner of his mouth twisted. "Unfortunately, what I want doesn't count for much."

All at once, I was cold, my whole body overtaken by a chill. It wasn't so much the cool October day as the bitterness I saw in his expression, a bitterness I could tell he hadn't done much to hide.

"Sorry to be such a burden," I said. "Don't let me waste any more of your time, Rafe. I'll go inside now."

I walked away, my head held high. With all my being, I hoped he'd hurry to catch up with me, apologies on his lips.

Of course, he didn't.

At least the casita was cozy and warm. My eyes had begun to prickle with the beginnings of tears, but I forced them away. Crying wouldn't fix this. About all I could do was hope that Rafe would begin to realize this was a done deal, and he'd have to make the best of it, just as I was.

In the meantime, I figured I might as well get settled.

First order of business was to unpack my bags. I took them with me down the hallway and saw that there were two bedrooms, one a little larger than the other, although they both shared the same bathroom, which turned out to be the door at the end of the hall. That bath was bigger than I'd expected, with a separate shower stall and sunken bathtub, and lots of cabinets painted in the same cheerful blue as the front door. I put my toiletries away, then headed toward the larger of the two bedrooms.

It had a big iron bedstead, the canopy hung with filmy gauze. The furniture in here was also rustic and hand-painted, in shades of green and rust and blue. There was even a small kiva-style fireplace in one corner, the dark metal basket next to it nicely stocked with logs. I'd have to try that tonight; there was nothing like a crackling fire to make a place feel homey, and right then I needed to feel at home.

Hanging up my clothes didn't take much time. Still, I had a sense of accomplishment when I was finished, a feeling that I'd done what I could to get settled here. This might be my home for only a week or so, depending on when Genoveva wanted the wedding to happen, but I might as well be comfortable in it while I could.

I realized then that I hadn't yet contacted my parents. They'd known there might be a delay in getting in touch, which had turned out to be the case, but I didn't have any reason not to message them now. Maybe this didn't exactly count as an emergency, but it was still important that everyone back home know I was okay…even if I really wasn't. I didn't want to think about that, though. I pushed aside that nasty little exchange with Rafe and tried to compose myself. The last thing I wanted was for my parents to hear any pent-up tears in my voice.

After I retrieved my phone from my purse, I recorded a brief message. "I'm here and I'm fine," I said. This was going to be a cheerful little note, nothing more than that. No way was I about to tell my parents that my husband-to-be apparently hated my guts. "They're letting me get settled, so I don't know for sure yet when the wedding is going to be. Everyone's been very nice, and Rafael is nice, too, and super handsome. It's all going great." Was that laying it on too thick? I couldn't be sure. I also couldn't know for sure whether my mother might be able to listen past the words of the message to hear the doubt and worry I was trying so desperately to hide. Well, there wasn't much I could do about it either way. "I'll get back

to you when I have more to tell. Love you both—
and love to everyone else, too."

I pushed the button to stop recording, then
hit Send before setting the phone down on the
table. The chill of my walk seemed to have settled
in my bones, so I thought what I should do then
was make some tea. I wasn't even that huge a fan
of tea, but wasn't tea the sort of thing you were
supposed to make when you needed some
cheering up?

An inspection of the pantry turned up several
varieties, including Darjeeling. I figured I could
use the caffeine if nothing else, so I pulled out a
bag of that, located a brightly painted mug in the
cupboard, then filled the kettle and set it down on
the apartment-sized gas stove.

Just as it was beginning to heat up, I heard a
loud and peremptory *meow* from the front door.
Startled, I went over and opened the door, and
saw a large long-haired black cat sitting on the
doormat, staring up at me. Without so much as a
by-your-leave, it walked past me and went into
the casita, then stopped by the pantry and
meowed again.

Was it hungry? I hadn't seen any cat food in
there, but then, I hadn't really been looking for
any, either. A search of the pantry didn't turn up
anything specifically cat-related, but there was a
can of chicken. I figured a little bit of that would

work, and a bowl of water. Or did cats prefer milk? I didn't know for sure, because my family had always had dogs, starting with Blue, the shepherd/heeler mix my parents had brought home from the shelter when I was barely four. But I didn't really want to think about dogs, either, since that would only make me miss home that much more, miss the way our dog Wheeler always ended up sleeping on the foot of my bed, even though technically he wasn't allowed on the furniture.

There wasn't any milk in the fridge, only nondairy creamer, which answered that particular question. I got a couple of bowls out of the cupboard and filled one with water, then put a few chunks of chicken in the other and set them down on the floor. Just in time, too, because the kettle began to whistle, and I had to hurry to turn off the gas.

The cat went to the bowl with the chicken and ate a few pieces, but casually, with the air of doing me a favor rather than because he was actually hungry. While I put the teabag in my mug of hot water, he drank from the water bowl as well, although not for very long. Once he was done, he ambled out of the kitchen and went over to the sofa, where he jumped up on the arm and stared out at the gardens.

Okay, then. I would be the first to admit I

didn't know all that much about cats, but this one was definitely acting as if he owned the place.

A knock at the door pulled me away from my bemused study of my feline visitor. Had Rafe come back to apologize? It didn't seem likely, considering the way he'd acted earlier, but maybe his mother had read him the riot act and had forced him to return and make nice.

When I opened the door, I saw Cat standing on the low stoop outside. I only allowed disappointment to surge for a second or two before I said, "Hi, Cat. Come on in."

"Thanks."

I stepped aside so she could enter the casita. Before she could say anything, I asked, "Is that your cat?"

She looked from me to the lordly feline specimen perched on the arm of the sofa, still acting like the king of all he surveyed. "No, I don't think I've ever seen him before. We don't have any animals—my mother says they leave too much hair everywhere."

Which I supposed they did, although that wasn't the first consideration one usually had in mind when it came to having pets. Then again, it did sound exactly like something Genoveva Castillo would say. "Do you mind that I let him in? He seemed so insistent—"

Cat grinned. "It's fine. Sometimes animals

find you, if you know what I mean. And my mother really doesn't come down here anyway, so I doubt she'd even notice that you had the cat around."

That was a relief. For some reason, I didn't want to be forced to shoo the cat away. Besides, if he was here in the casita with me, then I wouldn't feel quite so alone.

"Anyway," she went on, "I wanted to apologize for the way Rafe was behaving. Seriously, sometimes I want to smack him right upside the head."

Those words conjured a mental image that almost made me want to chuckle. Almost. Even so, I couldn't overlook the fact that it was his sister who'd ventured here to make the apology, and not the person who really needed to do so.

"It's okay," I said. "I understand why he's not thrilled about this whole thing. To be honest, I'm not that thrilled, either. I'm not saying that Rafe isn't good-looking or anything, but it's not exactly my dream to be married off to someone who can't stand me."

Cat surprised me then by taking a step toward me and giving me a quick hug. "I'm so sorry. And I don't think it's that he can't stand you personally…he just hates the idea of being forced into it. He'll come around."

Personally, I had my doubts on that score. Sure, hate turning to love was a popular theme in a lot of books and movies and television shows, but I wasn't sure that kind of dynamic worked so well in real life.

But since Cat had come here to apologize, the last thing I wanted to do was throw her apology back in her face. None of this was her fault. She was only trying to make me feel welcome, make me feel not quite so lost in this new world where I'd found myself.

"We'll see," I said, my tone neutral. I remembered that I'd left the teabag steeping in my mug, so I hurried back into the kitchen to pull it out before the tea got so strong that it was undrinkable. "I made some tea," I went on. "The water's probably still hot—you want some?"

"Sure." She watched as I retrieved a second mug and a teabag, then poured hot water from the kettle over it. As I handed it to her, she said, "I didn't come here just to apologize, actually."

"Oh?" I sipped at my tea and tried not to make a face. It was too strong, but at least it was warm and sort of soothing as it went down my throat.

"Well, it's Halloween, and it's your birthday," Cat said. "My mother made noises about all of us having dinner at the house, but I know that would probably be a disaster. Rafe needs some space to process, I can tell, and there's no point inflicting my mother on you any more than we have to. So I said I'd take you to my cousin Tony's Halloween party."

"His what?" Not that I had a problem with Halloween parties—who didn't like getting to have every one of her birthday parties be a costume party as well?—but I wasn't sure I was up to that sort of thing after the day I'd had. Back home, the McAllister elders and many of Jerome's witches and warlocks would be preparing for their Samhain observances. It didn't sound as though the holiday was observed in the same way here, which made sense. The Castillo clan was very Catholic, from what I'd heard.

"Halloween party." She looked at me with her arched brows lifted and her head tilted to one side, as though trying to gauge my level of enthusiasm for such an event. "It'll be a chance for you to meet more of the Castillos, and since the party is at my cousin's house here in town, my mother can't get too freaked about you going out. It's not like I'm taking you clubbing with a bunch of civilians or something."

Hopefully, the rest of the Castillos were a little friendlier than Rafe and his mother. But Cat had been nothing but kind to me, and I could tell she was trying to make a bad situation even just a little bit better. "I don't have anything to wear," I said slowly.

Her eyes danced. "That's not a problem. We're

about the same size—you can wear my costume from last year."

I had to hope last year's costume wasn't a sexy nurse or something. Then again, I doubted Genoveva Castillo would allow her daughter to walk out the door wearing something like that, even if Cat was legally an adult and therefore supposedly able to do as she wished.

And what was my alternative, really? To sit here and drink tea and brood over the way Rafe had behaved, my only company a cat? It was a little too soon for me to turn into the crazy cat lady. If Rafe didn't want me, then I had to act like it didn't matter. And right then it seemed as though the best way to accomplish that goal was to go with Cat to this Halloween party.

"Okay," I said. "I'll go."

4

HAUNTINGS

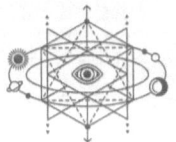

WE MADE A DETOUR ON OUR WAY TO THE party to pick up some cat food and kitty litter and a litter box at the grocery store, after which we grabbed a quick dinner at Blake's Lotaburger, then swung back toward Canyon Road, although not all the way to where the Castillo *prima's* house was located. This neighborhood was distinctly different from the one where Cat and her parents lived, still old, but with brick and wood homes that didn't look so different from the ones in Flagstaff's historic district, probably built in the late nineteenth century.

The driveway was packed with cars, and so was the street in front of the house. Cat had to park her SUV around the block but didn't seem to mind.

"If we'd been any later, we would've had to

park blocks away," she said as she locked the Mercedes. "Tony's parties are kind of legendary."

I wasn't sure if that was necessarily a good thing. Smoothing my voluminous ruffled skirts, I said, "So a lot of people come?"

"Yes, they do. Mostly Castillos, but there are usually some civilians mixed in. Tony has a lot of friends." She paused and gave me a faint frown. "And you don't need to keep fussing with that skirt. You look great."

Personally, I wasn't so sure about that. Cat had dressed me up as a Spanish señorita, complete with black lace mantilla and high hair comb, but I wasn't sure whether I was really pulling off the look. She herself wore the costume of an ancient priestess, in white draped robes and with a golden crescent moon resting on her brow, holding back her long black hair. The effect was pretty stunning, I had to admit, whereas I was just worried that my borrowed mantilla and comb were going to end up falling in my face by the end of the evening.

I didn't have time to argue the point, though, because she was already leading me to the corner, where we turned right and headed toward the party house. Even from half a block away, I could hear the music spilling out, and I wondered what the neighbors thought of Tony's "legendary" parties.

"His house is totally haunted," Cat told me. "But don't let that bother you. Victoria is completely harmless."

"Victoria?" I asked, a bit taken aback by her casual tone.

"The ghost who lives there. She was having an affair with the next-door neighbor because her husband traveled so much. But he found out one time when he came back early from a trip and discovered them together, and he shot her and the neighbor, and then buried them both somewhere in the backyard. Luckily, the bodies were found and moved to the cemetery before the Castillos bought the property."

This story might have been more startling if I hadn't already been used to this sort of thing. Of course I didn't have the talent to speak to ghosts— I didn't have a magical talent for anything, apparently—but when you're raised by a mother who could converse with the departed the way most people might talk to their next-door neighbors, communicating with the dead was no big deal. "How do you know all this?"

"Because Victoria told me. That's my talent, just like it is with your mother. And believe me, there are a *lot* of ghosts to talk to in this town."

I could definitely believe that. How many spirits must linger in a place that was more than 350 years old? Hundreds, probably.

"The jealous husband didn't hang around?" I inquired, wobbling my way around a large crack in the sidewalk. Cat had also lent me some fancy openwork boots, but her feet were a little bigger than mine. That meant I kept feeling as if the only thing holding the boots on was the laces, which I'd fastened as tightly as I could without cutting off my circulation.

She shook her head. "No, and neither did her lover. Just poor Victoria, alone in the house. Some Castillos bought it around the turn of the last century, and we've lived there ever since. Mostly Victoria doesn't do anything except move things from place to place, although she's very particular about the setup in the dining room. Tony's uncle lived there before he took it over, and when he tried to move the dining room furniture out and switch it over to a game room, he came home one night to find all his new furniture thrown in a heap in the backyard. He put all the original stuff back pretty soon after that."

"I can imagine," I remarked with a grin. Ghosts didn't frighten me. How could they, when my mother had explained to me from a very early age that they were simply people who'd remained in this world because they had certain issues they still hadn't quite figured out? "And Victoria doesn't mind the parties?"

"No. I think it's because Tony tends to go all

out with the decorating, and it amuses her. They've kind of worked out an arrangement."

It did sound as if they'd managed to attain a sort of peaceful coexistence. That was about the most you could hope for with ghosts. Sometimes they moved on, and sometimes they didn't—I know my mother was saddened when the ghost called Maisie had finally decided to leave Jerome after hanging around there for well over a hundred years. One day she was there, and one day she wasn't, and my mother couldn't really say why, but had only commented that sometimes you just knew when the time was right.

Cat's revelations brought another question to my mind. The music from the party was getting louder, and the distance to the house smaller, and I knew I didn't have much time left before we arrived and wouldn't have a chance to speak privately. "What's Rafe's talent?"

She paused on the sidewalk and gave me an odd look. Or at least, it seemed odd to me; it was full dark by that point, and so the only illumination was the uncertain light of the widely spaced street lamps. Still, she didn't hesitate as she replied, "He's a shapeshifter. His favorite is a wolf."

My eyes widened. "He's a werewolf?" I'd almost said "skinwalker," but I knew from my Navajo relatives that skinwalkers generally were connected with very dark magic, and I guessed Cat wouldn't have appreciated the insinuation.

Luckily, she gave a small laugh, apparently not offended at all. "No, a *shapeshifter*. He prefers changing into a wolf, says it's the easiest, but I've seen him become a coyote, a mountain lion, even an eagle and a raven. Something about the mass involved—he can't change into anything that's too much bigger or too much smaller than he is, so it's not as if he can change into a mouse or an elephant. Don't you have any shapeshifters in your clans?"

"Not that I'm aware of," I said. Inwardly, I was relieved that Rafe's shapeshifting talents weren't boundless, that he had his own constraints. It wasn't as if he could turn himself into a cat, for instance, and mysteriously turn up on my doorstep. Then again, why would he do that, even if he could? He'd made it plenty obvious that he wanted to spend as little time in my company as possible. I tried to tell myself I didn't care—if it turned out that he truly hated me, then maybe Genoveva would relent and I could go home— and yet, deep down I knew that I did care. My whole life already felt like one big failure. I didn't want to fail at this, too.

By that point we'd reached the front gate to the house, which stood wide open. The entire front yard had been turned into a graveyard, with fake headstones everywhere. Tony must have concealed a fog machine someplace nearby, because a pale mist wrapped around the faux tombstones, the chemical smell of the fog unmistakable.

Even though I knew it was all part of the decorations for the party, I couldn't help shivering a bit. The night was spooky enough on its own, with the high clouds overhead lit by a gibbous moon and looking like the scales of some enormous serpent wrapped around the sky. Deep down, I knew I really didn't need to worry about things that went bump in the night, because ghosts didn't scare me, demons had been permanently banished from this plane, and zombies were something for movies and TV, not anything I'd be likely to encounter here in Santa Fe.

Still….

As I followed Cat down the front walk, I reflected that I was probably feeling hinky because of the prospect of meeting a bunch of her Castillo relatives. That was scary enough without having to worry about made-up monsters.

People dressed as ghosts and vampires, mummies and Victorian ladies hailed her as we passed by. She cheerily responded to the greetings and called out, "This is Miranda!", which forced me to summon a smile and wave, even though of course I had no idea who any of these people were.

Then we were inside, and she was guiding me over to the punch bowl, where a guy doing a pretty decent Gomez Addams impression was ladling some sort of acid green, steaming concoction into those pressed-glass cups that are supposed to look like cut crystal. Pretty classy for a Halloween party, but I'd already figured out that the Castillos didn't do anything by halves.

"Tony, this is Miranda," Cat said, and he put the ladle back in the bowl, then reached out and took my hand. Before I could even react, he'd planted an extravagant kiss on my wrist.

"*Cara mia!*" he cried, then placed both his hands on his heart. "If only I'd known—I would have sent my Morticia costume over to you. You would have been perfect."

I was somewhat dubious as to my suitability to portray Morticia Addams, but maybe with the right wig and makeup…. Anyway, I just sort of gave him a lopsided smile, not sure how I should react.

Cat said, "I thought Noël was dressing up as Morticia."

"She is," Tony said with a grimace, his drawn-on pencil mustache crinkling as he did so. Despite the Gomez getup, he was very good-looking, tall and dark like Rafe, but with sparkling hazel eyes. I reflected that my afternoon walk probably would have gone much better if I'd been promised to Tony rather than the brooding Rafael. Tony seemed like the sort of person who could roll with anything, who might have looked on having an arranged marriage as just another adventure. "But since she's been stress-eating since she broke up with that civilian she was dating, she's about to rip the seams out on that dress."

Cat shook her head. "Don't be a jerk, Tony."

"I'm not," he protested, hazel eyes widening in a decent imitation of innocent surprise. "I'm just stating the facts." He reached for the ladle again, then picked up a cup and filled it with some of the neon-green punch. I thought I saw a couple of fake eyeballs floating in amongst the dry ice–generated fog, but it was hard to tell for sure. "Here you go, Miranda. This should make meeting the relatives a bit easier."

Despite my worry over that very thing, I couldn't help but smile at him as I took the cup. "Is it that obvious?"

"You do have a bit of a deer-in-the-headlights look going on, but I doubt anyone could blame you for that." He paused, then bent toward me and said in a conspiratorial whisper, "Don't worry. We don't bite…unless you want us to, of course."

Cat looked on in some amusement. Obviously, she was all too used to her cousin's flirtatious behavior. "You'd better chill it, Tony, or I'm going to tell Rafe that you're after his girl."

"'His girl'?" Tony repeated, looking around the crowded living room. It was packed to the gills with people, although it seemed as if their drinks were stocked for now, since no one had yet come over to interrupt us. "If he's that concerned, then where is he?"

"He…had something to do," Cat replied, her gaze not quite meeting Tony's.

Yeah, right, I thought, taking a sip of the punch and trying not to wince. It actually didn't taste that bad—sharp and citrusy, with a bit of effervescence—but I could tell it was *strong.* I sipped again, noting how the second swallow went down a bit easier. *I'll bet Rafe's at his house right now, sulking over how much his life sucks and reading Kierkegaard or something.*

It wasn't until that moment that I realized how angry I was with the man who was supposed to be engaged to me. He hadn't even *tried,* for God's sake. Spent ten minutes with me in the garden, then insulted me and let me go my merry way. Cat had done a pretty good job of distracting me—which was why she had dragged me to this party in the first place, I was certain—but sooner or later I had to come back around to the sorry fact that he didn't care one bit.

"Yeah, and I'm running for president," Tony

scoffed, then took a sip of his own glass of punch, which he had set off to the side while he played bartender.

I decided to play innocent, just to see what happened. "What, Rafe isn't into parties?"

Both Tony and Cat laughed. "Um, no," she said. "He's more the brooding Lord Byron type. It does get old after a while. But," she added quickly, maybe realizing that criticizing her brother might not be the best tactic when he'd already done his best to turn me against him, "he really is a decent guy. He's just not super social. You just need to give him some time."

About all I could do was lift my shoulders. I hadn't even been here in Santa Fe for an entire day, so I knew it probably wasn't a good idea to be making any set-in-stone judgments about my future. Even so, even a blind man could see that things between Rafe and me had gotten off to a rocky start.

Tony sipped at his punch again. It was pretty obvious that this wasn't his first cup of the evening, but he also didn't seem noticeably drunk. Just...relaxed. Then again, maybe he was like that all the time. I didn't want to think it was the alcohol that made him relaxed enough to tell Cat, "Well, he's acting like an idiot." Shifting his attention to me, he went on, "Maybe you should kick him to the curb. I'm sure there are plenty of other

Castillos who'd be willing to step up and maintain the family honor."

"That's not how it works," Cat said. She had a cup of punch in her hands now, too, and drank some, even as she sent her cousin a reproving glance. "It has to be Rafe. But thanks for volunteering."

"No problem." Tony put his free hand on his heart and leaned toward me. "I mean it, Miranda. I'd be more than happy to take over for my clueless cousin."

What could I do in response to such an offer besides laugh, or play it off as a joke? "I'll take it under advisement," I said soberly.

Cat looped her arm in mine. "That's enough, Tony. I'm going to take Miranda around, introduce her to everybody. You might want to cut back on that punch."

Her cousin's expression was wounded. "Are you insinuating that I'm intoxicated?"

"Something like that."

She didn't stay to hear his response, though, but led me away from the living room and into the dining room, where a long table was currently pushed up against the wall so it could serve as a buffet. I wondered what Victoria the ghost would have to say about that arrangement, then figured maybe she wouldn't mind so much, since the setup was clearly temporary.

It was just as crowded in here, with most of the group—well, those whose faces weren't concealed by masks or heavy Halloween makeup —sharing a strong resemblance to one another. Of course there were individual differences, but many of them had the same proud, high cheekbones, the same sculpted nose and strong chin. The Castillo blood clearly bred true, even after so many generations and what I assumed had to be some mingling with outsiders, so the clan wouldn't become inbred.

I met Tony's sister Noël, who was fairly curvy but who didn't seem inclined to burst out of the seams of her tight-fitting beaded dress anytime soon. And there was Tony's other sister Lisa, in an old-fashioned harlequin costume, and so many more who were only names, names that maybe one day I'd be able to put to faces—well, if I could recognize them without the Halloween makeup and the half-masks, of course.

The weird thing was, besides Tony, no one seemed all that surprised by Rafe's absence, that I was here with Cat as my "date." No one asked where he was, or thought it strange that he'd abandon me on my first day here, on my birthday, of all days. It was as if they'd known he'd behave this way.

And that surprises you why? I asked myself as I squeezed myself into an inconspicuous corner while Cat went to use the bathroom. *These people have known him all his life. I'd be shocked if he hadn't bitched about his arranged marriage to all of them, probably multiple times.*

That would explain the pitying looks some of the women had given me, and the speculative glances from some of the men. They all knew Rafe didn't want me, that I was only here because Genoveva insisted on following through on the ridiculous bargain her mother had made. And those speculative looks? Maybe they were thinking, like Tony had joked, that if their cousin decided not to go through with the wedding, then maybe they would have a shot at me.

Fat chance. I certainly wasn't going to trade one perfect stranger for another. If this whole thing fell apart, I'd be on the first flight back to Arizona. What I'd do with myself then, I had no idea, since I'd spent basically my whole life keeping people at a distance, thinking that I was going to disappear into Castillo territory and never be seen again, but I'd figure something out. Possibly I'd find a civilian who shared some of my interests and hook up with him. It seemed better to do that than be constantly reminded of my own lack of powers by being married to a warlock.

"That's an awfully long face to be wearing at a party," Tony said, approaching me with a plate full of hors d'oeuvres. Real ones, like you'd get from a restaurant, not bite-size quiches from Costco. For all I knew, he'd had the party catered.

Figuring I'd drunk enough steaming green punch on an almost empty stomach, I selected a puff of phyllo pastry stuffed with cheese and spinach, and put it in my mouth. Chewing gave me a little time to think of a reply. "Was it long? I guess I was just thinking."

"About nothing pleasant, looked like." He leaned against the wall next to me and popped a bacon-wrapped date in his mouth. I supposed I should be relieved that he hadn't brought any punch with him, had apparently decided it was time to soak up some of the alcohol with food. "I meant what I said, you know."

Oh, dear Goddess. Not that I wasn't flattered by his attention, especially after being rejected by Rafe, but still, I knew better than to encourage him. All things being equal, if I'd just met him at a massive convention for witches and warlocks— which wasn't even a thing, but maybe should be— then I might have wanted to get to know him better. As matters stood, however, I felt like we were treading on some very dangerous ground. Rafe might not want me, but somehow I guessed he'd be irritated to find out someone else did.

I cleared my throat. "Tony, I'm not sure—"

Luckily, I was saved from having to proceed any further by Cat reappearing, her pretty features twisted in annoyance. "Damn, Tony, can't you take a hint?"

"I didn't hear any hints."

"Then clean out your ears." Cat's gaze shifted from him to me, and she said, "The bathroom's free now."

"Thanks," I said, and I meant it. Not that I really had to go, but I was certainly grateful for the opportunity to escape.

However, the bathroom on the ground floor was occupied when I got to it. I looked away and caught sight of the stairs, which were decorated with garlands made of sparkly black tinsel and glow-in-the-dark skulls. Surely there had to be another bathroom upstairs. This house seemed to be of around the same vintage as my family's home in Jerome, and we'd had three bathrooms, one downstairs and two up.

I climbed the stairs, moving slowly because of my voluminous skirts and wobbly lace-up boots. At least it seemed as if most of the party was going on downstairs; no one passed me as I ascended to the second floor, and I was grateful for that. I needed some time alone to get my head together.

Sure enough, there was a bathroom just past the first bedroom on the left. I went inside and shut the door, then walked over to an antique cupboard that now served as a vanity and washed my hands, then touched my damp palms to my cheeks. I couldn't do much more than that or risk ruining my makeup, but even that cool, moist sensation helped to settle me a bit. In the mirror, my eyes looked huge and tragic. No wonder Tony had zeroed in on me, like a predator going after the one gazelle in the herd with a wounded leg.

No, that wasn't fair. He didn't seem like a predator. He'd just seen someone he found attractive and expressed his interest. Not all that appropriate, considering my status in his clan, but still—

A second pair of eyes stared at me from the mirror. I gasped and spun around, but I was alone in the bathroom. And yet, as I turned slowly back toward the mirror, my heart pounding, I could see her clearly.

She was probably about five years older than I, with a smooth oval face and big blue eyes. Her light brown hair was pulled up into a complicated arrangement of braids and curls, and drops of gold and seed pearls hung from her ears. In the quiet, cramped little chamber, I could hear the swish of her silk bustle gown against the tile floor as she took a step toward me.

"They're all the same, you know," she said sadly. "Full of compliments, praising you to the skies. But don't you ever expect them to follow through on their promises."

"Vic—Victoria?" I asked, somehow managing

to get the syllables out, although right then my mouth felt like sandpaper.

"Yes," she said. "This is my house. I let the Castillos use it because I don't have much of a choice, really, but I still make sure that they keep it the way I like it."

How was this happening? I'd grown up in one of the most haunted places in the world, but I'd never seen a single ghost, nor spoken to one. Even when I'd had a chance to observe my mother talking to one of Jerome's numerous spectral residents, it had seemed like a very one-sided conversation, since I could hear what she was saying but never was able to detect a single syllable coming from the ghost.

"It's a very nice house," I said, feeling like an idiot. Then again, what on earth was I supposed to say to her?

"Thank you," she replied, but her tone was absent, as if she was focused on something else. Possibly she was worried about the damage the party-goers might be doing to the place, although if Tony had these sorts of get-togethers on a regular basis, you'd think the ghost would be used to it by now.

She moved again, and I had to prevent myself from shrinking up against the vanity to get out of her way. This time she went over to the window and looked out into the garden, where orange

Japanese lanterns bobbed in the wind and a few brave souls stood outside in the cold, drinking and talking. It was the oddest sensation, because although I heard the rustle of her dress, I couldn't feel it as she went past, even though it looked as if her full, trained skirts had brushed against mine.

"Do you talk to a lot of people?" I asked. After all, just because I'd never participated in any of my mother's ghostly conversations, it didn't necessarily mean I was incapable of doing such a thing. There were hundreds of accounts of ordinary people—nonmagical people—having encounters with ghosts and spirits.

"Oh, no," Victoria responded immediately. She turned her back on the window and gave me a quizzical look, as though trying to determine why it was that she could talk to me. "Only Catalina, and there's another one who comes by every once in a while. Louisa, I think. She doesn't live here, though."

"'Catalina'?" I repeated, wondering who that was.

"The young woman who brought you to the party," Victoria said.

Oh, of course. Cat hadn't told me the full version of her name, but it made sense that it had been shortened from something else. *Catalina.* It was pretty, and unusual, although I thought that "Cat" suited her better. "Right. Well, I'm not sure why I'm able to talk to you, Victoria. My mother has that ability, but I've never shown any sign of it."

"Until now," Victoria responded, an enigmatic smile touching her Cupid's bow of a mouth. "Perhaps you have more of your mother's talents than you thought."

"No, I'm pretty sure — " I began, then stopped, because she'd disappeared, fading from view within the space of a second.

Rude. But then, I remembered how my mother had said that spirits didn't always follow our rules when it came to manners. They did as they pleased, often not staying around to answer direct questions. Or sometimes they simply went away because they felt like it.

Whatever the case here, I was clearly alone again. I looked in the mirror, and my dark green eyes stared back at me, cloudy and haunted.

I didn't know what the hell was going on.

And I wasn't sure I wanted to.

5

EXPLORATIONS

I DIDN'T SLEEP WELL THAT NIGHT—NO wonder, because I couldn't get that conversation with Victoria out of my mind. It wasn't that she'd said anything of any particular import. It was more that I shouldn't have been able to say anything to her at all. Why had I seen a ghost—spoken to a ghost—now? According to my mother, Jerome had been teeming with ghosts, but I'd never seen any of them, let alone had a conversation with one. What was different about Victoria?

The car ride home with Cat had been quiet. I hadn't volunteered anything about my encounter with her cousin's resident ghost because I was still processing what had happened. At least after that unsettling experience, the night had been fairly uneventful—Tony seemed to have taken the hint and backed off, and I met a bunch of Castillos I might or might not be able to identify if I saw them again. But, ghostly encounters or no, it had felt good to go out on Halloween, to do even a little bit of something to celebrate my birthday.

And that wasn't all. When I got back to the casita, I found a beautiful vase of cream-colored stoneware, bursting with blush-edged creamy roses, sitting on the front step. Tucked in among the roses was a plain white card. All it said was "sorry," in a strong masculine hand, but I knew it had to have come from Rafe. The gesture wasn't quite enough to melt all of my annoyance, and yet I knew I'd forgive him.

I had to.

Despite my weariness, it felt good to wake up the next morning and see the roses sitting in the center of the table where I'd left them the night before. Some coffee revived me, although I had to put off brewing a pot for a bit so I could pour some fresh water and put out some food for the cat. He settled in to eat right away, leaving me free to get back to my coffee.

As I sat down to drink it, the cat finished his breakfast and jumped up to perch on the little window seat next to the alcove where the table and chairs were located. The morning sun poured in through the window, awakening glints of reddish light in his black fur.

He really was a magnificent animal, clearly part Persian, with that long, luxurious fur. I had to wonder where he'd come from, because you'd think such a glorious cat would have a home. Although he ate with a healthy appetite, he was sturdy, his fur glossy. He definitely didn't look like a street cat.

Maybe later I'd see if Cat could help me make some posters with his picture on them, put them around the neighborhood just in case someone was looking for their lost pet. In the meantime, I thought I might as well give him a name, even if it was a temporary one. With the way he sat on the window seat and gazed out on the garden, dark lord of all he surveyed, I thought Lucifer might be a good name for him. But that seemed like a lot of baggage to pin on a cat, so I settled on Loki, although I hoped he wouldn't bring quite as much mischief with him as his namesake.

I didn't have time for much more than that cup of coffee and a muffin I'd found in a bag in the breadbox. It was probably one of the best muffins I'd ever had, cornbread with little chunks of green chile and whole kernels of corn, not really sweet at all, which was good, since it would have to sustain me until lunch with Rafe and I didn't want to deal with a sugar crash. At least, I assumed we'd have lunch somewhere in the midst of our sightseeing.

After my hasty breakfast, I showered and got dressed, and took more care with my makeup than I normally would. I wanted him to see me at my best, rather than the travel-weary girl who'd shown up on his mother's doorstep the day before. Nothing too fancy, since we'd be walking, but I thought I looked chic enough in my fitted leather jacket, slim jeans, and low-heeled boots. The final touch was the green tourmaline dangly earrings my parents had given me for my eighteenth birthday, and a plain silver ring on my right hand.

I'd just finished running the brush through my hair one last time when someone knocked at the door. A quick breath, a pause to tell myself that it would be okay, and then I hurried to answer that knock.

Rafe stood outside. Like me, he was wearing jeans and a jacket over his T-shirt, a nod to the chilly day. The first of November, hard and bright, with more of those thin clouds beginning to drift in. His eyes wouldn't quite meet mine as he said, "Ready?"

"Yes," I replied. "I just have to grab my purse."

As I went back to fetch the bag from where I'd left it on the table, Loki slipped past me and headed out the front door. Rafe watched the cat go, one eyebrow raised. "Who was that?"

"I don't know," I admitted, coming back to the door so I could shut it behind me. Because

Loki seemed like he could take care of himself, I hoped he would do all right on his own. At least this street was fairly quiet, and deep enough in the city that coyotes probably weren't an issue. "He was here yesterday. Cat said it was all right for me to keep him."

"I suppose so. I doubt my mother will come down to visit you at the casita and see the cat—she likes to summon people to her presence, like a queen."

He was frowning as he spoke. The last thing I wanted was to get on the subject of his mother, so I said hurriedly, "Thank you for the roses. They're really beautiful."

His expression didn't change much. "You're welcome. It seemed the right thing to do, considering." A pause and he added, "Well, let's get going. I'm parked out by the garage."

I followed him, trying to push back at the irritation that sought to raise its head again. It seemed he couldn't even accept a thank-you gracefully. However, I was determined to have this day turn out better than the day before—not that that would be too difficult—and so I decided I should just let it go.

He hadn't actually parked in the garage, only pulled into the driveway, blocking one of the bays. His vehicle was a sand-colored Jeep Wrangler, much older than the shiny Mercedes SUV

Cat drove. Was the slightly shabby vehicle a subtle hint from Genoveva that Rafe didn't have favored status, or did he simply prefer to drive something that didn't attract quite so much attention?

It wasn't a question I felt comfortable asking, so I only climbed into the passenger seat and buckled my seatbelt without comment. He backed out of the driveway, saying, "I figured we'd start in the Plaza and work out from there. You probably didn't get to see much of it yesterday."

"No," I replied. "Just a little as we were driving through."

"It's Friday, so it'll be crowded. Luckily, I already have parking arranged."

"Oh?"

A slight pause as he stopped at the corner of Palace Avenue and waited for an opening in traffic. "My father owns a bunch of restaurants around town. There's a parking lot behind one of them that he also owns, and he always keeps a couple of spaces open for family."

This was the first time I'd heard Rafe—or anyone else, really—mention his father. I figured he had to be around, but he didn't seem to have played much of a role in my coming here. "That must keep him busy."

Rafe shrugged. "It's something to do. I'm just glad he never tried to rope me into the business.

My sister Louisa and her husband Diego take care of that."

I couldn't really blame Rafe for feeling that way. Running just one restaurant, let alone several of them, was hard, demanding work. "So what do you do?" I asked.

He gave me a quick sideways look before replying, "I do pre-vis work for VR games."

Not exactly the most comprehensible of answers. "Um…what?"

This time he almost smiled. "Creating virtual reality games isn't that different from making films, in a lot of ways. Pre-visualization is just imagining what you want the world to look like, the backdrops, the characters…lighting, music. The companies often use freelancers for that part of the work before it goes to their in-house programmers. I like it because it's not dealing with tourists at a restaurant, or having some crappy desk job."

"Do many of the Castillos have crappy desk jobs?" I inquired, genuinely curious. The McAllisters tended to be an artsy bunch, since the clan stipend guaranteed they didn't need to have an income from a career to sustain their lifestyles, and Jerome was the kind of kooky place where no one batted an eye if you were a fiber artist, or made musical instruments, or whatever. More of the Wilcoxes worked at "real" jobs, just because they lived side by side with civilians, and it would have looked strange to have a nice house and car and all that without any visible means of support.

"A number of us. There are a lot of artists and musicians and writers here, because this is Santa Fe and that's what people tend to expect. And we have people in other parts of the state who run wineries or are ski-lift operators or whatever, but there are also a lot of teachers and lawyers and insurance adjusters."

By this point we'd turned down a narrow street a few blocks away from Palace Avenue. We turned again, and there was the parking lot Rafe had mentioned, not much more than an open area with a gravel surface and some outbuildings off to one side. Obviously, the woman sitting in the parking attendant's booth knew him, because she waved us through before he'd barely had a chance to begin braking.

As promised, there was a trio of empty spots under a sort of carport on one side. Rafe pulled into one of them and turned off the ignition. "It's just a block to Loretto Chapel from here," he said. "I figured we'd start there, since it's a landmark and everything. Then we can decide what to do next."

"Sounds good," I replied, unfastening my seatbelt. Generally, I wouldn't have been all that eager to go visit a church, since my upbringing had been more pagan than anything else, but right then I was just glad to be out with Rafe. I'd learned a little bit more about him, about his family, and that made me feel better. He hadn't tried to keep any information from me, but it also wasn't as if I'd asked any truly personal questions.

We got out of the Jeep, and he led me across the parking lot and through a sort of covered arcade between two buildings. On the other side of the arcade was a large courtyard with huge old trees and beds of flowers, now nearly dormant. Some patio furniture remained, although covered against the snows and wind of winter. There was something forlorn about the scene, as if the courtyard mourned summer's passing and the knowledge that it wouldn't come alive again until late the following spring.

However, I didn't get much of a chance to linger, because Rafe kept walking, heading toward the street. Now we were back on Palace Avenue, on a block filled with all sorts of intriguing stores. I itched to explore some of them, to pause and look in the windows at the Native American jewelry and the fancy belts and shoes and who knows what else. But we had a destination in mind, so I didn't say anything, hoping there would be time for shopping later. Then again, maybe that was something better saved for an outing with Cat. My relationship with Rafe was rocky enough. The last thing I wanted to do was drive him crazy by dragging him from shop to shop.

The chapel was less than a block away from Palace Avenue, its gothic spires pointing toward the sky, a stained-glass window overlooking the street. All around it were carefully tended shrubs and trees, and in fact it appeared as though there was a park to one side. I didn't have much of a chance to stop and look, though, because Rafe kept walking and headed in through the chapel's front door, and I could only follow him.

Lofty ceilings arched overhead, and the pale November sun gleamed through stained glass windows. At one end of the chapel was an impressive spiral staircase carved from wood, and the altar gleamed with gold.

To my surprise, Rafe paused after we entered and dipped a finger in the font of holy water near the entrance, then made the sign of the cross. This quiet observance made me a little uncomfortable, even though I knew the Castillos were still fairly devout Catholics, just like the de la Paz clan in southern Arizona. Genoveva had assured my mother that no one would try to make me convert, but still....

Speaking quietly, Rafe said, "The staircase was made without nails, and doesn't have any support from the walls of the chapel. Some say it's a miracle in itself."

I glanced back at the staircase, now even more impressed. Before I had merely thought it was beautiful, but now I could see why some people might think it was a miracle. Or, lacking miracles, a pretty amazing feat of engineering.

"Do they still have services here?" I asked, noting that tourists seemed to outnumber worshippers about two to one.

"Not regular mass—it's used only for weddings and funerals now. But it's also open to the public. Sort of like Notre Dame in Paris, although I've never been there." He offered me a humorless smile after making this statement, as if he understood the implausibility of his making a trip to France. Witches and wizards very seldom ventured out of their home territories even to go to a neighboring state, let alone a whole other country.

"It's beautiful," I said honestly. I could admire the chapel for its architecture and its artistry without getting hung up on the religious reasons for its existence.

"Yes, it is." He was silent for a moment, gazing up at the flying buttresses that held up the roof. Had he used elements of this architecture for his pre-vis work? I could see how they might lend themselves to fantastic fantasy worlds, and I supposed he must look for inspiration everywhere. It really did sound like a fun job. Maybe, once we'd gotten to know each other a little better, he'd show me some of his work.

After that, he walked me around the chapel, showing off more of its design features and explaining the reasons behind them. I could see why he'd wanted to come here first; he seemed more relaxed as he spoke, more comfortable with himself and possibly even me. It was a good starting point, and I hoped we could just pretend that the day before had never happened and move on from here.

"If you jog back down to Old Santa Fe Trail, you'll come to the oldest house," he said as we left the chapel. We'd spent more than a half hour inside, and when we emerged, the sun was higher in the sky, the day a little warmer, although I was glad of my jacket.

"What's the oldest house?" I asked.

"One of Santa Fe's original buildings. They claim it's one of the oldest houses still standing in North America. Those witches in Salem don't have anything on us."

He was smiling slightly as he spoke, and I realized he was making a bit of a joke. It was true, though; most people probably had no idea how old Santa Fe was, how it had a history just as long and complex as the original thirteen colonies.

"That sounds interesting," I said. "We don't have anything like that in Flagstaff or Jerome. I mean, they're old compared to some places, but not like this."

"Good," Rafe replied, looking almost relieved. He was probably glad I was willing to do the touristy stuff, because then he could talk about neutral topics like Santa Fe's history rather than having to get into the far more fraught subject of our future together.

And I was fine with that. I still had basically no idea what Genoveva had planned for us, whether she was going to allow things to develop organically no matter how long that might take, or whether she intended to get us married off after an appropriate amount of time had elapsed. Sooner or later, I'd have to bring up the subject with Cat, mostly because I hated to have everything up in the air. Not knowing was always the worst part. True, I had a hard time visualizing the man who walked beside me as my husband, but this was only my second day here. We both had to ease into this. At least he seemed to be trying today, and I couldn't deny the thrill I got when I looked up at him, took in the fine, strong features and the breadth of his shoulders.

The oldest house wasn't spectacular like Loretto Chapel, but it was still fascinating to stand within its walls and realize it had been there for almost four hundred years. I could almost feel the weight of those years in the thick adobe walls, the residue of the lives that had been lived there.

Were there ghosts? I couldn't say. Certainly no one came out and introduced themselves the way Victoria had, but a sense of heaviness in the air, of something lingering within those walls, made me think there might be. For all I knew, I was trying to manufacture something simply to prove that last night's encounter with Victoria hadn't been a fluke. I wanted to believe that I had inherited my mother's talent, that it had only slept within me until I had come here to Santa Fe. It felt so much better to believe that my magical gifts had only been dormant all these years, rather than to think I had none at all.

Maybe that was why Rafe's grandmother had been so insistent about having me marry her grandson, make this place my home. Maybe she had seen that the only way for my powers to develop was to come here, for whatever reason.

It was noon when we came out of the oldest house. I knew without even glancing at my phone, because the cathedral a few blocks away was chiming the hour, the sonorous carillon drifting out over all of downtown Santa Fe.

"Lunch?" Rafe asked, and I nodded.

"Sounds great." I'd noticed several restaurants as we'd walked over here, and all of them had looked interesting. In fact, there was one almost right across the street.

Rafe didn't take me there, however. No, he passed that restaurant and several others, heading back almost to the Plaza. To my surprise, he led me inside the La Fonda Hotel, an impressive-looking structure that took up basically an entire block.

"The food here is good," he said, "and it's a pretty setting. I think you'll like it."

Even though several groups were waiting ahead of us, as soon as the hostess saw Rafe approach, she made a show of looking down at the screen at her station, as if confirming something there. "Hello, Mr. Castillo," she said, and picked up two menus. "I have your reservation. This way, please."

I could feel my eyebrows lifting, but I knew better than to comment as she took us over to a table in the corner. Rafe had been right—it was kind of spectacular here, because the restaurant was set in a spot where the ceiling was at least two stories high, with glass enclosing the roof and natural light falling on the tables and the plants clustered around them. After murmuring a thank-you, I took the menu the waitress had handed me and waited until she was out of earshot before I said, "Reservations?"

"The people at La Fonda know my family. They take care of us."

He spoke with an assurance that was almost arrogance. I supposed he was so used to his family getting preferential treatment that he really didn't even see it as such. Anyway, I wouldn't comment, because I'd seen much the same thing in Flagstaff when I was with my Wilcox relatives. Things were much more casual in Jerome, probably because the McAllisters wouldn't presume to take advantage in such a way...and the civilians who lived there wouldn't put up with it, either.

"The Castillos don't own this hotel?"

"No. It's not good for one family to control too many places. Even in Santa Fe, that sort of thing gets noticed." He took up his own menu and began to scan its contents, although I got the feeling he already knew everything that was written there.

Something about his comment made me think about all those restaurants we'd passed. "That place across from the chapel—is it one of your father's?"

A muscle in Rafe's cheek twitched. Without looking up from his menu, he said, "Yes."

"So why didn't we eat there?"

"Because there's plenty of time for that later. I thought it might be better to have lunch some-place more...neutral."

I wasn't sure how to respond to that comment. His expression was studiously blank, and even if it hadn't been, I didn't know him well enough yet to be able to accurately read his moods. Still, the question lingered. Was he trying to keep me away from his father for some reason? That didn't even make any sense. We'd have to meet eventually.

But since I didn't feel like starting an argument over the situation, I merely shrugged and went back to my menu. When the waitress came over to take our drink orders, I asked for iced tea, while Rafe wanted only water. We also ordered our food at the same time, mostly because he went ahead and did so, and therefore I was kind of forced to make a quick decision. Luckily, it's pretty difficult to go wrong with an enchilada.

An uneasy silence fell. I picked up my napkin and put it on my lap, but doing so didn't exactly use up enough time to make much of a difference. I pretended to look around at the architecture, at the ficus trees in planters that helped enhance the open-air feel of the place, at the stained glass, at the people seated at the other tables. Tourists mostly, I guessed, since we were, after all, eating in the restaurant of a hotel.

The waitress returned with our drinks and disappeared again. Then Rafe said, "I heard you had a good time at the Halloween party last night."

I wondered who he'd heard that from. Cat, I hoped, and not their cousin Tony. The Goddess only knows what he might have said about me. My tone noncommittal, I said, "It was nice of Cat to invite me. I had fun meeting more of your family."

"Including Tony?"

Startled, I looked up from squeezing some lemon into my iced tea and met Rafe's gaze. His face was still mostly expressionless, but I thought I saw an angry glint in his brown eyes. "Tony seems like a fun person."

"As opposed to me, I suppose."

Anger flashed through me. Still, my tone was level as I replied, "I didn't say that."

"You didn't have to."

My chin went up, and I narrowed my eyes at him. "It's all right, Rafe. I'm sure you had much more important things to do with your time than provide some company for a stranger on her first night in Santa Fe."

Rafe looked almost pleased by my response, as if that was exactly the way he'd hoped I would react. "So you are still pissed off about it."

"'Pissed off' is probably too strong. Annoyed, maybe." I lifted my glass of iced tea and sipped some through the straw, hoping by doing so that I had signaled I really didn't want to talk about this anymore.

"You look a little more than annoyed."

I took a breath. I didn't exactly count to ten, but I did allow myself a small pause before I said, "Why are you trying to get a rise out of me, Rafe? Does it really matter one way or another? Yes, I was angry about it, but you apologized. Or," I went on, struck by a sudden thought, "were the roses your mother's idea, or maybe Cat's?"

Clearly, I had struck a nerve, because he looked away from me then. Voice almost a mutter, he said, "Cat might have had something to do with it."

Of course. I probably should have guessed, but I'd been trying so hard to believe that Rafe had realized the error of his ways that I'd refused to consider the most obvious explanation.

This whole thing was impossible. Why should I try to play nice with someone who obviously disliked me, didn't want me to be a part of his life? He wouldn't attempt to meet me halfway...not even a quarter of the way. Better to just walk away and say sorry, your grandmother's vision or whatever it was obviously was wrong. You go back to your life, and I'll go back to mine. In a way, it would be a relief to dismiss the whole thing. Surely the Castillos would have to back off once they realized the failure of this stupid bargain had everything to do with Rafe and nothing to do with me.

I didn't even realize what I was doing until I'd plucked the napkin from my lap and stood. Rafe looked up at me with some alarm. "What are you doing?"

"Leaving," I replied, bending down so I could retrieve my purse from where I'd slung it over the arm of the chair. "I think we're just wasting each other's time."

"But—"

"Goodbye, Rafe."

I hurried away before he could say anything. Not much chance of him turning into a wolf or a mountain lion in a public place like that. About all he could do was get up from his seat and chase after me, but even doing that might have caused a scene.

But, just like the day before, he didn't attempt any sort of pursuit. I emerged onto the street alone, and looked around.

This might be my last day in Santa Fe. I might as well take advantage of it while I could.

6

UNEXPECTED ENCOUNTERS

WHAT I REALLY WANTED WAS A DRINK. OH, I could have gone into any of a number of nearby stores and indulged myself with some retail therapy—I still had access to my bank accounts via my phone; at least Genoveva Castillo hadn't asked that I give those up...not yet, anyway—but shopping seemed like a frivolous endeavor right then. Since it seemed as though there was a good chance I might be heading right back to Arizona, I didn't think it was a good idea to load up on stuff I couldn't possibly fit on a plane. As to how my parents would react to such a precipitous return, I really didn't know. I hoped I could make them understand that I'd tried, but I'd worry about that later. For now, I needed to do my best to get my head together. My hands were shaking, and I knew I had to calm down, find a quiet place where I could take some time to get my rattled nerves in order.

I didn't even know where I was going. How could I, when I knew hardly anything about Santa Fe? I started heading west on San Francisco Street, figuring sooner or later I'd come across someplace that looked promising. Across the street there was a bar, but it looked a little seedy, especially with the bright light of noontime beating down on its front window and revealing some battered-looking furnishings, with even more battered-looking people sitting at those seen-better-days tables and chairs. It wasn't exactly the sort of place where I'd want to go in alone.

There. Just a few doors down from the bar, I came upon a wine tasting room, and figured that should work nicely. I wouldn't do a tasting, of course, but only order a glass of wine, one which I hoped I could nurse for a while at a table by myself while I tried to decide what I should do next.

No one was tending the bar when I walked up to it. Down at one end of the long, copper-covered counter was a couple in their early thir-ties, the woman looking a little tipsy. She smiled as I approached and said, "He's just in back getting some bottles for us. I'm sure he'll be right out."

"That's fine," I replied. "I'm in no hurry."

There was an understatement.

I set my purse on the countertop, took a seat on one of the counter-height chairs provided, and looked around. While I hadn't been of legal drinking age until the day before, I'd been to all the wine-tasting rooms in Jerome and always liked to see how they were decorated. This one was similar enough in appearance to the ones back home, with its racks of bottles behind the bars, the small tables where you could sit and do a tasting, or cut straight to having a glass of wine the way I planned to. But the place had a fun decorative copper ceiling to match the counter, and black and white photos of Santa Fe's past on the walls. It was good to look around, just because doing so helped to distract me from the real reason why I was there.

Then the man working the counter came out from the stockroom with a bottle of wine in each hand, and I almost fell off my chair.

It was Simon, the guy I'd met on the Railrunner train.

He recognized me, too; his eyes widened as soon as our gazes locked. But then he seemed to shake his head, as if reminding himself that he needed to attend to his work first, and went over to the couple who were waiting for their wine. Working quickly and efficiently, he wrapped the bottles in paper sleeves to protect them and then slid them both into a gift bag. The woman handed over her credit card, nattering away in her tipsy Texas twang about how much fun it was to discover new wines, especially local ones that nobody had heard of. Simon offered her a polite smile, ran the card, and told the woman her receipt was being emailed to her. Then, mercifully, the couple took their bag of wine and disappeared, no doubt in search of more wine tasting rooms…or maybe just more wine.

"Miranda." Simon came over to where I sat, then took a closer look at me. "Are you okay?"

It was so nice to see a sympathetic face, to hear the concern in his voice, that I almost burst into tears right then and there. However, I didn't want him to think I'd completely lost my mind, so I summoned a smile and said, "I'm not sure. But I would like a glass of wine."

"I can do that. What would you like?"

"Something dry. Dry red. Whichever you think is best."

He looked somewhat surprised at my request —probably dry red wine wasn't a common choice for twenty-one-year-olds—but my parents had allowed me to drink wine at home after I turned eighteen, since they were of the opinion that if you were old enough to vote, or be considered legally an adult, you should be able to drink. They collected wines from all over Arizona, and had helped to train my palate.

"Try this," he said, after pouring a nice garnet-colored wine into a glass, then pushing it across the counter toward me. "It's a Cinsault. The grapes do really well here in New Mexico soil."

That was a variety I hadn't tried before, which was fine by me. If I concentrated on tasting the wine, on analyzing it, then I might not have the headspace left over to brood about that lovely little scene I'd just shared with Rafe at the La Fonda Hotel.

The wine was good, fruit forward without being heavy, not tannic at all. I took a second sip, then nodded. "That's really nice." I paused, and gave Simon a considering look. "You didn't card me."

"Well, judging by the expression on your face, I thought that getting carded was probably the last thing you needed to deal with right now. But you're twenty-one, aren't you?"

"As of yesterday."

His eyes widened. They were such a dark brown that you almost couldn't see the difference between the iris and the pupil, unlike Rafe's, which were a warm tea color, almost amber, striking against his dark hair.

But I shouldn't be thinking about Rafe, and especially what he looked like. That was the only thing I really found appealing about him. So what if he was good-looking, when he also happened to be a raging jerk?

Anyway, Simon was attractive, too, just in a completely different way. But again, I probably shouldn't be thinking about his looks, either, although for another reason entirely. I might have mentally kicked Rafe to the curb, but in the eyes of both our families, we were meant to be together. Flouncing out of the La Plazuela restaurant wouldn't change anything in their eyes, although I felt as though I was now done with the whole sad charade.

"I should be pouring you champagne to celebrate your birthday, not Cinsault," Simon said, and I blinked, bringing myself back to the here and now.

"Oh, well." I made a deprecating gesture with one hand, then picked up the glass of wine and sipped again. "This is very good, even if it isn't champagne. Besides, I don't feel like I have all that much to be celebrating."

He hesitated, as though he knew we were still barely acquaintances, and not really in a position to be sharing confidences. But apparently he decided that wasn't enough of a reason not to speak, because he said, "Do you want to talk about it?"

I did, but I knew I really shouldn't be pouring

out all my woes to a man I'd only met the day before. "It's...complicated."

That comment elicited a grin. "Isn't it always?"

"I suppose so." I fiddled with the stem of the wine glass, then glanced over my shoulder. No one had come in to replace the couple from Texas, but still, more customers could arrive at any moment. Even if I did work up the nerve to try to give Simon a carefully edited version of what was going on, I ran the very real chance of someone coming along just as I was picking up a head of steam.

"Most of the time it's pretty slow until after three, even on a Friday," he said, then added, "If that's what you're worried about."

"Partly, but...." I drank some more Cinsault. It was starting to do a number on my mostly empty stomach, but right then I didn't much care. There was a burger place a few doors down; I could always get some solid food after this if I needed to.

And what then? It would be simple enough to call one of the automated Ryde cars, have it take me back to the casita. After that, though...my imagination really didn't want to venture into what might happen once I got there. Genoveva was sure to be furious, and it wasn't as if she was the most pleasant of people to be around, even when she was in a good mood. Whether she'd be angrier with me for walking out, or with Rafe for provoking me in the first place, I couldn't know. Either way, it probably wasn't going to be pretty.

"Did you have a fight with your relatives?" Simon asked, and I blinked. His tone patient, he clarified, "You told me yesterday you were coming here because of family. If you're here drinking alone the day after your birthday, well…it doesn't take a rocket scientist to do the math."

"Something like that," I replied, figuring it couldn't hurt too much to make a few comments on the subject, as long as I kept the phrasing vague enough that he couldn't possibly determine who I was actually talking about. "Let's just say we had a difference of opinion."

His tone sympathetic, Simon responded, "Family can be a pain."

"But now I'm stuck here," I continued. "So I have to figure out a way to make things work."

"Stuck here how?"

He only looked politely curious, or at least, that was how I chose to read his expression. Still, he'd asked a question, so I needed to come up with some way to answer him without giving away too much. "It's sort of an arrangement my family made. I can't really go back. But I'm not getting along with anyone here, so I have no idea how I'm supposed to make it all work."

"That sucks." Now his face reflected more

confusion than anything else. "But…why is it you can't go back to Arizona? I mean, you're an adult. You can do what you want, right?"

The way he said it, the situation sounded so simple. If all things were equal, then yes, I should have been able to pack up and leave, and not have anyone give me any trouble over my decision. Problem was, I had no idea what Genoveva would do if I went back to the casita to get my things and announced I was returning to Arizona. My instincts told me that she would use her *prima* powers to prevent me from doing such a thing—for all I knew, she could lock all the doors so nothing would open them, would tie me to a chair until I was forced to marry her obnoxious son, or whatever else the situation required.

"Not really," I said, then took a large swallow of Cinsault. To my surprise, the glass was almost empty.

Simon reached under the counter, pulled out the bottle, and filled my wine glass. "Consider it a birthday present."

I was already a little fuzzy-headed, or I might have stopped to consider the ramifications of having so much wine on a nearly empty stomach. As it was, right then I was just glad that I apparently didn't have to worry about running out of booze. "Thanks, Simon."

"Not a problem. I wish I could join you, but I can't drink while I'm on duty."

"How late do you have to work?"

"Until six."

That was a long time from now, considering the clock hanging on the wall behind the bar told me it wasn't even one o'clock yet. No way I could stay here and drink that whole time, waiting until Simon was done with his shift. I'd have to be carried off on a stretcher.

If I'd been a little more sober, I might have also asked myself why I thought it was a good idea to hang around until Simon was off work. But because a pleasant cloudiness had begun to take over my brain, I wasn't prone to much self-analysis. I only thought that I liked talking to him, and that it might have been fun to go get something to eat, go see a movie. Something normal, like regular people our age did. I'd never been on a date. What would have been the point in cultivating any kind of a relationship when I knew it would only get torn apart as soon as I turned twenty-one and had to leave my whole life behind?

At least I had enough presence of mind not to voice any of these thoughts aloud. I sipped some more wine, then asked, "Is that when most of the shops around here close?"

"Mostly," he replied as he fetched a rag from

under the counter and went over to where the couple from Texas had been sitting. He rubbed at some marks I couldn't even see from my vantage point, then returned the rag to its anointed spot beneath the counter. "Obviously, the bars and the restaurants stay open later, and some of the shops do that, too, on Friday and Saturday nights. But because we don't serve any food, the owner decided it was okay to close at six. He's been talking about having some cheese plates to serve with the wine, but that hasn't happened yet."

"Oh," I said. Too bad about that, because I probably could have used some cheese right then. Or a burger. Anything to soak up the alcohol pooling in my stomach. "Do you work Saturday nights, too?"

"Yes. I have to get as many hours in over the weekend as possible, because I have a couple of days during the week where I don't get back to Santa Fe until really late in the afternoon. Luckily, the owner is a family friend, so he lets me be flexible with my schedule."

"That's nice of him," I replied, thinking how refreshingly normal all that sounded. Going to school, working, trying to make everything fit. I realized I'd never had that kind of experience, because I'd never had a job, beyond babysitting for relatives from time to time. Even the babysitting wasn't really a job, since I hadn't gotten paid for it. That was just part of being in a tight-knit clan—you pitched in where you could. "Have you worked here long?"

"About six months. It's a decent gig." He grinned again, dark eyes lighting up with some kind of secret amusement. "Especially when you get people who've been drinking all afternoon and who tip you on the price of the bottles they buy, not just the cost of a wine tasting. It can add up pretty fast."

"Well, here's hoping you get enough of those this weekend that you can pay for your car repairs," I said, lifting my glass in a sort of salute before I took another sip. Well, all right, it was more a large swallow than a sip. The room tilted slightly, and I blinked and grabbed the counter with my free hand, the copper cool and smooth beneath my fingers.

Simon's grin abruptly faded. "Are you all right, Miranda?"

"S-sure," I replied, even though I was beginning to get the idea that I might not be so all right after all. "I just haven't had anything to eat. I was supposed to, you know," I added, my voice dropping conspiratorially. "But I got so pissed off at him that I just walked out."

"Him who?"

I shook my head. "No, I can't tell you. I wish I could, but that's just the way it is."

Now Simon was starting to look downright alarmed. "Maybe I should text Ryde for you—"

"No, I'm okay." I blinked. Was I okay? Judging by the way I now seemed to see two Simons in front of me, maybe I wasn't. That Cinsault was some strong stuff. "I mean, I think I'm okay. Maybe I should just go."

I began to slide off the tall chair where I sat, but my legs felt like rubber, and the next thing I knew, I was falling in a boneless heap to the wooden floor. Rather than being mortified, I sat there and giggled. "Oops."

"Oh, shit." Simon came around the counter, grasped me by the arms, and somehow managed to haul me to my feet. "You are really wasted, Miranda."

I tilted my head to one side, considering his words. "You know, I think you may be right."

"Okay, I'm texting Ryde." Still holding me up with one hand, he reached into his jeans pocket with the other. "Where are you staying?"

"Nope," I told him, somehow retaining enough of my faculties to realize that I couldn't possibly give him the address of the Castillo *prima's* house. "I can't tell you that."

"Miranda, I need to know where to have the Ryde take you."

"I already told you, I can't tell you." I hiccuped, and rather than be completely mortified, I giggled again. Somewhere deep within, I realized that as soon as I was sober I would recall this incident and want to die at the memory, but right now I just found the entire situation enormously funny.

"All right," Simon said. He cast a quick glance at the door, but the people passing by on the street kept going and didn't show any interest in entering the wine tasting room. "I'm taking you upstairs."

"What's upshtairs?"

"My apartment. You can lie down there until you sleep off the alcohol."

I cast a glance at the pressed-copper ceiling above us. "You live here?"

"I live up there. Most of the stores along this block have apartments above them. Come on."

He slipped an arm around my waist, grabbed my purse with his other hand, and guided me back behind the counter and into a storage area. All around were cases of wine, several of them sitting on a table with a stack of mailing labels next to them. I saw a bulletin board, a few large metal casks, doors that maybe led to an office or an employee restroom. Past all this, however, was another door, one that opened on a little foyer with a narrow staircase off to one side. Simon pushed me toward those stairs and then half-carried me up them, since I was in no shape to do anything as complicated as lift one foot and then the other.

Upstairs was a small landing, with a door off to the right. He fished some keys from his pocket, unlocked the door, and brought me inside. The place was small, with wood floors and walls painted a cheery butter yellow. I didn't have time for much more of an impression than that, however, because he led me to a worn blue couch and pushed me down on it. Apparently his intentions were pure, because he remained standing, looking down at me with an expression that was simultaneously befuddled and concerned.

"Try sleeping it off," he said. "I'll be back up a little after six."

I opened my mouth to tell him that I couldn't possibly stay here that long. The words didn't seem to want to come out, though, and the last thing I remembered was him shaking his head as he went back out through the door.

After that, everything was darkness.

7

BEST-LAID PLANS

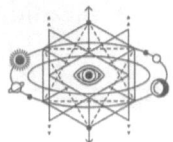

Rafael Castillo

CAT SAT ON HIS COUCH, FROWNING SO fiercely that Rafe almost wanted to tell her to stop before she ground a permanent line into her forehead. "I cannot *believe* how badly you screwed this up."

Rafe wanted to argue with her, except he knew that he really had screwed up. Fucked up, really. No point in sugarcoating it. The problem with self-flagellation, though, was that it really didn't get you anywhere. He could analyze everything he'd done wrong, tell himself all the things he should have done differently, but the point still remained:

Miranda was missing.

At the time, he'd been so angry about her

walking out on him that he'd sat at the table for a good five minutes before finally realizing that letting her just go like that was a very bad idea. Setting aside the reason why she was here in Santa Fe in the first place, she was still a young woman on her own in a town she didn't know. His first thought had been that she'd call for a Ryde and go back to the casita, but then he'd guessed that she wouldn't do any such a thing. Her pride wouldn't allow it.

Which meant she was probably somewhere downtown. He'd gone out and walked the streets around the Plaza, looking for a slender figure with a rich fall of dark brown hair and wearing a dark green leather jacket, but he hadn't found her. Even when he'd cut down to Water Street and searched the shops there, he hadn't seen her. If he'd been able to shift into wolf or coyote form, he might have been able to pick up on her scent and track her that way, but since it was broad daylight and Santa Fe's downtown was packed full of civilians, that option had been denied him.

He tried to tell himself that she was perfectly safe, that the only danger she faced was being parted from some of her cash in one of the overpriced shops around the Plaza that catered to tourists. Problem was, he couldn't know that for sure. People got mugged down here. It didn't happen all that often, but it was a danger. And there was that girl from Oklahoma who'd been abducted from the bathroom of one of the city's nightclubs just a week before. The police still hadn't found her, or her kidnapper. Rafe thought that Miranda would present quite the prize to someone who was on the prowl and looking for defenseless young women, especially since she didn't have any magical talents to protect herself.

When he couldn't come up with a coherent plan as to what he should do next, he'd called Cat. Not so much because he thought she could help remedy the situation, but because he needed to talk to someone, and he could trust her not to go blabbing to their mother. If Miranda didn't resurface, then Genoveva would have to be told what had happened, but Rafe would prefer to put off that evil day for as long as possible.

"Yeah, okay, I know I screwed up," he told his sister. "You can give me crap about it as much as you want, but that's not going to help me find Miranda."

Cat crossed her arms, and Rafe had the uncomfortable impression that she fully planned to take him up on that offer. However, her next words were sensible enough, not accusatory at all. "Have you tried calling her?"

Not quite looking at his sister, he replied, "I don't have her number."

"Oh, for God's sake." She rummaged through

the embroidered backpack that served as her purse, then pulled out her phone and said, "Call Miranda."

Rafe watched, thinking, *Please God, let it be this easy....*

But the phone just rang and rang, and eventually he could hear Miranda's voice coming through the tiny speaker, saying, *Hey, I can't take your call right now, but leave a message. Or text me. Thanks!*

Cat was frowning, but she kept her voice light and pleasant as she said, "Hey, Miranda, it's Cat. I'm worried about you. Give me a call when you get this, but I'll try to text you, too." She pushed a button to end the call, then said, "Text message."

The phone's screen lit up, and Cat dictated more or less the same message she'd left on Miranda's voicemail. When she was done, she sent a significant glance in Rafe's direction. "Well, that's about all I can do on that front. I already called Marco, and he's driving down from Taos, but he won't be here for a while."

Marco Ruiz was a Castillo clan warlock whose talent was locating things, both people and inanimate objects. Rafe was sure his cousin would be able to find Miranda once he got here; he just wished Taos wasn't an hour and a half away.

And he also wished he'd thought of Marco while he was frantically trying to find Miranda somewhere in the shops down by the Plaza. His brains were so fried, it had taken Cat's suggestion to get their cousin on the case.

In the meantime, though, there had to be something else they could do.

"What if we try asking some of the shop owners if they've seen anyone matching Miranda's description?"

Cat shook her head. "That would take forever. Besides, enough of them know us that word would get back to Mom soon enough. Then we'd be wasting our time explaining ourselves to her instead of trying to find Miranda."

True enough. Rafe found himself somewhat relieved by the way Cat had said "we" and "us." It meant she felt like she was part of this, instead of backing off and telling him to clean up his own mess. Of course, he hadn't really expected her to behave in such a way, because that wasn't Cat. Family loyalty wouldn't allow her to abandon him. He supposed he should be glad that her loyalty seemed to be more to him than the clan at large, or their parents in particular. That was partly due to their being closer in age, while both their older sisters were in their early thirties. Anyway, Genoveva wasn't exactly the world's most sympathetic mother, and Eduardo, their father, was so busy with his restaurants that he'd gladly relinquished most of his parental duties to his wife once all his children were of age.

Their parents' relationship was downright weird, no matter how you looked at it. They spent much of their time apart because of Eduardo's schedule, but when they were together, they seemed affectionate enough, stealing kisses, sharing discreet little touches on the arm or hand. Whether all those gestures were signs of true affection or only some biochemical byproduct of their consort bond, Rafe really didn't know. What he did know, despite those public displays of affection, was that his parents' marriage wasn't exactly a great advertisement for the institution, which only cemented his desire to avoid it for as long as possible.

Especially when said institution involved a girl he didn't even know.

An image of Miranda flashed into his head then, of the angry spark in her green eyes and the way her full mouth had pressed itself into a furious line right before she turned and walked away from him. As much as he'd been set against marrying her, he had to admit she was gorgeous, far more beautiful in person than in the images Angela McAllister had sent to his mother. If he'd met her in the usual way, at a friend's party or out on the town somewhere, he probably would have tried to ask her out. What he hated about this entire situation was the way he'd been forced into it. He really didn't have anything against Miranda as a person. How could he? He barely knew her. In a way, her walking out had shocked him so much simply because before that moment, he hadn't even thought of her as a person, only an obstacle to the life he wanted to make for himself. But in that moment, he'd realized she probably wasn't any happier about the situation than he was, had her own hopes and dreams that had been forced aside to fulfill the bargain their parents had made.

And he knew he really hadn't intended to upset her so much, but Rafe was aware that he did have an unfortunate habit of tripping over his own tongue.

"If we're not going to ask around, then what do you propose we do?" he asked his sister.

"Oh, we're going to ask around, but we're going to do it my way."

"Your way?"

She'd been playing with the edge of one of the brick-colored throw pillows that had come with the couch, but now she pushed it away and got to her feet. "I'll ask the ghosts. There are a bunch in this part of town, and they see everything. I mean, what else do they have to do except hang around and watch what the living are up to?"

The notion hadn't even entered his mind, but

Rafe thought Cat's idea was a good one. As she'd said, the ghosts would have seen everything going on in their immediate vicinity, and, unlike mortal shopkeepers, they wouldn't be inclined to let Genoveva Castillo know that her son and daughter had been asking odd questions about their house guest.

"Okay," he said. "Where do you want to start?"

Cat paused for a moment, considering. "Well, there's Alfonso. He hangs out on the corner of San Francisco Street and Old Santa Fe Trail. Did you notice which way Miranda left the hotel?"

"Definitely the side entrance, the one on Santa Fe Trail. That is, it looked like she was headed in that direction. I guess she could have cut through one of the shops, like Detours or Mama's Minerals and gone another way, but I sort of doubt it."

"Then Alfonso would have seen her." A smile touched Cat's lips, revealing her one-sided dimple. "Alfonso's a sucker for pretty girls."

It was somewhere to start. And as Rafe followed his sister out of the house, he reflected that sometimes it was a good thing to be part of a witch clan. If Miranda had been an ordinary missing girl, and he and Cat civilians with no magical powers, they'd have a much harder time finding her.

At least, he hoped that Cat's magic could bail him out. If not, he was going to have a lot of explaining to do in the very near future.

They got in her Mercedes, mostly because it was parked out front and provided a quicker getaway than having to pull his ancient Wrangler out of the garage. As Cat pointed her SUV downtown, she tapped her fingers impatiently on the steering wheel, clearly annoyed that she had to let the vehicle do the driving for her, which meant obeying the local posted speed limits.

Sometimes, Rafe reflected, *it would be nice to be able to actually ride broomsticks. It would be so much faster.*

That was a talent he didn't possess, and neither did anyone else in his clan. He'd heard that Miranda's parents had the talent to instantly teleport from place to place. That would be a helpful ability to have, but again, it certainly wasn't a gift he or anyone else he knew actually possessed.

All the damn rules about self-driving cars were part of the reason he kept driving the Wrangler. He'd sought it out, knowing that vehicles more than ten years old were exempt from the local ordinances about not being able to manually operate a car in the zone near the Plaza. More than once, Genoveva had lamented his dislike for following rules, for always questioning authority, but Rafe didn't care. Some rules were meant to be ignored.

Eventually, they did reach downtown, although traffic was thick, thanks to the usual influx of tourists coming in on a Friday afternoon. Cat parked in the garage at the La Fonda, since hunting for street parking would have only wasted more precious time, and neither of them wanted to go to the lot their family owned in case they ran into someone they knew. Without speaking, they got out of the Mercedes and took the stairs down to the ground floor, then hurried through the crowded lobby of the historic hotel and out to the street on the other side.

The corner of Old Santa Fe Trail and San Francisco Street where Cat hoped to find her ghost was occupied by a high-end clothing store. They didn't go inside, but lingered on the corner, and Rafe could only be glad for that bit of discretion. He hated having to fend off salespeople.

But apparently Cat didn't see any need to go into the store. She paused on the corner and drew her phone out of the backpack that served as her purse, pretending to be occupied with whatever was on its screen. Good idea—that way she wouldn't look quite so crazy when she started talking to thin air.

"Alfonso," she said, her voice low and clear. "Are you there?"

A long pause, during which Rafe could only stand off to one side and do his best to keep watch. None of the tourists passing by seemed to show much of an interest in the two of them, but you never knew. He'd seen his sister contact ghosts before, and so the experience had lost some of its novelty. Actually, in a lot of ways it was sort of boring, because of course he couldn't actually see or hear what the ghosts were doing, could only observe his sister's reactions.

Cat spoke after a long pause. "Hi, Alfonso. Yes, I know it's been a while. I've been busy. And you?" Another pause. "Oh, well, I hope for your sake they decide not to go ahead with the remodel. I know that would be disruptive." She was silent for a few seconds, then said, "Alfonso, my brother and I are looking for a friend. We were supposed to meet her down here, but she hasn't shown up. We were wondering if you'd seen her." A shorter pause this time. "She's a little younger than I am, with long wavy brown hair and green eyes. She was wearing a green leather jacket. Did you—Are you sure…? Well, thanks, Alfonso. It's okay. We'll keep looking." Disappointment was obvious in her expression as she turned to Rafe. "Alfonso says he hasn't seen anyone like that today."

"He's sure?"

"Sounds like it. He says he would have

remembered her because green is his favorite color."

And if it wasn't to begin with, it might become a person's favorite color after seeing the deep, moody green of Miranda McAllister's eyes. Rafe wanted to shake his head at himself for that thought. If he'd spent a little more time letting himself get lost in Miranda's eyes rather than trying to pick a fight with her, they wouldn't be in this mess.

"Well, hell." Rafe ran a hand through his hair and looked around, hoping against hope that he might see her somewhere in the crowds around them. "This was the most logical direction for her to go, based on where she seemed to be heading when she left the restaurant."

"True, but she could have stayed on the same side of the street as the hotel, which means she wouldn't have gone past Alfonso's hangout." Raising a hand to her eyes to shield them from the afternoon sunlight, she, too, looked around at their surroundings, clearly wishing she could see some trace of their lost McAllister witch. "Or she could have cut across San Francisco Street and gone directly to the Plaza. Maybe she went up to Palace Avenue to look at the shops there."

"You have any ghostly friends in that area?"

Cat grinned. "Of course I do. Let's go take a look."

They waited for the light to change, then crossed back to where they'd started, and again so they'd end up in the Plaza. Despite the chilly air, plenty of tourists and locals out for an afternoon constitutional filled the walkways there. Once again Rafe scanned the crowds, but he didn't see any sign of his wayward would-be wife.

They cut across the Plaza on the diagonal, ending up on Palace Avenue not far from the cathedral, and one of the restaurants their father owned. Rafe supposed he should have known there were some ghosts hanging out in the building, because the properties here also belonged to the family, but he had never asked his sister for a complete catalogue of Santa Fe's ghosts. That would have been a lot to keep track of, and he'd always thought he had better things to do with his time. Now, though, he could only be glad of Cat's otherworldly contacts, even though the last one hadn't been of much help.

Once again she paused in a quiet spot and took out her phone as camouflage. Rafe pretended to look in the shop window, staring at the expensive Native American jewelry without really seeing it. What if Cat struck out here, too? How long would it take to interview all the ghosts in the area to see if any of them had spotted Miranda?

Cat was speaking in a low voice, reaching out to someone called Gabriela. Once again she asked the same question, whether the spirit who lingered in this area had seen someone matching Miranda's description. It was easy enough to see that Miranda hadn't come this way, either, judging by Cat's responses to the ghost's replies.

"Well, crap," she said, after she thanked the unseen Gabriela and shoved her phone back in her purse. "Nothing here, either. It's like she disappeared into thin air."

If it had been anyone other than Miranda McAllister, Rafe might have entertained that as a possibility, since some witches and warlocks did have that talent, including her own parents. But Miranda was a *nunca,* someone with nothing more than the most basic of powers, like opening locks and touching flame to candles. She couldn't disappear.

Did that mean the worst had happened? Had someone actually taken her?

Cat's phone buzzed within her backpack/purse, and she pulled it out. The expression of worry she'd been wearing turned to one of relief as she read the words on the screen.

"Miranda?" Rafe asked, trying to quell the flare of hope that awoke within him.

"No," Cat replied. "Marco. He's just coming into town now, so he should be down here in a few more minutes." She lifted the phone and typed in a quick text, then hit Send. "I told him where we are and to meet us here. We'll have to hang tight for a few minutes."

Hanging tight was the last thing Rafe felt like doing, but he knew if Cat's ghosts weren't going to come through for them, then their cousin Marco was their best hope. "He made good time," he said, his tone neutral.

"Yes, he did. He must have sped the whole way. Or at least," she added, "as fast as anyone can go through Española."

Which wasn't very fast, since the whole town seemed designed to catch you at every light. More than once pressure had been brought to bear to create a relief route for the little town in the Rio Grande Valley, just as had been done here in Santa Fe for those who didn't intend to go into the heart of the city. But the local tribal elders kept putting their foot down, and so the traffic situation in Española remained pretty much as it was. Whenever he went to Taos, Rafe used the high road, which cut through the mountains and avoided Española altogether. Problem was, it really wasn't any faster...it just felt that way.

He shrugged, and they fell into a waiting silence, Cat checking her phone again, as if she thought that Miranda might suddenly want to reach out and make contact. From the way his sister sighed and put her phone away, however, it was pretty obvious that she hadn't received any useful information.

The chimes in the cathedral began to boom. One...two...three.... Hard to believe that it had been three hours since Miranda had stormed out of the restaurant. What on earth could she have been doing all that time?

"Too bad we can't hack into Ryde, see if she went someplace else," he said. For all they knew, Miranda had given up on the Plaza and its surrounding shops hours ago, and had gone to the Railyard to watch a movie in the theater there.

Cat made a derisive noise. "We're witches, Rafe, not the NSA."

It would have been more useful if they had been government agents. Right now they could only rely on the motley talents that had been with them since birth. He had to hope that Marco's gift would be more useful than Cat's had turned out to be.

And there was his cousin now, coming down the street from the direction of the parking lot behind Rafe's father's restaurant. Probably Marco had taken advantage of one of the Castillo clan's reserved spots, rather than hunting for street parking.

"Hey," he said as he approached Rafe and Cat, a little out of breath. A year younger than Rafe, Marco was much huskier, thanks to a fondness for tamales and little inclination for physical exercise. "I got here as soon as I could." He looked up at Rafe. "You have a picture of her?"

Nodding, Rafe got out his phone and found one of the images of Miranda that his mother had emailed to him. The photo had been taken somewhere outside, maybe in Sedona, since you could see red rocks and blue, blue skies off in the distance. Miranda was smiling, looking very different from the guarded young woman Rafe had met only yesterday.

Marco's lips pursed, as if he wanted to whistle and then realized that sort of reaction probably wouldn't be met with much enthusiasm. "Okay, got it," he said. His eyes shut, and Rafe guessed his cousin must be reaching out with his talent, trying to find the girl he'd just seen in the picture.

Cat moved a little closer to their cousin, doing her best to block him from the people passing by. Good idea. Rafe shifted his position slightly as well, shielding him from those who were coming down Palace Avenue and heading to the Plaza. If someone came right up to them, of course they'd still be able to see a man standing there in front of the store, eyes closed, but at least the casual observer probably wouldn't notice anything particularly strange about what Marco was doing.

Then his eyes opened, and he shook his head. "I'm not getting anything."

Rafe tried to ignore the worry that surged in him once again. "What do you mean, you're not getting anything? I thought your gift was for finding lost people, missing stuff."

"It is." Marco glanced from Rafe to Cat, possibly hoping she'd come to his defense. "I've never had this happen before. If I know what something looks like, I know how to find it, even if it's far away. When I shut my eyes, it's like I can see where the thing I'm looking for is, and I just *know*. But right now?" His chubby shoulders lifted. "I got nothing. I don't know what to say."

Cat put on a sympathetic smile. "Can you try again? Should we go someplace quieter? Maybe all these people are distracting you—"

"No," Marco said at once. "I've never had a problem like that. Hell, I found the diamond out of my Aunt Sophia's wedding ring at her daughter's *quinceañera,* and there were hundreds of people at that party, stomping all over the dance floor. But I suppose I can try again, just in case."

"Please," Cat said.

Marco's eyes closed again, and Rafe saw the way his cousin pulled in a deep breath, trying to center himself, trying to tap into the power he'd been given. A minute passed, an excruciating one during which Rafe didn't even want to move for fear he might interrupt the waves or whatever it was that sent the pertinent information into Marco's brain.

But then he shook his head. "Nope, sorry. When I try to think of your girl, all I see is swirling darkness. She's just not there."

Hell. Rafe jammed his hands in his pockets, attempting to push back against the wave of despair that went over him upon hearing his cousin's words. Cat's ghosts hadn't seen Miranda, and now Marco the infallible object-finder had also fallen down on the job. It was as though she'd disappeared completely from the face of the planet. Once again Rafe thought of how Miranda's parents could teleport. Had she called them, told them how she'd been treated? Maybe they'd come to fetch her away.

That seemed the most likely explanation. Actually, he hoped that was exactly what had happened, because even though today's events would paint him in a very bad light with the Arizona witch clans, at least if Miranda was with her parents, then she was safe.

Of course, that begged the question as to what he should do now. He didn't have the Arizona clan leaders' contact information, which meant he'd have to get it from his mother. Which meant she would then find out what had happened…which meant she would be royally pissed off.

Terrible as it sounded, it might be better if he

didn't do anything right away. Surely if Miranda had gone home with her parents, they'd reach out at some point to let Genoveva know the marriage was off. He'd still have to deal with the fallout, but he would have gained a little time to figure out how to deal with it.

And what if she isn't home? he thought then. *What if someone has taken her? What if she's hurt, frightened?*

Damn it. He didn't want to think about that. No, she had to be okay. Even if she wasn't, what could he do about it? He'd done his best to find her. He could go to Genoveva right now and tell her the whole sordid story, and there probably wasn't anything else she could do, either. Not if Marco's gift was useless. Not if Santa Fe's resident spirits hadn't seen a damn thing. Rafe had never heard of someone's magical talent failing so utterly, and that it was happening now made Miranda's disappearance all the more upsetting.

Where the hell *was* she?

"It's okay," Rafe said at length, knowing that both Cat and Marco were watching him, waiting for him to respond. "Thanks for trying."

"Sorry, man."

Rafe knew he should offer something to his cousin as a thank-you for driving all the way down here—at least buy him a beer or something —but he didn't feel like doing that. All he wanted to do was go home and see if he could figure out what to do next. He needed some peace and quiet. The noise in the street here was starting to make him crazy.

"Thanks, Marco," Cat said. "Do you want to grab something to eat?"

Oh, God no. Even though he hadn't eaten anything since breakfast, Rafe was pretty sure he couldn't handle going out for a mid-afternoon snack with their cousin.

"No, I'm good," Marco replied. "I called Tony and told him I was coming down here. We're going to try this new brewpub he found out in Tesuque."

"Sounds like fun," Cat said. She was still smiling slightly, although the expression made her face look strained, as though she was doing her best to keep that smile from cracking into a thousand pieces.

"Hope so." Marco glanced over at Rafe. "Again, I'm sorry, man. I hope you find your girl."

He waved at both of them before turning and heading back to where his car was parked. As soon as he was out of earshot, Cat said, "What now?"

"I don't know," Rafe replied dully. "I just don't know."

8

SECRETS

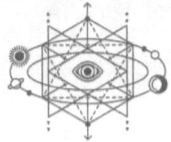

Miranda

OH, GODDESS, MY HEAD WAS KILLING ME. I sat up on the couch and looked around the unfamiliar room, a panic-induced adrenaline rush moving through me as I tried to remember where the hell I was.

Then I saw Simon come toward where I sat, a glass of water in his hand. He didn't try to sit down on the sofa, but only extended the water to me.

"Are you doing better?"

"I don't know." I took the water from him with a shaking hand and gulped it down, my body as dehydrated as though I'd just walked fifty miles in dry desert heat. The water didn't exactly get rid of the headache, but the pain did settle down to a dull pounding. "Maybe."

Facing the sofa was a plain wood cross-back chair with a blue cushion. Simon picked it up and moved it a little closer to the couch, then sat down. "I didn't like leaving you here, but I was the only person scheduled to work this afternoon, so—"

"It's okay," I cut in. "All I did was sleep." *And I must look like hell, too, after spending five hours passed out on some strange guy's sofa.*

"Well, it seems to have helped a little. I—I'm sorry about what happened," he added, the words coming out in a rush. "If I'd known the wine would affect you like that, I never would have poured you a second glass."

I frowned. "It really shouldn't have," I said. "I mean, it's not like it was my first drink or something—my parents let me have wine at home, as long as I didn't get carried away." I sighed, thinking of those family meals at the big table, which had felt a lot bigger the last few years, with both Ian and Emily settled and moved into their own homes. But it had still been fun with only my parents and me, because they'd bring home wine from one of the local vineyards and talk about it, and tell me why they'd decided to pair it with whatever we were eating that particular night.

Thinking about home probably wasn't a very good idea. Just the memory of our dining room in the Jerome house, with the wrought-iron chandelier overhead and the sideboard flickering with candles, made a sharp ache start somewhere in my chest. It couldn't be a heart attack, because I was way too young for that sort of thing. No, the discomfort was something much more mundane, but no less painful.

I really hadn't thought I would be this homesick. I'd thought I would come to Santa Fe and become part of the Castillo clan, and they would become my new family. Not once had I entertained the idea that Rafe might reject me, that I wouldn't fit in at all. Faced with that unhappy reality, I wasn't sure what I should do next.

"It was probably that you hadn't eaten anything," Simon said. He rubbed his chin, then added, his tone diffident, "Can you eat now? Because I think it would be a good idea…if you can manage it."

There was a question. I drank a few more sips of water and sat quietly, doing my best to assess my current condition. Although my head hurt, it seemed to be rapidly improving, and the water didn't appear to have upset my stomach. In fact, thinking about my tummy seemed to have woken it up, because it came alive then, letting me know in no uncertain terms that it needed food, and now.

"I could eat," I said cautiously. Was he asking me out to dinner?

Apparently he was, because he said, "Then let's go to El Sótano. It's less than half a block from here, and the food's good."

"Okay," I replied. Even as I agreed, I inwardly vowed that I would pay for this meal. I knew Simon wasn't exactly rolling in cash, and I could afford to cover our dinner. Besides, I owed him one. He'd made sure to get me someplace safe where I could sleep off my weird drunk. Some guys would have just let me walk out of that wine tasting room to fend for myself.

"The bathroom's down that hall, if you want to tidy up first."

Which was probably Simon's polite way of letting me know that my hair needed brushing and my lip gloss some reapplication. I murmured a thank-you, then grabbed my purse and went to the door he'd indicated. Inside was apparently the apartment's sole bathroom, since the tile counter had some of his toiletries ranged across it, and a razor was plugged into the electrical outlet on one wall.

But everything was neat and clean enough, especially for guy in his twenties living on his own. I set my purse down on the counter, then hunted through it for my brush. My hair was definitely smashed on one side from lying on the couch, but a few vigorous strokes from the brush livened it up a bit, and the loose curls I'd put in that morning seemed to be holding. Thank God I'd inherited some wave from my mother and didn't have stick-straight hair that wouldn't cooperate with a curling iron.

Some gloss on my lips, and careful blotting under my eyes to get rid of any mascara smudges. After I was done, the Miranda who looked out at me from the mirror did seem to be immeasurably improved, if a little wan and tired-looking. Some food should help with that, though.

And afterward?

I honestly had no idea. By this point, more than six hours had elapsed since the time I'd walked out of the La Plazuela restaurant. I didn't try to fool myself that Rafe would be sick with worry, but I knew Cat probably was, and I hated to have her suffer for no reason. At some point I'd have to go back and face the music, but for now, it seemed the best thing to do was at least let her know I was alive and okay.

After pulling my phone out of my purse, I found Cat's number in my nearly empty contacts list and sent her a quick message. *I'm okay,* I typed. *I'll be in touch later.* After the text had been safely sent, I put the phone on "do not disturb" mode so I wouldn't have to worry about her interrupting dinner. We could sort out everything after Simon and I were done eating.

When I returned to the living room, I found him also on his phone, although he seemed to be surfing the web, not checking his email. He closed the browser window and stood as I approached.

"Ready?"

"Yes," I said. Was I? I didn't actually know for sure. I felt steadier now, and a little more composed now that I'd let Cat know I wasn't dead in a ditch somewhere, but my hands and legs were still shaky. Some food should fix that problem, though.

He paused at the door. "Are you going to be warm enough? It'll be pretty cold now that the sun's down."

"It's all right if we're just going across the street."

My reply didn't seem to reassure him all that much, but he didn't argue, only shrugged slightly before he grabbed his own jacket from the coat rack by the door. We went downstairs and out through the door in the little foyer in the rear of the building, and so we had to jog down to the alley in order to cut back over to San Francisco Street. All the maneuvering meant we had to walk a bit further than that "just across the street" Simon had mentioned, and I was starting to shiver as we hurried over to the side of San Francisco where the restaurant was located.

But soon enough we were inside, partly because our destination occupied the lower floor of the mercantile building, and we had to take a set of stairs down from street level to get there. The sound of Spanish classical guitar came to my ears. I glanced over at Simon.

"I forgot—they have live music Thursday through Saturday," Simon said. "If you don't like it, we can go someplace else."

"No, this is fine," I said quickly. "I love classical guitar."

He smiled then, and took me over to the hostess station. The girl working there seemed to know him, because she smiled and called him by his name, and guided the two of us over to a secluded table in one corner. The guitarist, a man in his thirties with his black hair pulled back in a severe ponytail, was sitting in the opposite corner, but because the restaurant wasn't very big, the music was still loud enough, just on the verge of being too loud for Simon and me to have a decent conversation but not all the way there.

I looked around before I picked up the menu, liking the lively color scheme of the place, from the bright lime green paint on the walls to the canvases of local art that had been hung everywhere, Technicolor pieces depicting pueblos and churches and deep green valleys with rocky red walls on either side. There were three tables and six booths in all, about half of them occupied.

No one was paying any particular attention to Simon and me, and I liked it that way. Also, I could tell that no one else in the restaurant was of witch-kind, something I found reassuring. I didn't have any real talents, but at least I had the same inborn ability as all other magical folk to be able to tell when there were others of my kind in the immediate vicinity. Since I didn't sense anything, I didn't have to worry about whether some of the other diners were members of the Castillo clan, and therefore possibly people who would report my whereabouts to Genoveva.

I didn't dare order a glass of wine, and Simon took his cue from me, also asking for just water. Some of the menu items weren't familiar to me, since the restaurant seemed to have a South American slant to its food, but luckily, everything had a description. We ordered pupusas as an appetizer, and I opted for a cheese enchilada, hoping that something so bland wouldn't do too much damage to my stomach. Simon ordered carne asada and I was glad, because it was one of the more expensive menu items and therefore well-suited for me to show him just how much I appreciated the way he'd let me crash at his place for the afternoon by paying for dinner.

"You want to talk about it?" he asked after the waitress had brought us our water and then disappeared into the kitchen to place our orders. "If you don't, that's fine, but it's pretty obvious that you've got a lot weighing on your mind."

There was an understatement. He'd done so much to help me—surely it couldn't hurt if I gave him just a bit of information. Obviously, not anything about my being from a witch clan, or revealing that another, larger clan lived in Santa Fe and had for generations, but I didn't have to mention any of that to let him know I'd been sent here to marry someone I'd never met before.

"It's—it's going to sound kind of crazy."

He smiled, his fingers touching his water glass, although he didn't lift it to his mouth to take a drink. "I'm from Santa Fe. Crazy is kind of in the air around here."

You have no idea, I thought, remembering the ghost I'd met at Tony's Halloween party. I wasn't even supposed to be able to see ghosts, let alone talk to them.

So why had I encountered Victoria?

"I came to Santa Fe to get married," I said in a rush, and at once Simon's face fell. Although I hated to be the source of any kind of disappointment for him, in a way I was also flattered. If he hadn't felt some form of attraction toward me, then he wouldn't have cared whether or not I was supposed to be married to someone else.

"Oh," he said, his tone flat. This time he did pick up his glass of water and took a big swallow. "When's the happy day?"

"I don't know," I replied honestly.

His eyebrows lifted. "Huh?"

"It—it was arranged," I told him. "I'd never even met the guy before yesterday. Supposedly we're going to get married after we've had a chance to get to know each other a little better, but since about all we've done since we met is fight, I'm not sure how well that's going to work out."

"Arranged?" Simon pronounced the word as if he'd never heard it before, his thin but somehow elegant mouth flattening in disapproval. "Isn't that kind of, I don't know, old-fashioned?"

"Very. But it was something his mother worked out with my mother before I was even born. I didn't have any say in the matter."

"Well, you must have had some, because you're here now. It's not like they locked you in a basement or something."

Wait until tomorrow, I thought, but I didn't say the words aloud. Right then, it seemed entirely possible that Genoveva would lock me up somewhere until I was safely married to her son. Oh, come on—she really wouldn't do that…would she?

Unfortunately, I got the feeling that there wasn't much Genoveva Castillo wouldn't do, if sufficiently provoked. Oh, I didn't think she was evil or anything, didn't think she practiced dark magic like the warlock who'd caused so much trouble for my parents before I was even born, but I could tell Genoveva was used to getting her own way, using her role as *prima* to move the people around her like pawns on a chessboard. It wasn't that hard to imagine her keeping me in the casita until Rafe's and my wedding day rolled around… and I thought she'd probably move that day up as soon as she found out about my disappearance this afternoon. Allowing the two of us time to get to know one another was one thing, but if she learned I'd used that time to get to know someone who wasn't her son, she probably would throw those noble sentiments right out the window.

"They're trying to be nice," I said, then sipped some of my water. "Give me my space, you know? But I don't think that's going to go on for too much longer."

Simon gave me a sympathetic nod. "What are you going to do? Go home?"

"No," I replied. The strange thing was, as terrible as this day had been, I hadn't once thought of calling my parents, hadn't once considered contacting them to ask if they could take me home. I supposed I could have, but this was my problem, and I needed to work it out. The first two decades of my life I'd had Mommy and Daddy making sure I was okay, looking out for me. It wasn't their fault; I knew they still carried the guilt of agreeing to hand me over to the Castillos in the first place, and so they overcompensated by doing their best to make sure my life was smooth and serene, and as free as possible from any uncomfortable bumps. My childhood had been a happy one, but I would be the first to admit that it hadn't done much to prepare me for living in the real world...not that coming here to Santa Fe to be a member of the Castillo witch clan was exactly living in the real world, either.

A frown touched Simon's brow. He fiddled with his fork and couldn't seem to look at me directly. "You're going to marry this guy?"

"I...I don't know."

This time Simon did look up, his dark eyes boring into mine. We might have only known each other for a day and a half, but I was fooling myself if I thought he wasn't interested...and also hurt and angry that I might be considering marriage to someone I didn't love. "Well, if you don't want to go home, and you don't know if you're going to get married, then what are you planning to do?"

"I don't know," I said again, hating that I must sound like a complete idiot, even though I had no other response to give. "I guess I need to see if we can make this work. If not...well, then I guess I will go home. I don't have a lot of options."

Simon traced a forefinger along the edge of his plate. Again he wasn't looking at me, and I couldn't blame him. He must have been feeling even more confused than I was. "I'd like to be one of your options."

Gratitude—and more than a little shame—washed over me. "Simon, I can't ask you to look out for me. We barely know each other."

"So what?" he said. "I like you, Miranda. You're—I've never met a girl like you before. I don't want to see you go back to Arizona. And I also don't want to see you hooking up with this guy you're supposed to marry, because he sounds like an asshole. But...I also get it. Your parents made a promise, and you don't want to be the one to break it."

He still wasn't quite looking at me, but I could hear the sincerity in his voice. And oh, right then I wished we didn't have the table separating us, because I would have reached over to give him a hug. Then again, maybe hugging him wasn't the best idea. I could tell I was attracted to Simon, but we'd had basically zero physical contact. It was probably better to keep it that way, for fear of starting something I knew I couldn't finish.

"Yes, that's exactly it," I said, glad that my

voice sounded so steady. I knew I needed to try again with Rafe, no matter what kind of tenuous attraction existed between Simon and me, if only because I didn't want to admit to failure so soon after coming here. Very likely, I was only reaching out to him because I'd been so careful not to allow any real connection to any of the guys I'd known back home. Now that I was off leash, so to speak, I'd glommed on to the first man my age I'd met. I didn't know if any of this was real, or merely a reaction to circumstance. "I—I really appreciate what you've done for me, Simon. I could have been wandering the streets like a drunk if you hadn't taken me in."

"Yeah, and you wouldn't have been drunk if I hadn't been pouring those glasses of wine for you," he returned, his expression troubled. "I'm not sure I did you any huge favors. But I'm glad I could give you a place to crash."

A place where I'd crashed for hours and hours, while Cat and Rafe and, for all I knew, the entire Castillo clan was looking for me. I'd only extended my disappearance by going out to dinner with Simon, but I told myself my body needed the food. I would have been a wreck if I'd tried to meet with Rafe on an empty stomach, all that alcohol still churning around in my guts with nothing to soak it up.

As soon as the thought crossed my mind, I

realized that was what I needed to do. I needed to see Rafe, try to get this worked out, and the sooner, the better. I supposed I could have gone back to the casita and gotten a good night's sleep first, but that seemed the coward's way out. No, I needed to confront the situation head on.

"And I appreciate it," I said. "I really do. But now...."

"Now you need to go to him."

Thank the Goddess that Simon was so perceptive. I didn't have to explain myself to him; he seemed to instinctually understand what I had to do. "Yes, I need to have a long talk. But can I have your number? I'd still like to be friends, if that's okay."

A hesitation that was impossible to ignore, but then his shoulders lifted slightly, and he got his phone out of his pocket. "Sure."

I got out my phone, too, and we touched them briefly so our information would be transferred to each other. As much as I would have liked to linger in the restaurant and put off the evil hour of the coming confrontation for as long as possible, I knew that wasn't a good idea. I needed to get this over with, if for no other reason than the desire to know exactly where I stood. It was hard to plan for the future when you didn't have any idea what your next step was supposed to be.

"I guess this is it," Simon said. He had a few bites of carne asada left on his plate, but from the way he pushed them around without lifting any of them to his mouth, I figured he was done.

"Unless you want dessert," I replied, trying to lighten the mood and failing miserably.

He shook his head. "No, I think we're finished."

The waitress seemed to realize we'd reached a stopping point, because she came over and asked if we wanted anything else. I told her no and asked for the bill. She pulled her tablet out of a pocket of the apron she wore, and I quickly handed over my phone so she could scan it.

This all happened so fast that Simon really didn't have a chance to intervene. Once the waitress was gone, he said, "I would have paid for dinner."

"I'm sure you would, but this is the least I could do to say thanks for taking care of me this afternoon."

His mouth drooped. "Am I ever going to see you again?"

"I don't know," I said honestly. "I hope so. Like you told me, Santa Fe isn't that big a town."

I got up from my seat then, and paused next to him for a moment so I could lay a reassuring hand on his shoulder. After that, I made my way to the entrance and climbed the stairs to street level, at the same time using the app on my phone to summon a Ryde vehicle. They must have cruised the downtown area in decent numbers, because I got confirmation that one would be in my location in less than two minutes.

So I stood at the curb, phone in hand, and waited. I honestly didn't know whether I was doing the right thing.

I only knew that I was doing what needed to be done.

9

MISUNDERSTANDINGS

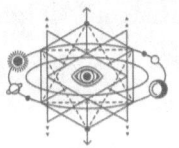

As soon as I climbed in the back seat of the Ryde—a late-model Toyota—I spoke, telling the AI that controlled it what I wanted. "Can you just circle the Plaza for a few minutes? I'll have my actual destination after that."

"Certainly," said the mechanical voice, and the car headed east on San Francisco Street at a leisurely pace. "You understand that certain portions of the streets immediately adjacent to the Plaza are blocked to vehicle traffic and are not accessible."

"Yes, I know," I replied as I went to my contacts list to find Cat's information. I would have to contact her manually, without using voice commands, or I risked confusing the AI that controlled the vehicle where I now sat. "Just stay in the general area."

"Of course."

Texting seemed safer than making a phone call. It turned out that she had replied to the hasty text I'd sent from Simon's apartment—replied a total of five times, all of the messages variations on "where the hell are you?" I ignored all that and wrote, *I need to talk to Rafe in person, but I don't know where he lives. Can you give me his address?*

The answer came back almost at once. *We've been worried sick. Where are you?*

I'm down near the Plaza. I'm fine. But I need to see Rafe.

This time she didn't reply as quickly. But after a gap of about thirty seconds, the answer came back. *All right. He lives at 318 Magdalena Rd.*

Thanks, I responded. *I appreciate it.*

Another pause. Then, *I hope you can work it out.*

So did I.

I put my phone in my purse and told the Ryde, "We're going to 318 Magdalena Road."

"Yes, ma'am."

The car accelerated slightly, then jogged to the right so it could turn left on Alameda. After that, I lost track of all the twists and turns we made, although it seemed we were headed to an area that was located slightly to the north and east of the actual downtown area. The Ryde headed down a narrow street with large adobe-style houses on either side and came to a stop next to one of them, a two-story structure with autumn-bare aspens clustered around it. Most people probably would have wondered how a twenty-six-year-old man with an odd vocation could have afforded a place like this, but it was par for the course in witch families, especially for someone closely connected to the *prima*. Money was not a problem.

My phone chimed, indicating that the Ryde had sent the bill to me. Since I had the app set up for auto-pay, I ignored the chime and got out of the car, then followed the sidewalk until it led me to the front door of the house. I could see a few lights inside, but the place still seemed dark and dim. What if Rafe wasn't even home? He might have decided to work through his anger by getting together with some friends, going out to get something to eat, or a few beers.

But I was here now, and I had to try.

Before I could lose my nerve, I put my finger on the button for the doorbell and pressed it. At once I heard it ring inside the house. I held on to my purse with my other hand, hanging on to it for dear life as though it was a life preserver, the only thing keeping me from drowning.

No one came to the door, and I pulled in a

breath. I wasn't that worried about being stranded here, because of course I could just call another Ryde and have it take me to the Castillo house on Gonzales Street. It would be an anticlimax, that was for sure, but I could always try again later. After all, just because Cat had given me her brother's address, it didn't mean she'd known for sure that he would be home.

Then the door opened and Rafe stood there, staring down at me. In the dim light from the wrought iron and amber glass fixture next to the doorway, he looked very tall, very brooding. He said briefly, "Cat told me you were on your way over," and stepped aside so I could enter the house.

I wasn't quite sure what to make of his greeting. True, he hadn't told me to get out, so that was a good sign, but on the other hand, he'd certainly sounded cold and curt. But then, what had I expected? For him to welcome me with open arms after I'd walked out on him?

"Yes, I needed to get your address from her," I said, then steeled myself to enter the house and walk past him.

"This way," he said. He shut the door and led me down a short corridor, into the living room. In contrast to the traditional adobe style of the home's exterior, the furniture and art here was modern and spare, two couches of beige linen facing each other across a travertine coffee table. The only real color was in the brick-colored throw pillows on the couches and the abstract art on the walls. And yet, because of the honey-toned wood floors and the wooden beams on the ceiling above, the effect wasn't cold, but subtly calming.

I wondered if Rafe had decorated the place, or whether he'd hired someone to do it. No, I couldn't imagine him relinquishing that kind of control to a decorator. Maybe to his sister, or someone else he really trusted, but not a stranger.

"You want a glass of water?" he asked.

Considering how dry my mouth was, water sounded like a good idea. "Yes, please."

"Go ahead and sit down. I'll go get some."

Clearly, he didn't want me to follow him into the kitchen. Since I knew I was on thin ice already, I didn't try to ignore his request. Instead, I went and sat down on one of the couches, and clasped my hands on my lap. The air smelled faintly of wood smoke, as if he'd had a fire in here during the last couple of days. There was a rounded kiva-style fireplace in one corner, a well-stocked wood basket next to it.

I wondered what the room would look like with a fire going, the flickering light from the flames dancing over the abstract art on the walls. Would the pictures seem to move, take on a life of their own?

Rafe returned, a glass of water in either hand. He gave one to me, then sat down on the couch opposite the sofa where I was perched on the edge of the cushions. His expression was impassive and the light in the room dim, coming from several burnished steel sconces on the walls, so I really couldn't get a read on what he was thinking.

Maybe that was a good thing. Maybe I really didn't want to know what he thought about me.

He spoke first. "You want to tell me where you've been all afternoon?"

"I—" The syllable seemed to catch in my throat, and I drank some of the water Rafe had given me. "I was safe."

"That's not a real answer." He shifted on the sofa so he sat on the edge of the cushions, the same as I had, his hands clasped over one knee. Tension seemed to thrum along every limb, and his dark eyes glittered despite the room's dim light. "We looked for you. Called my cousin Marco down from Taos, because his talent is finding lost objects, missing people. He couldn't find you, and he's never had a problem using his talent before. The ghosts downtown claimed they'd never seen you. It was like you'd disappeared into a black hole."

While all that was strange, and I had no ready answers for why I had been so difficult to locate, it didn't change the fact that I'd been safe and nearby the whole time. "I was right here, in down-town. I was angry when I left the restaurant, and I thought a drink might calm me down. So I went to that tasting room over by the Lensic Theater. I met a friend there, and—"

"A friend?" Rafe cut in, still with that dangerous glitter in his eyes. "You just got here yesterday. You don't know anybody in Santa Fe, except the people you met at the party last night, and they would have let me know that they'd seen you."

"Well," I said disingenuously, "I know one person who isn't a Castillo."

From the way Rafe stiffened, I knew that had been exactly the wrong thing to say. "Who is it?"

This conversation was not going the way I'd planned—or hoped—but I knew I needed to be honest. There wasn't any point in lying, anyway, because since I'd already told Rafe that I'd been in the tasting room by the Lensic, it wouldn't be that difficult for him to visit the place and see who worked there. "His name is Simon. I met him on the Railrunner yesterday as I was coming up from Albuquerque."

None of this information seemed to mollify Rafe in the slightest. "Simon who?"

"I don't know his last name. I never asked. He lives here and goes to school in Albuquerque, at

UNM, and he works part-time in the tasting room."

"So you went to see him because you were angry with me?"

"No," I said at once. I needed make him understand that I hadn't purposely sought out Simon as a sort of refuge. "That's not how it happened. We talked on the ride up from Albuquerque, but he never told me where he worked. I went in to get a glass of wine, and he was there. Total coincidence."

Rafe's fingers tightened on the knees of his jeans. "There's no such thing as coincidence."

"Well, in this case, there was."

Silence for a moment. I could see the way his eyes narrowed, and I guessed that he was trying to look for anything suspicious in what I had just told him. Well, he could look all he wanted, but he wouldn't be able to poke holes in my story because I was telling him the honest truth.

Then he said, "I've been to that tasting room several times, and I've never met anyone named Simon who worked there."

"Which proves what, exactly?" I shot back at him. "Places like that always have lots of part-time help. Just because you haven't bumped into Simon doesn't mean he doesn't have a job there. Also, he's only worked there for about six months. When was the last time you dropped in?"

"I don't know. Maybe close to a year. Some friends and I went there right after they opened."

"Well, then." Judging by the way Rafe had looked away from me, I could tell he didn't like to admit the possibility that he might be wrong about Simon.

"Still…." He reached for his glass of water and sipped, then put it back down on the table. No coaster, which went against all my upbringing, but it was his table. Besides, I doubted a few drops of water could hurt the travertine. "Maybe all that's on the up and up. But I find it hard to believe that it took you more than seven hours to drink a glass of wine."

This was the part of the story I knew would probably bother him the most. However, I knew that I had to tell him the truth. "I was upset. I had a glass of wine, and then another after that. My stomach was empty. I got pretty wasted, so Simon let me crash upstairs at his place."

"You went to his apartment?"

The question was asked in an even enough tone, but that dark glitter was back in Rafe's eyes. I swallowed, then replied, "Yes. It's upstairs from the tasting room. Nothing happened. I passed out on his couch, and he went back downstairs to finish his shift. I didn't wake up until he came back to his apartment after he was done for the day. At that point, I did text Cat to let her know was okay, but I was starving, so Simon and I went across the street to El Sótano to have a quick dinner. After that I contacted Cat to get your address, and I came here. That's the whole story."

"And you never thought to call her before that? She would have come to get you. Better that than sleeping it off in some strange guy's apartment."

Put that way, it did seem as if I'd made one bad decision after another. Problem was, I'd been so far gone that the thought of reaching out to Cat hadn't even crossed my mind. It had been about all I could do to make it to the refuge of Simon's apartment, and I'd only been able to manage that much because he'd helped me up the stairs.

Also, even though I would never admit this to Rafe, I guessed that, deep down, I hadn't wanted to contact Cat because I'd known that I needed some time away from the Castillos. All of them, even the one person I'd begun to think might be a friend.

"I'm sorry you were worried," I said in a small voice. "I didn't mean to upset you, or to cause any trouble. Please tell your cousin I'm sorry he had to come here to try to find me."

Rafe shrugged. "Marco? I think he was glad of the excuse to get out of Taos. He and Tony are going out to party tonight. I'm sure Marco will end up crashing on Tony's couch."

This reply made me feel a little better about the situation, but despite his off-hand manner, it was obvious that Rafe was still angry, less than happy at the story I'd produced to explain my disappearance that afternoon. Driven by an impulse, I got up from the sofa and went to sit down next to him. His eyes widened in surprise, although he didn't attempt to move away from me.

Being this close to him, close enough that I could sense the heat of his body, made a little thrill go through me. My own body didn't appear to have gotten the message that we always seemed to be at odds with one another, because every time I got close enough to Rafe, I reacted with little shivers, or a speeded-up heartbeat, or a flush of warmth. Certainly Simon didn't cause me to respond in anything close to the same way. I felt some kind of attraction for him, but it was nothing like this, something visceral, something I couldn't begin to explain.

"I really am sorry," I said.

For a moment, he didn't speak, didn't move. But then he moved his hand so it could rest on mine, heavy, warm. A bracelet of leather cord and cut hematite beads glittered on his wrist. Had Cat made that for him, or had he picked it up in one of the shops downtown?

"Don't be," he said at last. "You had every right to walk out. I was being an asshole."

"I don't know—" I began, but he shook his head.

"Well, I do. I was so busy being wrapped up in how pissed off I was at my mother, at the whole situation, that I forgot you were caught in the same trap. And it's worse for you, because you had to come to a strange place, had to uproot your life and leave everyone you knew behind."

This little speech was so close to what I'd told myself hundreds of times that tears suddenly stung my eyes. How could he be so compassionate, so understanding, and yet such a jerk at the same time?

"Rafe, I—"

I didn't have the chance to say anything else. He shifted on the couch so he faced me, then reached out and cupped my face in his hands, brought his lips to mine.

The heat I experienced at his nearness was nothing compared to the flood of sensation that swept over me then. I'd never kissed anyone, had held myself as aloof as any *prima*-in-waiting who hadn't yet begun to search for her consort, and right then I was glad I'd held back. I was glad, because my abstinence had meant that my first kiss would be shared with Rafe, the man who seemed to have awakened every nerve ending in my body, leaving me tingling and alive in a way I never had been before.

After a long moment, he pulled away, his dark eyes watching me intently. I somehow knew he wanted me to be the one to speak first, to let him know if I was all right with what he'd just done.

"Wow," I said at last. Not terribly articulate, but I hoped that single syllable would be enough to tell him that it definitely was all right.

"'Wow' is right," he said with a smile. "I was looking at you, looking at how beautiful you are, and I realized how stupid I was for not kissing you before this."

"You were too busy being angry, I guess."

"Again, stupid." He paused, then reached up to touch my hair where it fell over my shoulder. Another little shiver went through me, even more delicious than the first. "You're not going to disappear on me like that again, are you?"

"It depends," I replied, slanting a look at him up through my lashes. "Are you going to be an emotionally distant jackass again?"

To my relief, he chuckled. I hadn't been sure how he would respond to that irreverent question, but it needed to be put out there. He needed to know that I might have come here meekly enough, following our parents' wishes, and yet my actions didn't mean that I intended to let him walk all over me.

"I'll try not to be," he said. "I might backslide every once in a while, though—I've got about twenty years of resentment I need to work through."

"I'll keep that in mind."

He smiled, and lowered his mouth to mine again. All the weariness and worry of the day seemed to disappear the second our lips touched. No, he wasn't my consort, but close enough. Even these few kisses told me that our union could be almost as intimate, almost as deep.

When he drew away from me as the kiss ended, however, the next words he spoke didn't exactly inspire confidence. "What are you going to tell this Simon person?"

Was Rafe jealous? I didn't want to flatter myself, but then again, he wouldn't be asking if he wasn't concerned about the possibility of me seeing Simon in the future. "I already told him I was going to try to work things out with you. Oh, don't worry," I added quickly as I saw a flare of alarm work its way over his features. "I didn't give any specifics. I'm not so stupid that I'd go blabbing about clan business. But it wasn't too hard to talk about what was going on without bringing any witchy stuff into it."

His hand covered mine again. "Good. I mean,

I trust you not to tell strangers what's going on, but…."

"But I'd had a lot to drink. I know. Still, nothing slipped out. He knows I was going to do my best to be with you."

"He must have been disappointed."

"I—I don't know for sure. It's not like anything was going on between us."

"I know it wasn't. You told me. I believe you."

Three simple words, and yet they meant so much to me right then, especially after all our previous bickering. Some of my gratitude must have shown in my face, because Rafe reached out and pulled me close, holding me against his chest. He didn't try to kiss me, just kept his arms wrapped around me, let me listen to the strong, regular beat of his heart.

It felt good. Because I'd made sure never to be intimate with anyone before now, I hadn't realized exactly how good it would feel to be held like this, safe and warm and protected. I wanted the moment to last forever.

Of course it didn't. After a little while, Rafe let go of me, although he touched my hair as I drew away, as if to prolong the moment of contact.

"I should probably take you back," he said, and I blinked up at him, confused.

"Back?"

"To the casita."

"What if I don't want to go back?" I wasn't sure why I was being so bold, but I knew I wanted to stay here with him. I wanted him to kiss me again and again, to take me upstairs to his bedroom. We were already promised to one another, so what difference did it make when we slept together?

"Oh, Miranda." He touched my cheek, his fingers gentle, caressing. "Don't tempt me. But I'd never hear the end of it if I didn't do everything I could to make sure you were 'pure' on our wedding day."

I tilted my head at him and lifted an eyebrow. "Seriously? What year is it?"

"The year doesn't matter to my mother. And, considering how good she is at making your life miserable if you dare cross her, better to go along for now. It won't be that long." He bent and kissed me again, but very softly this time, barely more than a brush of his lips against mine. "Besides, it wasn't so long ago that you seemed more interested in giving me a kick in the nuts than going to bed."

True enough. And intellectually, I understood the reason for his forbearance now. Witches and warlocks didn't care all that much about virginity, unless you were talking about a *prima*, whose "purity" had to be maintained so she could bond correctly with her consort once he was found. Or

I should say, McAllister and Wilcox witches and warlocks didn't care all that much. The Castillos, on the other hand, were extremely Catholic.

Did that mean Rafe was still a virgin?

Despite the intimacies we'd just shared, I didn't think I was up to asking that question. I'd made sure to keep a careful distance between myself and any guys who'd seemed remotely interested, and I didn't want to know if Rafe hadn't practiced that same forbearance.

"All right," I said. "You can take me back to the casita and maintain my purity so your mother doesn't freak out. But I'm not going to wait around forever."

"Neither am I," he replied, his gaze lingering on my lips. "And if I know my mother, she'll kick things into high gear as soon as we give the word."

I assumed by "high gear," he meant that the wedding preparations would be set into motion. Another little shiver went through me, but this time one of worry rather than arousal. No matter how much I liked kissing Rafe, knew that we were intended for each other, the thought of being married in the very near future stirred a flicker of anxiety within me. Marriage was a big deal. In the witch clans especially, marriage was supposed to be forever.

And although I tried to reassure myself that my reactions to Rafe only proved we were supposed to be together—witches and warlocks had a better chance of finding their "one" than most people did—I wondered if it was a good thing to rush the whole process. Going to bed was one thing, but once we were married....

"Then I suppose it's better if I get a good night's sleep," I said lightly, doing my best to push my worries aside.

"Exactly." He got up from the couch, extended a hand to help me get to my feet. I really didn't need the assistance, but it was nice to see that small gentlemanly gesture from him.

We left the living room and turned down a short hallway that ended in a door. On the other side of that door was the garage, with Rafe's ancient Wrangler sitting in solitary splendor in the middle. Without speaking, we both got in, and he opened the door and backed out.

The drive from his place to his mother's compound only took about five minutes. I was glad of his presence, glad that I wouldn't have to come back here by myself, sneaking in like a thief in the night.

He held my hand as we let ourselves in through the gate and headed toward the casita. Solar lights picked out the path, so it wasn't that difficult to find our way.

Unfortunately, the path was blocked before we'd even gone ten paces. Standing there was a very angry Genoveva, her arms crossed, a dark cape thrown over her shoulders to ward off the nighttime chill.

"I hope you have an explanation for all this," she said.

10

DOUBTS

Even with the reassuring pressure of Rafe's fingers on mine, I couldn't prevent a stab of fear from moving through me. Genoveva did look very forbidding as she stood there and blocked our way, the dark cape flowing from her shoulders, her features harsh in the dim light of the solar lamps that lined the path.

However, it seemed that Rafe was used to this sort of thing, because he only smiled and said, "An explanation for what? Miranda was over at my place. I just drove her home. Wasn't the whole point that you wanted us to spend time together?"

Genoveva's lips thinned. In the semidarkness, the dark lipstick she wore looked almost black. "She might have been at your house just now, but she certainly wasn't there all afternoon. I heard how she disappeared."

Oh, hell. I risked a quick glance up at Rafe, but his expression hadn't changed. He still wore a faint smile, one side of his mouth quirked slightly higher than the other. No doubt he'd had years of playing cat and mouse with his mother.

"She needed to cool off for a while," he said. "My fault entirely—I was being a jackass. But she's fine, as you can see. We've worked everything out. It's all good."

"I hardly think that disappearing for hours and hours, and having to call your cousin Marco down from Taos to help out, can be classified as 'good.'" Her gaze moved from Rafe to me, and I made sure I stood there tall and straight, my chin lifted. I might not have had any more powers than your run-of-the-mill civilian, but I was still the daughter of a *prima* and a *primus*; I wasn't about to let Genoveva Castillo cow me. "Where did you go, Miranda?"

"I was downtown the whole time," I replied. Even if Genoveva was somehow magically able to detect a lie, she wouldn't be able to find fault with that reply.

"Doing what?"

"This and that." The *prima* might have been Rafe's mother, but she wasn't mine, and I was damned if I was going to allow her to give me the third degree when I hadn't done anything wrong. There was no need for me to feel like some kid caught sneaking back into her room after breaking curfew. "None of your business, frankly. Rafe doesn't have a problem with how I spent my afternoon, and neither should you."

His smile was gone now, replaced by a faint expression of shock, as if he'd never before witnessed someone talking back to his mother in such a way. Maybe no one had...except him, that is. Apparently Genoveva wasn't too happy with me, because her mouth tightened and she said, "That may be. However, you should learn some respect, young woman. I am the *prima* of this clan."

"And I'm the daughter of a *prima*. Maybe you should show me some respect as well." Before she could reply, I turned to Rafe and said, "I'm getting cold. I think we'd better get to the casita."

He nodded and took me by the arm. "We'll discuss this later...Mother."

Her face was pale in the darkness. "There is nothing to discuss. Since you two seem to be getting along so well, I'll go ahead and get the preparations moving. I think a sunset wedding on Sunday should do very well."

After delivering that salvo, she stalked off toward the house, her back stiff as a ramrod.

Rafe shook his head. "That's my mother. Always has to have the last word."

"Did she really mean it?" My voice was very small.

"Oh, she definitely meant it. Hey," he added, bending down so he could kiss me on the cheek, "it's going to be fine. You want this, don't you?"

I thought I did. All I had to do was recall the way I'd felt when he kissed me, and it seemed as if I couldn't ask for anything more in the world than to be married to Rafe Castillo. It was why I had come here, after all. What I was feeling now was simply nerves, and probably some anticipatory stage fright at the thought of having to stand up in front of all those Castillos and not completely botch my part of the ceremony. I'd been to plenty of weddings, but we McAllisters were kind of a freewheeling bunch. Getting married to Rafe in the splendor of Loretto Chapel—for I had no doubt that the service would take place in no less grand a spot than that—was an entirely different proposition.

"Yes," I said. "It's just…can she really pull together a wedding in two days?"

"Oh, yeah," he replied, his tone somewhat grim. "You haven't really seen my mother in action yet."

I didn't answer, only shook my head and let him lead me toward the casita. The light next to the front door was on, although everything looked dark within. Rafe touched his hand to the latch, and the door swung inward. A moment later, several of the lamps in the living room flared to life.

"I'll leave you here," he said softly. "If I go inside, I'll be way too tempted to stay. But I'll come by in the morning and take you to breakfast, get you fortified."

"Fortified for what?" I asked, although I thought I already knew the answer.

"God, let me think...dress fittings, cake tastings, you name it. My mother's had everything lined up for months. I'm sure she's calling the bishop right now to confirm the time for Sunday afternoon."

My head was spinning. "You sure do know how to reassure a girl," I said, my voice shaky.

"You'll be fine. And Cat will be with you the whole time. She'll help you out."

That piece of information did make me feel a bit better. I didn't think I'd be able to survive a day alone with Genoveva Castillo, but Cat's presence should make the experience bearable... although I doubted it would be much fun.

Rafe bent and kissed me, a deep, thorough kiss, one that made me tingly all over. "Is nine-thirty too early to pick you up tomorrow?"

"No," I said, a little breathless from that kiss. "I'll be ready."

"I'll see you then." A flash of a smile, and then he turned and headed back down the path.

Time to go inside. I started to walk over the threshold to the casita, then almost tripped and went sprawling, thanks to my adopted cat choosing that moment to make an appearance and rush past me to get inside.

"Goddammit, Loki!" I snapped, hanging on to the doorframe to keep myself from doing a face plant. Even as the rebuke left my lips, I realized I shouldn't be too angry with the cat. It was now past eight o'clock; the poor thing had to be starving.

I hurried into the kitchen and poured some food for him into a bowl, then freshened his water. He fell to eating right away, and my feelings of guilt intensified. What with everything that had happened that day, I'd completely forgotten about Loki. I needed to make sure he was taken care of in the morning, too. It sounded as if the next day was going to be crazy busy, and although cats didn't need the kind of attention a dog might, I'd still taken on the responsibility for making sure he had food and water.

Ah, Goddess. I wandered into the living room and collapsed on the sofa. So much had happened, I didn't know whether I'd be able to get my mind around it. Rafe, and Simon, and ghosts, and now a wedding. Right then, I wanted more than anything to be able to talk to my mother, to have her tell me this was all going to be okay. We'd always been close, closer, I thought, than she'd been with my older sister, who'd always seemed more attached to Ian, her twin, than to either of our parents. Maybe my mother had done all she could to wring every drop out of the hours we spent together, since she'd always known that one day I'd have to be sent away, that I wouldn't be close by the way Emily was, or Ian and his family.

The longing for home was so intense that I almost fancied I could see the living room in my parents' house in Jerome, the worn but infinitely comfy leather sofas, the coffee table made of one lovingly polished chunk of twisted juniper. Even the scent of wood smoke from the fireplace and the little bucket of cinnamon pine cones my mother kept there from October through the beginning of January seemed real, inviting and aromatic.

Wait a second....

Drifting into the living room from down the hallway came the sound of voices.

My parents' voices.

I wasn't imagining this. I really was standing in the living room of the Jerome house. The casita where I'd been sitting just a moment before had vanished as if it had never been.

To reassure myself that I wasn't going crazy, I reached down and touched the glossy varnished surface of the coffee table. It felt all too solid, distressingly real. If this was a hallucination, it was the most detailed one I'd ever heard of.

I looked around. Everything was just as I'd remembered it—except for a new photo sitting on the mantel, wrapped in a frame of burnished rosewood. I knew that photo even though I'd never seen it before, because it was one my father had taken of my mother and me just the day before as we'd stood in the dark at the train station in Flagstaff. The flash had washed out some of the color in both our faces, making us appear far paler than usual.

Or maybe we'd been that pale because we knew we weren't going to see each other ever again.

At any rate, that photo hadn't been there the last time I'd been in the Jerome house. I supposed there was a chance my imagination might have conjured it into existence, but I didn't think so. It was real, just as this house was real.

Somehow I'd traveled here, covering hundreds of miles in the blink of an eye.

I turned toward the hallway, took a few hesitant steps in the direction of the voices I'd heard. I needed to talk to my parents, needed to convince myself that I really had managed to teleport here, that I wasn't experiencing some strange fever dream brought on by the crazy day I'd just survived.

My foot caught on the edge of the runner that covered most of the hall's wooden floor. I looked down at it—and that seemed to be all the distraction I needed, because in the next second I was falling, landing palms down on the Saltillo tile floor of the casita with enough force that the wind was knocked out of me for a second.

Coughing, I rolled over on my back and stared up at the ceiling. It was definitely the casita, with the wood slats and thick logs crisscrossing overhead in traditional Santa Fe style. Whatever had sent me to the house in Jerome apparently had decided to yank me right back here.

I didn't have time for much more analysis than that, because a second later, Loki jumped on my stomach and stared down into my face with big, gleaming amber eyes, thus managing to knock the air out of me all over again.

"Goddammit, Loki," I said for the second time that evening, once I'd caught my breath. Maybe at another time I would have been glad to see that the cat was so comfortable with me, but right then I needed a chance to get my bearings. I put my hands on his belly and lifted him off, then deposited him on the floor. Breathing still a little rough, I pushed myself to my feet and went over to the couch so I could sit down again. My hands shook, and my knees felt pretty rubbery, too.

This was all so insane, I didn't even know how I should react to what had just happened. I knew with every ounce of my being that I'd been back in Jerome. Only for a minute, but long enough for me absorb all those familiar sights and smells and sounds, enough to let me know I was home. And that was just flat-out impossible. I didn't have any kind of magic at all, let alone the sort of immense powers that would let me jump from one location to another in the blink of an eye.

My parents had that gift, though. Or rather, they possessed an almost bewildering collection of talents, far more than any witch or warlock should have had in their arsenal. They'd explained that it had something to do with the bond they shared, so much stronger and more mysterious than the connection between a *prima* and her consort, and that on their own they weren't nearly as powerful.

I hadn't seen most of those talents in action. Certainly they hadn't used their gifts of teleportation to blink the whole family to Prescott for the afternoon, or anything close to that. We traveled the old-fashioned way, by car. I remembered how I'd asked my father one time why the two of them never did anything interesting with their gifts, and how he'd chuckled and said, "One of the most important things you'll learn about possessing magical abilities is knowing when to use them... and when not to."

At the time I'd only been seven or eight, several years away from having my witch powers begin to manifest. Little did we know that those powers would decide never to show up.

Is that what was happening to me now? I judged myself steady enough to stand, so I pushed off the couch and went to get some water from the fridge. Standing in the kitchen and trying to wet my dry throat, I wondered if, by some strange chance, my absent abilities had decided to make an appearance ten years later than they should have.

In a way, it made sense. I'd spoken to Victoria, an ability my mother possessed. And now I'd teleported, something that my parents could only do together, not on their own.

My father's innate gift was one of illusion, specifically, being able to change his own appearance. Still clutching my glass of water, I went into the bathroom and stared at my reflection. I looked tired, shadows under my eyes and my mouth seemed a little swollen from Rafe's kisses, but otherwise it was pretty much me. But what if I tried to make myself someone else?

Something easy. My father couldn't make himself look like someone radically different from him physically, and I wasn't going to try anything drastic. But Cat was around my height and build, and dark-haired as well, so attempting to make myself take on her appearance shouldn't be too difficult.

I stood there in the bathroom, trying to recall every detail of her appearance, from the glossy sheen of her long near-black hair to the one little freckle, almost like a beauty mark, high on one cheekbone. The clear gloss she wore on her full mouth, and the leather cord with the crucifix that hung around her neck.

And…nothing. My same old face stared back at me, completely unchanged.

"This is crazy, isn't it?" I asked my reflection. Luckily, it didn't answer. I wasn't sure if I could handle that on top of everything else.

I tried again, this time closing my eyes so I could see Cat's face like a reflection on the inside of my eyelids. For the longest moment, I stood there, breathing quietly, doing my best to turn this into a meditation of sorts.

When you open your eyes, you'll look like Cat.

I opened them. Still me.

"Well, shit," I said, then took my glass of water with me back to the living room, where I set it down on one of the coasters on the coffee table. Loki had curled up on the rug next to the fireplace and was giving me the evil eye, as if demanding to know why a fire hadn't been lit.

It did feel rather chilly in there, although maybe the shiver that walked its way down my neck had more to do with all the craziness of the day than the actual temperature. Still, logs had already been set in the grate, which meant I wouldn't have to do much to get a fire going.

The simplest of talents, one that even I possessed. I knelt down and touched my fore-finger to one of the logs, sending a line of flame running along its length. The thin kindling sticks beneath the logs caught first, jumping up, bright and lively. Almost at once I could feel the warmth flow out from the hearth, soothing my chilled limbs.

Loki seemed to appreciate my efforts, because he rolled over on his side and stretched luxuriantly before curling himself into a ball once more.

"Happy?" I asked, but his eyes had already closed.

Shaking my head, I went back over to the couch and sat down, then made myself drink some more water. Why hadn't I been able to work the illusion the way my father could have? If I could talk to ghosts like my mother did, and teleport the way both of them could when they were together, why wasn't I able to also create an illusion, my father's talent?

Because I was trying too hard? When Victoria approached me in the bathroom at Tony's house, I certainly hadn't been attempting to talk to any ghosts. She'd appeared out of thin air, so to speak. And the same thing with my little unscheduled jaunt to Jerome. I'd been thinking of my parents, sure, and of home, but never in a million years had I believed I would be able to travel there. It had just…happened.

Well, if that was the case, I was in trouble, because a witch who couldn't control her talents was worse than a witch who didn't possess any at all. I'd always wondered whether it was a sort of safety mechanism that made witches and warlocks start to develop their powers at ten or eleven, rather than years earlier. Yes, a ten-year-old was still very much a child, but one far better-equipped to manage their magical gifts than a four- or five-year-old.

My hands still shook, and I wondered if I should try to call Cat, get her advice. No, that wasn't a very good idea. She'd be bound to be sympathetic—or at least I hoped she would—but I also worried that she might say something to her mother, since she'd probably be way out of her depth with something like this. Genoveva Castillo might be an utter pain in the ass, but she was also the *prima* of a very old and powerful clan. She was the natural person to go to with any questions about magic and its workings.

I could call my parents. They might have some words of reassurance. At the very least, they'd probably offer to research my strange situation, to find out if any of the records of the various Arizona clans had stories remotely similar to mine. Anyway, it would be good to hear my mother's voice, to have my father tell me it would all be okay. Genoveva hadn't specifically forbidden me from contacting them, had only said she thought it would be a good idea to put some distance between us so I might acclimate to my new environment more quickly, and that it would be better if I kept my calls to a minimum.

My purse was still sitting on the kitchen counter where I'd set it down as I first came into the casita. I rose from the couch and went over to dig my phone out of the depths of my bag, then lifted it to my lips.

"Call home," I said.

No sooner had the words left my mouth than Loki appeared in the kitchen, meowing loudly and taking a swipe at my leg. His sudden arrival startled me so much that the phone dropped from my already shaky hand, crashing on the hard tile of the kitchen floor.

"Oh, shit. *Shit.*" I dropped to my knees and reached for the phone, but I could already tell it was a total loss, the screen smashed to bits, the plastic casing itself cracked. Nevertheless, I lifted it to my mouth and said, "Call home."

Nothing, of course. And when I tried to push the button to get me to my contacts list so I could punch in the number manually, nothing happened. That phone was dead.

Great. Just great.

I pulled in a breath and got back to my feet, then put the ruined phone on the counter as I glared down at Loki. "What the hell was that all about?"

He stared up at me with innocent amber eyes and meowed softly.

If I had been back home and that had been our dog Wheeler, then I would have known he was asking for a treat. Did cats beg for treats? I really had no idea, and even if I did, it wouldn't have mattered, since all I'd gotten at the grocery store was regular cat food. No treats. No catnip or whatever else it was that cats liked.

"I don't have anything for you, big boy," I said. "But thanks for wrecking my phone. What the hell am I supposed to do now?"

In response, Loki looked around the kitchen once, meowed again, and then stalked off majestically, his tail in the air. Clearly, if I didn't have any treats, he didn't have any use for me.

Stupid as the feeling might have been, I

wanted to cry right then. I hated the idea of not having a phone. No, I wouldn't have abused it to call my parents day and night, but without the phone, I felt completely unmoored. The casita didn't have a computer, and I hadn't been allowed to bring my laptop with me. Some rudimentary connectivity was possible through the television, but it wasn't the same thing.

No booze in the cupboards, either. At that point, it seemed as if about all I could do was have a drink to settle my nerves, but obviously Genoveva had feared I might try to self-medicate, and so there wasn't anything stronger in the tiny pantry than coffee. All coffee would do was have me bouncing off the walls until two in the morning.

About all I could do was call the day a loss and go to bed. I didn't know where these powers were coming from, but I figured that I should be safe enough if I was asleep. I had a big day tomorrow, after all. Shopping and dress fittings and flowers and the Goddess only knew what else.

And the day after that I would marry Rafe.

Maybe if I kept repeating that crazy sentence over and over in my head, it might finally seem real.

11

PREPARATIONS

AT LEAST I DIDN'T TELEPORT IN MY SLEEP, OR set the casita on fire, or any of a hundred other gruesome scenarios that flitted through my head that night before sweet oblivion finally claimed me. I didn't have the alarm on the phone to wake me up, but the morning sun did a good enough job, filtering through the loose-weave curtains in the bedroom and letting me know it was time to get out of bed.

I took extra care getting ready, not to please Genoveva, but so I would look good for Rafe. Yesterday I'd done much the same thing, but an afternoon of sleeping on Simon's couch and all of the day's worry and strain had mostly erased the special effort I'd put into getting dressed and doing my hair and makeup. Even though I hadn't had a chance to look in a mirror after I left Simon's apartment, I knew I'd been pretty much a mess by the time I went to see Rafe at his house. Today I knew I wouldn't have to worry about such complications. Rafe and I had ironed out our differences—at least for the moment—and I vowed that I'd do my best to be civil to Genoveva. She was going to be my mother-in-law, after all. We'd be in each other's lives from here on out, and so I needed to make an effort to get along with her, difficult as it might seem.

And I'd have to do something about getting a new phone. Were there even any electronics stores near the Plaza? I somehow doubted it. Maybe Rafe and I would be able to carve out a little time to go to a different part of town and do some phone shopping. I supposed I'd just have to wait and see.

Rafe was about five minutes late, but I didn't mind. He was frowning when I opened the door, though, which didn't exactly give me a good feeling about how the rest of the day was going to go. To my relief, he revealed the source of his irritation as soon as we locked eyes.

"Didn't you hear your phone? I called to say I was running a little late—I got bogged down in a chat with a client."

"Oh, sorry about that." I stepped aside so he could enter the casita, then gave a helpless shrug.

"I had a mishap with the cat last night, and I dropped the phone. I think it's dead for good."

The frown intensified, his brows drawing together. "Are you sure? Let me take a look."

I thought I could recognize a dead phone when I saw one, but I didn't protest, only went to the kitchen where the broken phone was still sitting on the counter. He took it from me, turned it over, tried entering a few voice and touch commands, then shook his head.

"I guess it is dead." With a shrug, he put it back down on the counter. "We'll try to get you a new one as soon as we can, but it isn't that big a deal."

"I was afraid your mother would be very angry about it."

"This?" He shook his head. "It's just a phone. If you're worried about the cost, please. Genoveva spends more than that on a facial. And it's not like we have to worry too much about getting in touch —you'll either be with me or with Cat and my mother all day today and tomorrow. Once everything is settled down, you and I can go shopping for one, if we haven't gotten a replacement before then."

The tension that had been knotted inside me ever since I'd dropped the phone eased somewhat, although not all the way. Yes, I was glad the phone apparently wasn't a big deal, but there was still the far more pressing issue of those weird bursts of magic I'd experienced during the past few days. I didn't even know how to bring up the subject.

Well, I'd survived the night. Probably it was better to wait to talk about my little problem until the right opportunity presented itself. "All right," I said.

He smiled, the frown gone as if it had never existed. "Hungry?"

"Starved," I replied, because I was. The dinner I'd shared with Simon was long used up, and I hadn't eaten anything this morning, since I knew I was going out.

"Then I'll take you to my favorite breakfast place. Come on."

We drove downtown and parked in one of the structures there, one almost across the street from Simon's wine tasting room. I shot a surreptitious glance at the storefront as we passed by, but of course at that hour of the morning, the place was closed. Thank the Goddess. Rafe didn't even spare a look in that direction, although he probably hadn't wasted the effort simply because he knew the shop wouldn't be open yet. Still, I was glad there would be no chance of a confrontation. The two of us would be long gone before Simon showed up for work.

The restaurant Rafe took me to was a little hole in the wall squeezed between two shops. The man who seated us greeted him by name and smiled at me, and took us to what he proclaimed was the best booth in the house. I didn't know about that—they all seemed pretty much the same to me—but it was clear that everyone there knew Rafe and his family, because the waiter asked after Cat, and whether Louisa or Malena would be stopping by any time soon.

Rafe didn't appear put off by any of these friendly intrusions and answered the questions with a smile, his expression so sunny and open, he almost seemed a different man from the one who had sent me fleeing from La Plazuela the day before. Once we'd ordered some coffee and the waiter had left, I bent toward Rafe and whispered, "Do they know?"

He didn't bother to ask what I meant by that particular inquiry. "No. They're all civilians, as I'm sure you can tell. But we Castillos have been here a long time, and they know us, know the family. We can't avoid involvement with regular folks, so to speak. Not that I would want to. It can get kind of crazy-making, being among only our kind."

I nodded, although it seemed my experience had been quite different from his. But then, in Jerome, the civilians we allowed to live in our little town knew about the McAllisters, although they were sworn to secrecy. It wasn't the same in

Flagstaff, a much bigger city where you had to guard your tongue. I knew I would miss that about my hometown, even while I'd also known that I could handle myself in Santa Fe after so many years of learning to be cautious during the months of the year the family spent in Flagstaff.

"How many Castillos are there in Santa Fe?" I asked.

"I haven't counted. Around six or seven hundred, I think, and of course there are many more of us scattered around the state." A glint entered Rafe's dark eyes, and he added, "Don't worry—you won't have to remember all their names until you've lived with us for at least a month."

"You say that like you're joking," I replied, "but I have a feeling your mother will expect more or less exactly that from me."

"Oh, you're being too hard on her. I think she'll give you at least two months, maybe even more."

About all I could do was chuckle. The waiter came back with our coffee, and we ordered our meals—a breakfast burrito for Rafe, huevos rancheros for me. I'd barely glanced at the menu, but that sounded like a good choice, tasty without being too heavy. The last thing I wanted was to be all bloated while squeezing into wedding gowns.

The mere thought of trying on dresses made me tense up, although I tried to tell myself it would all be fine. After all, I'd known from the beginning that I would be marrying Rafe, and I also knew that a wedding required a wedding dress...or at least, any wedding that involved the Castillo *prima's* only son would require a gown. No quickie ceremony at the courthouse for us, that was for sure. Even so, I couldn't look on the upcoming preparations with anything less than trepidation. What if Genoveva had picked out a bunch of hideous gowns for me? I wouldn't have the luxury of saying no to all of them; I'd have to choose something, no matter how ugly, since I had a tight deadline breathing down my neck. And for all I tried to tell myself I was just borrowing trouble, I couldn't be sure I was wrong. Genoveva seemed like the sort of person who might take perverse pleasure in making sure her new daughter-in-law didn't look all that great on her wedding day.

"Stop stressing," Rafe said. "It's going to be fine."

"Is it that obvious?"

A smile touched the corners of his mouth, but I thought I saw understanding and more than a little sympathy in his tea-brown eyes. "Basically, yes. While I'd be the first person to admit that my mother is an excellent source of stress, she should be pretty mellow now. After all, she's getting her way."

"Does that bother you?" I asked, not sure whether I wanted to hear the answer or not.

His gaze met mine, deadly serious now. "It might have...if the other person involved in this whole thing had been anyone except you."

Warmth curled in the pit of my stomach. I could have blamed the sensation on the coffee I'd just drunk, but I knew it wasn't that, only the effect Rafe seemed to have on me.

Was now the time to tell him about what had happened to me last night, or even the night before, at Tony's party? I didn't want to keep any secrets from him, but at the same time, we were sharing a cozy, friendly moment. The last thing I wanted to do was to worry him. Anyway, the booth behind us was occupied by a retired couple who seemed more intent on their breakfasts than on having a conversation, so they were both silent. It would have been far too easy for them to over-hear what Rafe and I were saying.

No, better to wait until we could talk in private. I hadn't experienced any strange flare-ups this morning, and neither had I been able to summon a lick of magical talent to do anything except light the scented candle that sat on the dresser in the casita's bedroom. Whatever had been happening to me over the past few days, it seemed to have gone dormant again...at least for now. Strangely, I was almost disappointed by its disappearance. Those strange bursts of magic had frightened me, but they were also almost...exhilarating, like being blind your whole life and then suddenly being able to see flashes of color.

"I'm glad," I said. "I mean, I'm glad that it doesn't bother you. I've had my whole life to prepare for this, but...."

"But what?" His voice was soft, almost caressing.

"But now it almost doesn't seem real. You don't seem real. You're just too...perfect."

That comment made him laugh out loud, even as he shook his head. "Damn. Good thing I wasn't drinking coffee when you said that, or you might have gotten sprayed." He reached across the table and touched my hand. "Miranda, I am far from perfect. My little outburst yesterday should have told you that."

"It wasn't all your fault. I wasn't exactly making things easy for you."

"No, Miranda, I'm not going to let you make excuses for me." His fingers tightened on mine in a reassuring squeeze before he withdrew his hand. "Just accept my apology, okay?"

"All right, Rafe, I accept your apology." I didn't want to argue with him. If he wanted to accept all the blame—and most of it really should rest on his shoulders, if I was going to be entirely honest about the situation—then it seemed better for me to just let the matter go. "So…what's the plan for today?"

"After breakfast, I'll drop you off at the house. I think Cat is going to play chauffeur, but I'm not sure where you're going first. I didn't ask about the itinerary."

No, he probably couldn't have cared less about whether I would be sampling wedding cake first, or trying on gowns. Even now, when he was no longer regarding our upcoming nuptials in horror, he still most likely hadn't wasted much time on the particulars of the ceremony, as long as it happened.

I wondered who his best man was going to be. For that matter, who would be my bridesmaids? I assumed Cat would be the maid of honor, since that made the most sense, but I had no idea about the rest of them, or even how many there would be. Castillo cousins, I assumed, handpicked by Genoveva. It didn't matter, I supposed. What really mattered was that Rafe and I would be married, and afterward….

Well, afterward we would go live in his house, I supposed. It wasn't exactly my style, at least the small part of it I'd seen so far, but that really didn't matter so much. I'd get used to it. Just as I'd get used to living here, to being a part of the *prima's* immediate family. Maybe sooner or later my grand destiny would reveal itself. Or not. It was entirely possible that what Isabel Castillo had seen all those years ago was only the awakening of my talents, as if, for whatever reason, I'd had to come to Santa Fe in order for my magical gifts to show themselves. I wanted to believe that was the truth. At least then what was happening to me would make some sense.

"I suppose I'll find out where we're going soon enough," I said, then fell silent as the waiter returned with our breakfasts.

Rafe waited until he was gone to respond to my comment. "Exactly. And while you're off doing all that, I'll drive down to the electronics store and get you a new phone. That way, we can get it set up once you're done with all your running around, and you won't have to wait too long for a replacement."

"Sounds like a plan."

He smiled, and we dug into our food. It was nice to have had an ordinary, pleasant exchange like that, planning our day, no drama, no fuss. The circumstances surrounding my presence here might be strange, but I wanted things to be normal, wanted to at least act as if there was nothing out of the ordinary about what we were doing. It hurt to know that my parents wouldn't be able to attend the wedding, though. Just another one of Genoveva's edicts, a detail we'd all known about for a long time but was still difficult to accept. She had condescended to offer a full set of wedding photos of the blessed event, so at least my parents would have that much.

In every way, though, she'd done her best to make sure I knew this was my family now, that there would be no returning to Arizona and the world I'd once known.

That thought made me somewhat melancholy. I pushed it aside and concentrated on my excellent huevos rancheros, since there really wasn't anything else I could do. Rebellion was out of the question. I'd weighed the concept many times, mostly during the second half of my high school years, when I'd wanted to date, wanted to find some way to create a different future for myself than the one that had been planned for me. However, flat out refusing to come to Santa Fe would only have destroyed relations between the Castillo clan and my own, and although the witch world had been peaceful enough during all the years of my life so far, it never was a good idea to burn those sorts of bridges. I hadn't been born yet, but I'd heard about the one-time feud between the Wilcoxes and McAllisters, an enmity that had lasted for generations...and I'd also been told about the war between the California-based Santiagos and the Arizona clans. No one wanted something like that to happen with the Castillos.

So here I was.

Here with someone who was handsome and smart and talented. Rafe might have a temper, but at least it seemed as though he was the type to flare up and burn out quickly. I much preferred that sort of personality to someone who would hold a grudge indefinitely. And oh, the way he made me feel when he kissed me....

Yes, despite my adolescent gloom and doom, I thought all this was turning out pretty well.

While we ate, we chatted about ordinary enough things—how he wanted to take me up to Taos after the wedding for a sort of honeymoon, about the resort where we'd stay. It did sound romantic, and any plans that involved an extended time away from Genoveva Castillo could only appeal to me.

After we were done with breakfast, he took me to the house, where she and Cat were waiting for me. This morning, Genoveva might have been a different person, because she was all smiles, happy that everything was progressing the way she wanted. I couldn't quite forgive her for her past behavior, but I did my best to be pleasant, to smile at her as well and tell her I was looking forward to all the preparations.

Cat wasn't quite as effusive as her mother,

since she remembered all too well my disappearance of the day before. To my relief, though, she didn't seem inclined to bring it up, only said briefly that we'd better get going, since we had an appointment at the wedding gown shop at eleven.

After getting a goodbye kiss from Rafe, I went with Cat and Genoveva out to her SUV, which took us back downtown, to a street so small that I probably would have passed it by, thinking it was only an alley. Midway down the block was the store in question, an elegant little space where an equally elegant woman, her dark hair up in a French twist, welcomed us and offered tea, or coffee, or sparkling water.

Since I'd already had coffee with breakfast, I asked for water, while Cat and Genoveva both took tea.

"Excellent," said the woman who'd greeted us. "I'm Tess, and over here I have the dresses I've pulled for you."

She led us to a private little alcove off to one side where at least a dozen filmy white concoctions hung from a rolling steel rack. Looking at them, my heart sank a little. Not because they weren't beautiful, but because there were so many of them. Did Genoveva really expect me to try on all those gowns?

Apparently, she did. The alcove had also been outfitted with a beautiful antique carved screen, creating a dressing area. Tess brought the first dress to me, and the ordeal began.

I say "ordeal" just because even the most inveterate shopper might get worn down by having to try on so many dresses at once, and I was far from an expert shopper, given the limited options available in Jerome and Cottonwood or even Flagstaff. Still, I gritted my teeth and did what I was supposed to, rejecting this gown for being too ornate, and the next for being too plain, and shooting down yet another because it didn't fit well and I didn't possibly see how it could be altered in time for the ceremony.

But then I came to one that, while simple, seemed to mold to my shape as though it had been custom-made for me. The bodice was embroidered with silk flowers in the palest shade of blush imaginable, picked out with pearls and crystals. And I loved the way the skirt flowed behind me, with enough of a train to do justice to Loretto Chapel, but not so extravagant that it couldn't be bustled up out of the way for dancing at the reception.

"Oh, yes, that's the one," Genoveva said, watching me with a critical eye as I turned from one side to the other.

Cat clasped her hands together, the dubious expression she'd worn back at her mother's house now long gone. "It's perfect."

Smiling, Tess brought out a long veil and a tiara whose pearls and crystals echoed the ornamentation on the gown. "Try this."

A tiara? I raised an eyebrow.

Genoveva seemed to sense what I was thinking, because she said, "You will need it, to go with that gown. Shouldn't you look like a princess on your special day?"

How could I argue with that remark? Besides, I had the feeling that the Castillo *prima* did rather look on her family as royalty, and so she probably didn't see anything strange about her future daughter-in-law wearing a tiara for her wedding.

I gave a helpless shrug, and Tess set the tiara on my head. My hair was a little windblown, and so the effect wasn't quite the same as it would be once I was all done up for the ceremony, but I had to admit the overall impression was nice.

"All right," I said. "Tiara it is."

After that, we only had to attend to odds and ends like shoes and the correct petticoat and corset-like bustier to wear under the gown, and then we were out the door, with Tess promising that the dress and its accoutrements would be sent over to the house on the morning of the big day.

"The baker," Genoveva announced grandly, and we were off to the races once more.

The bakery wasn't too far from the dress shop, and there I got to taste all kinds of amazing samples of cake, although I was warned that the cake's decorations wouldn't be too elaborate, since the staff at the shop would start making it basically the second we left the store. I didn't mind all that much; after all, a cake was meant to be eaten, not hung on a wall and admired. Genoveva told me red velvet cake was Rafe's favorite, and so of course we had to have a layer of that, and another layer of chocolate with fudge ganache filling, and then another layer of red velvet for the very top, the part of the cake we were supposed to take home and freeze so we could eat it on our first anniversary.

First anniversary. I could barely wrap my head around the thought of marrying Rafe the next day, let alone being married to him for an entire year.

But I didn't have time to ponder that astonishing notion, because once we were done at the bakery, we headed over to one of the restaurants Rafe's father owned. This was the first time I'd even gotten to meet him, and I knew I sounded nervous and tongue-tied as he shook my hand and gravely welcomed me to the family. Eduardo Castillo was a handsome man, tall like his son, with an impressive head of gray-streaked dark hair. He bent and gave Genoveva a kiss on the cheek, and hugged Cat, before he took us to the restaurant's banquet room, an elegant space with square beams on the ceiling and an enormous fire-place on one wall. They'd already started deco-rating in here; beautiful little white-branched trees hung with fairy lights lined the walls, and a garland of leaves and fairy lights and pale roses bedecked the mantel of the fireplace.

"It's beautiful," I said, and Eduardo smiled.

"I'm glad you like it. Of course it isn't done yet, but I hope you can tell something of what it will all look like when it's finished."

"It will be perfect," I told him, quite sincerely.

"Speaking of getting things done," Genoveva put in, "we must be off to the florist now. I already gave him some direction, Miranda. I hope you don't mind."

"No, I don't mind," I replied, which was only the truth. What I knew about floral arranging could fit in a thimble.

"Excellent." She put up her cheek for another kiss, which Eduardo fondly bestowed on her. It seemed they were a happy enough couple, despite her sometimes overbearing personality. I wondered if there was something about the *prima*/consort bond that smoothed out many of the personality differences between those involved. Maybe, although I'd never thought the same thing about my parents. They'd always gotten along so well and seemed so blissfully happy together that I'd never questioned the source of their happiness.

Off to the florist's, where I could only nod at the photos Genoveva and the owner of the business, a woman named Liana, showed me. Everything looked lovely, and I especially liked the theme of shades of white and cream with little touches of blush, just like the wedding gown I'd chosen. Had Genoveva planned for me to pick that dress all along? I wouldn't put it past her exerting a little *prima* influence to get exactly what she wanted, although I couldn't argue with the final result.

And I couldn't wait to see the expression on Rafe's face when he saw me in my wedding dress.

On the way back to the house, we stopped at Loretto Chapel. I wasn't sure how Genoveva had managed it, because I knew the chapel was open to the public when it wasn't being used for weddings or funerals or baptisms, but the place was empty when we arrived, warm afternoon sunlight slanting through the stained-glass windows.

The bishop himself came out to meet us, an older man with cheekbones so proud, you'd think he was also a member of the Castillo clan, although I could tell right away that he was a civilian. Still, he was very pleasant, smiling at me and offering his congratulations, all deference to Genoveva as she told him what she had planned for the ceremony.

The two of them walked away, Genoveva pointing at the pews and at the altar, the bishop nodding in apparent agreement with everything she said. Once they were safely out of earshot, Cat grinned and shook her head. "Have you ever been to a Catholic wedding?"

"No," I replied. Neither the McAllisters nor the Wilcoxes practiced that religion, and although there were a good number of McAllisters who'd ended up marrying into the de la Paz clan, who were overwhelmingly Catholic, I'd never traveled to Phoenix or Tucson to attend any of those weddings. At the time, I'd thought it was only because they were distant enough relatives that my presence wasn't really required, but I realized now it was probably more that my parents had done everything they could to keep me in northern Arizona, away from awkward questions. I still didn't know whether the de la Paz *prima,* a woman named Zoe, had any idea of the bargain my parents had made with the Castillos.

"Well, at least they won't be doing the service in Latin, but it will still be long. Make sure you eat a good breakfast." The twinkle in Cat's dark eyes faded somewhat, and she added, "Seriously, I'm really glad you and Rafe were able to work things out. I was worried there for a bit."

"I know, and I'm sorry. I didn't mean to upset anyone."

"It's all right." She glanced toward the altar, where her mother and the bishop had paused. Genoveva was making a grand waving gesture with both arms, as if indicating the size of the floral arrangements that would be placed there. "If I'd been in your shoes, I probably would have taken off, too. Rafe's a good guy, but he does know how to get under your skin."

"Sometimes that's not such a bad thing," I remarked, remembering that first kiss we'd shared, the way he'd made my blood run both hot and cold.

Cat raised a hand in mock horror, even as she chuckled and said, "Spare me the gory details. While I've heard he can have that effect on women, I'd rather not know all about it."

"Oh, he does, does he?" I asked, a trickle of doubt beginning to work its way through me. Rafe had never spoken about being with other women before me, but I supposed I'd been naïve enough to believe—or hope—that he'd held himself aloof from the opposite sex, just as I had.

The expression of alarm that flared in Cat's dark eyes told me she'd just realized her gaffe. "It's —it's not what you're thinking. I don't think he was ever really serious about any of those girls."

"'Any'?" I echoed. "Just how many are we talking about here?"

"Oh, hell." Once again she looked toward the

altar, but it appeared that Genoveva and the bishop were still safely involved in their conversation. "All right, Rafe's had a few girlfriends over the years. Our mother didn't approve, but he didn't care. To be honest, I only met two of the girls he dated. He did his best to keep them away from the family."

"So they were civilians?" To my relief, I sounded absolutely calm as I asked the question. Inwardly, though, my insides were roiling with resentment. How typical that Rafe would go out and have all kinds of girlfriends, while I was practically living like a nun, saving myself for him.

"Yes," Cat replied. "He figured that was safer."

"Safer why?"

"Because he knew those relationships would be doomed from the start. There are plenty of Castillos who've married civilians, but our mother would never allow any of her own children to do the same thing. I guess Rafe worried that if he ever got serious about someone who was a witch, it could cause all kinds of problems, since he was already promised to you."

I knew I shouldn't let these revelations bother me. It wasn't as if he'd had a secret engagement with any of those women, had wanted any of them to replace me. I also had no way of knowing whether he'd been intimate with them. But then, why wouldn't he have been? A lot of progress had been made on that front over the years, but there still tended to be a double standard when it came to sexual activity. It would have been okay for Rafe to sleep with those girls, as long as he was honest with them about where the relationship was headed. On the other hand, I was sure Genoveva would have freaked out if I'd arrived in Santa Fe and announced that I wasn't a virgin, had had a long string of boyfriends back in Arizona.

Unfortunately, the more I told myself not to worry about it, to let the matter go, the angrier I got.

"Miranda—" Cat began, her tone openly pleading, worry clear on her features. No doubt she was kicking herself for bringing up the topic in the first place.

I didn't want to hear her make excuses for Rafe. Honestly, I didn't want to hear any excuses from him, either. Right then I just wished I could get away from Cat and from the drone of Genoveva's voice in the background, describing in minute detail everything she had planned for tomorrow's ceremony. I needed some space to think, to figure out what I should do about this—if anything.

And then, before I could even begin to react to what was happening, the cathedral blinked out of existence.

12

SUSPICIONS

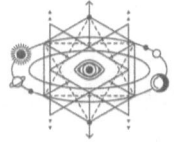

Rafe

HE HURRIED TOWARD CAT, WHO LINGERED near the entrance to one of the high-end jewelry stores that fronted on the Plaza. Even from several yards away, he could see how pale she looked, how her fingers were tightly wrapped around the strap of her purse/backpack. As he approached, she said, "Thank God."

All he'd gotten was a terse text ten minutes ago. *Miranda's gone. Meet me in front of Domenico's.*

Miranda was gone? How the hell could that have happened, when she was supposed to be with his sister and mother? It was one thing to walk out of a restaurant and blend in with the crowd before disappearing for the afternoon, but Rafe couldn't think how his fiancée could have managed the same feat when accompanied by the clan's *prima*.

"What's going on?" he demanded.

"I don't know," Cat replied. She glanced around them; although there were plenty of passersby on this section of covered sidewalk in front of the jewelry store, no one seemed to be paying any attention to the pair who lingered in front of one of the display windows. "Seriously, Rafe, it was the craziest thing I ever saw. One minute I was standing there in Loretto Chapel, talking to Miranda, and the next she was just gone. Vanished into thin air, even as I was looking at her."

None of this made any sense. How could Miranda disappear like that? She didn't have any magic. "So, what, just poof and gone in a puff of smoke?"

"There was no puff of smoke." Cat's gaze shifted away from him, toward the gleaming jewels in the shop window, although he got the impression she didn't actually see any of them. "I —I kind of screwed up, might have said some-thing about you dating other people in the past."

Oh, great. While he certainly didn't believe that having previous relationships was a punish-able offense, he could see why Miranda might think that way, considering how she'd apparently avoided any connections with the opposite sex. And he could also see why realizing he hadn't kept himself "pure" might have upset her.

"Thanks, Cat," he said, and she sent him a pleading glance.

"I'm really sorry. It just sort of slipped out. I didn't think it would upset her so much."

"And it was after you made this revelation that she disappeared?"

A shame-faced nod. "Yes."

Should he be angry with Miranda for being so unreasonable about a situation that really had nothing to do with her...or should he be annoyed with himself for cavalierly assuming that the girl being forced to marry him might be upset by his earlier indiscretions? Either way, Rafe wasn't sure what to make of his sister's admission. Was there a connection between what Cat had said and Miranda's disappearance, or was it simply coincidence? How had Miranda managed to disappear like that, anyway? He'd been told she had no magical talents; he could sense she was of witch-kind, but that extra little tingle he got when meeting another warlock or witch for the first time only let him know he was in the presence of someone with magical blood, not how strong that person might be.

"Did Mother see?"

Cat let out a little breath. "No, thank God. She was in the middle of telling the bishop all her grand plans for the ceremony, and Miranda and I were standing at the rear of the chapel, where it was pretty dark. I went outside to look for her, thinking that maybe I'd blinked or turned my head or something, and that was why I hadn't seen her slip out. But she wasn't outside. She was just…gone."

He supposed he should be relieved that Miranda had vanished when Genoveva wasn't looking, but at the moment he was more worried about where she might have gone. Even so, Rafe hated to think what would have happened if his mother had managed to witness Miranda's disappearing act. Still, they'd have to come up with some sort of explanation as to why she was suddenly not around.

Seeming to pick up on what her brother was thinking, Cat went on, "I slipped out and came down here. Then I sent Mom a text, telling her that Miranda and I were shopping for some jewelry to go with the wedding dress, and that we'd meet her at home later. It wasn't the best cover story, especially since I know that Mom was already planning to lend her something to wear, but it was all I could think of right then."

"No, it was a good idea," Rafe said, hoping his

reply might reassure his sister, if only just a little. Actually, he'd thought that was fairly quick thinking on her feet. He didn't know if he could have done the same thing. "I assume she bought it?"

"I think so. She texted back for us to enjoy ourselves, and said that she'd take a Ryde home once she was done going over everything with the bishop. It bought us a little time, but what if Miranda is gone as long as she was yesterday?" Cat glanced around again, clearly hoping she would see his runaway bride somewhere in the crowds around them. Unfortunately, she'd been almost impossible to locate yesterday, and Rafe had no reason to believe she'd be any easier to find today.

And there was also the pesky question of how she'd managed to accomplish this feat in the first place. Had her family been lying all along about her lack of talents? If so, why?

"Let's go to my Jeep," he said in an undertone. "Too many people around here."

Cat didn't argue, but followed him to the side street where he'd parked the Wrangler. They both got in, although he made no move to turn on the vehicle. He'd mostly brought his sister here so they would have a place where they could talk in private.

During the short walk over to the Jeep, he'd pondered the situation, trying to come up with a reasonable explanation for what had happened. "Miranda's parents are teleporters, aren't they?"

A frown as Cat considered his question. "Um…I might have heard Mom mention it once or twice. Yeah, I guess they are. What, you think Miranda's inherited their talent?"

"I don't know," he replied. "From what I heard, they made a pretty big deal about her not even having any talents. I think they tried to use it as a reason to call off the whole bargain, even though Genoveva wouldn't go along with it. But what if it wasn't Miranda at all, but her parents taking her away?"

"That's kind of a stretch—" Cat began, but he cut her off.

"Maybe not. From the things Genoveva has said, it sounds as though the McAllister *prima* and her *primus* consort have access to all kinds of powers that most witches and warlocks don't. Who's to say that they couldn't sense their daughter's distress somehow, and then called her home? It would make sense." Yes, it would make a lot of sense, although he hated the thought of upsetting Miranda so much that her parents felt compelled to extricate her from her current situation.

Cat frowned and fiddled with the strap of her backpack. "If she's with them, how would we ever know?"

"We'd have to contact them somehow.

Genoveva has their number in her phone,
I think."

"Which means it might as well be sealed up in
Fort Knox, thanks to the retinal lock on her
phone." Cat frowned and tapped her fingers on
the armrest built into the door, mulling over their
options. "But maybe there's another way."

"What's that?"

"She backs everything up to the desktop
computer in her office. It would probably be
easier to get the number from her address
book there."

That did seem like it might be simpler, since
the computer was only password-protected. Still,
he wasn't a hacker, and if anyone in the clan
possessed those sorts of talents, they kept quiet
about it. "You know anyone who can manage
that?"

For a second Cat looked at him blankly, and
then she chuckled. "I don't mean hack into it. I
was thinking more of trying to catch her while she
was working on the computer, then distracting
her for long enough that one of us can slip in and
get the information out of her address book. It
shouldn't take more than a minute."

That plan did seem to make more sense. Rafe
doubted it would be easy, but certainly this
strategy must be easier than attempting to dupli-
cate his mother's retinal patterns. Trying to get her

phone when it was unlocked would be almost impossible, since it locked itself after thirty seconds of non-use.

"How do you want to do it?" he asked. "Are you going to distract her, or should I?"

"Better let me do it. I can manufacture something about the bridesmaids' dresses, or some kind of other wedding crap." Cat paused there, looking somewhat distressed, then hurried to add, "I didn't mean it that way. But there are a lot of details to manage."

"No, I get it," Rafe said. "You're probably right." He was silent for a moment, trying not to think what would happen if they didn't manage to locate Miranda in time. The wedding was now barely twenty-four hours away.

Cat's phone chimed, indicating she had a text message. She yanked it out of her purse, read the message on her home screen, and seemed to relax slightly.

"Is it—?" he began, and she shook her head.

"No, it's not Miranda. That was a text from Mom, saying she was done at the cathedral and was on her way home. We might as well head over there, too—she was closer, so she'll get there before us. I'll go in to talk to her, tell her that Miranda is in the casita resting. That should explain why we're not together."

"And how do you propose to get her on the

computer?" Unlike most of the people Rafe knew, the *prima* of the Castillo clan didn't spend her days with her eyes glued to a screen. She viewed her computer and her phone as the useful tools they were, but they certainly didn't dominate her existence.

"I'll figure something out," Cat said. "I'll ask to look at the seating chart or something—God knows she's spent enough time obsessing over the damn thing. You just need to be ready to get in there on my signal."

This all sounded very clandestine. However, he knew they needed to reach out to Miranda's parents for their help, and they couldn't do that without their phone number. "Got it," he responded. "Let's go."

He eased the Wrangler away from the curb and then took a circuitous route to the house where he'd grown up, making sure the Ryde vehicle his mother had summoned would have plenty of time to get her home before he and Cat arrived. Rather than park in the driveway and therefore give his presence away, he stopped around the corner from the house and left his Jeep there. Thank God his mother didn't have the ability to sense when someone was on the property; like all *primas*, she knew if a witch or warlock from another clan had passed into their territory, but that talent didn't extend to knowing when her children might be lurking nearby.

"I'll just text 'now' when the coast is clear," she said. "Be ready."

"I will."

She gave him a thumbs-up, then headed off toward the house. Rafe followed at a safe distance, making sure he always had some hiding place where he could duck, just in case his mother appeared out of nowhere. This wasn't very likely, since once she was home she tended to stay inside, especially if the weather wasn't fine, but he knew he couldn't trust mere luck to protect him. He certainly hadn't been very lucky so far, with the woman he was supposed to marry disappearing at the most inconvenient times.

Well, maybe not the most. He was pretty sure the worst would be if she disappeared into thin air as she stood next to him at the altar tomorrow evening.

No, that wasn't going to happen. They'd fix this, track down where she was and make sure she came back. If she was angry about the women in his past life, he'd explain to her that he'd indulged in those relationships just as much to piss off his mother as he had to bring a little companionship into his world. Not the most mature behavior, but he wanted to be truthful. He hadn't loved any of them, although he'd done his best to treat them well and make sure they had a good time during the weeks or months they were together.

By this time of day, the sun was low in the western sky, obscured by the trees on the property that faced theirs across the street. Rafe was glad of the shadows the late afternoon light provided, because he wanted to skulk as close to the house as he could without being in direct view of any of the windows that faced out on the gardens. He glanced down at his phone, which he held clutched in one hand, but it remained mute, the screen blank except for the current time and temperature.

And what if the McAllister *prima* and the Wilcox *primus* didn't want to help him, decided it was better for their daughter to stay with them than remain someplace that made her so unhappy? Rafe wasn't sure what he'd do then. It wasn't as though he could confess his undying love for Miranda. He'd begun to care for her, but he couldn't call the tentative tenderness he now felt a love for the ages. Perhaps one day their connection might be exactly that—something about her kisses aroused him in a way no other kisses had— and yet he didn't want to oversell the situation between them.

Especially not to her parents.

His phone buzzed, and he looked down at the screen.

Now.

He hurried to the side entrance off the kitchen, since it was closer to his mother's study than the front door. Also, he couldn't know for sure where Cat was taking Genoveva, and there were more places to try to hide himself in this part of the house—the laundry room, the oversized closet used for cleaning supplies and the vacuum cleaner and so on. Once he was inside, he paused, hoping he could hear his sister's voice so he would have a better idea of where she might be.

Unfortunately, he couldn't hear a damn thing. All he could do was inch his way down the corridor toward his mother's study and pray that Cat had come up with a really good excuse for drawing Genoveva away from the room.

When he peeked into the study, he saw that it was empty, the big screen of his mother's computer alive with a series of images showing Santa Fe in the autumn. Good. If the screensaver was activated, then the computer shouldn't be locked.

He hurried over, touched the keyboard, navigated to the digital phone book she kept on the hard drive. It only took a few seconds to find the listing for Angela McAllister. Rather than waste time keying in the number, he took several photos of the entry with his phone, then engaged the screensaver again.

Voices began to drift down the hallway. "… couldn't find her shoes, and I don't know if we'll get the replacements here in time."

Cat, speaking a little louder than usual, clearly for his benefit. Rafe slipped out of the study and back down the hallway to the kitchen, then let himself out the side door. It was probably safest to keep going; they could maintain the façade of normality as long as it seemed he was off somewhere with Miranda, which meant he needed to make himself scarce and meet up with Cat once she got away from the house.

He breathed a sigh of relief as he let himself out the gate, and he was even more relieved once he'd climbed inside the Wrangler and turned on the engine. A quick text—*Got it. Meet me at Antonia's when you can*—and he was off, pulling away from the curb faster than he should have. Right then he didn't care. He just wanted to put as much distance between his mother and himself as he could.

Antonia's was a little gastropub on the northeast end of downtown. There was a public parking lot half a block away, so Rafe left the Jeep there and went into the pub to wait for his sister. At this hour, not quite five o'clock yet, the place was fairly deserted.

He didn't know the girl working behind the bar, which was a relief. Right then, he didn't feel like engaging in any small talk. He ordered a local pale ale and took it to the most secluded booth in the place, one off in a corner, and allowed himself a small swallow of beer. It took a considerable amount of willpower to keep himself from looking at Angela McAllister's number and calling her right then and there, but he figured that wouldn't be fair to Cat. She'd put herself on the line, too, and deserved to be present when he made the call.

To his relief, Cat walked in only a moment or two later. She spotted him in the booth, but first went to the bar and got a brown ale, then came over and slid into the seat next to him.

"Now I know why I never wanted to work for the CIA," she said. She lifted her mug to her lips, drank a large gulp of the ale, and set the mug back down. "I was so sure Mom could hear my heart pounding away as I told her lie after lie. Thank God detecting lies isn't her talent."

Rafe had thought much the same thing over the years. He nodded. "You did great. Do you think she suspected anything?"

"I doubt it. She's pretty distracted with the wedding. Sounds like she wants to make it her crowning achievement."

"You'd think it wouldn't matter so much, since she's already married off Louisa and Malena."

Cat made a face, then drank some more of her

brown ale. "Yes, but now she's marrying off her only son. It's a big deal. Or at least," she added, "it will be a big deal, assuming we can locate the bride in time."

Right now, that seemed like a fairly large assumption. Still, they had to try. He got out his phone and went to the clearest of the photos he'd taken of Angela McAllister's number, then stared at it for a moment, imprinting the digits on his brain. "I guess I'd better go ahead and call."

"What are you going to say?"

"The truth," he replied. "What else can I do? If Miranda really is with them, I'll only look like an even bigger asshole if I try to hand them some b.s. story."

"True."

Before he could lose his nerve—or forget the digits he'd just memorized—he went to the phone's keypad and quickly entered Angela McAllister's number. It rang once, rang twice.

Please don't go to voicemail, he thought. *That would be too anticlimactic.*

But then the ringing stopped, and a pleasant female voice said, "Hello?"

"Is this Angela McAllister?"

A pause. When she spoke again, her tone was altered subtly, laced with an edge of suspicion that hadn't been there the moment before. "Who is this?"

"My name is Rafe Castillo."

Another pause, this one more shocked than anything else. Then she said, "Rafe Castillo? Is Miranda with you? Is she all right?"

This question was followed by the murmur of a man's voice, probably Miranda's father, although Rafe couldn't make out anything of what he was saying.

"Well, um," Rafe said, feeling more wound up than ever, "I was kind of hoping she would be with you."

Dead silence.

"Angela?"

When she spoke, it was in slow, hesitant words, as if she wasn't sure how to respond. "Rafe, why would she be with us? Your mother specifically said we were to have limited contact with our daughter. She wouldn't even allow us to come to Santa Fe for your wedding. Has it happened yet?"

"Um, no. It's set for tomorrow at five, but…."

"But what?"

"But Miranda's disappeared. She was talking with my sister, and she just—went away."

A long pause. Then the McAllister *prima* said, "I don't understand."

"She disappeared into thin air. It was like she teleported, but that's impossible, isn't it? I mean, she doesn't have the ability to do that…or does she?"

"Hang on."

There came a sort of clicking sound. Rafe wasn't sure what it might be, but he guessed maybe it was the clatter of a ring against the plastic of the phone as she covered the microphone. He could faintly hear a murmured conversation of some sort, although he wasn't able to pick out the actual words.

A man's voice. "Rafe, this is Connor, Angela's father. You're saying she teleported right in front of your sister?"

"Yes, sir." Might as well be respectful. Rafe didn't know how much the show of deference would earn him in the long run, but he figured it couldn't hurt. "I thought—that is, I knew that you and your wife were able to teleport, so I was wondering if you'd taken Miranda away for some reason."

"No, we haven't." A brief pause, and Connor went on, an edge to his tone that hadn't been there before, "In fact, we've done everything your mother asked of us, and now you've gone and *lost our daughter?*"

Oh, hell. Rafe wished he could pick up his glass of pale ale and take a fortifying swallow, but that didn't seem like a very good idea at the moment. "I'm not sure if 'lost' is the right word. But if she's not with you, is there even a possibility that she could have done this on her own?"

"I don't see how. She's never shown any sign of true magical ability. For her to develop such a powerful gift, and at such a late age...." Connor's words trailed off. When he spoke again, he sounded almost confused, uncertain. "That is, I've never heard of such a thing happening before, but I can't say for sure that it's not impossible. I'll have to look into it. But what are you going to do to find Miranda?"

"We'll...." Jesus Christ, what *could* he and Cat do? They'd already learned the day before that when Miranda wanted to stay lost, that's exactly what she did. There was no good way to track her down, magical or otherwise. Luckily, Connor Wilcox didn't know that. "I have a cousin, someone who can find missing people. We're going to call him to come help us."

"Well, it's a start," Connor said, his voice grim. "But you need to find her. Now. Or Angela and I will come to Santa Fe to help you."

That was an outcome Rafe knew he couldn't risk. He could just imagine the explosion if the McAllister *prima* and the Wilcox *primus* showed up in Santa Fe out of the blue and confronted his mother about their missing daughter. The fireworks could probably be seen all the way to the Four Corners region.

"Oh, we'll find her. Thanks for letting me know she's not with you. Now we can start searching here around town. You have a good evening." God, that sounded terrible. The last thing Angela and Connor would probably have was a good evening, now that they knew their daughter was missing. He added quickly, "Don't worry—we'll find her."

He jabbed the keypad to end the call, then dropped the phone on the tabletop, halfway expecting it to ring as soon as he let go. Cat raised an eyebrow at him.

"That doesn't sound as if it went very well."

Now was the time to take a swig of his beer. Rafe lifted the glass and drank, thinking that the bitterness of the pale ale was an accurate reflection of his current mood. "It could have gone worse. At least they haven't shown up to start looking for Miranda."

Yet.

Cat was eyeing the phone as if she thought it might suddenly lift off the tabletop and grow fangs. "I'm surprised they let you go that easily."

"So am I. But they think I'm going to get Marco on the case, so I suppose they're willing to wait and see what happens. They've been in charge of their clans for a long time, which means they know it's not a good idea to go barging into another witch family's territory." He pushed his hand through his hair and let it flop back over his forehead. It was getting too long, but cutting it was the least of his worries right now.

"And what happens when they find out Marco can't help?"

Good question. Rafe shook his head. "I have no frigging idea."

13

SAFE HARBORS

Miranda

I WAS STANDING IN A HALF-FAMILIAR apartment, one with warm yellow walls and a mishmash of furniture that somehow managed to be charming in its eclectic clutter. Blinking, I put out a hand to touch one of those walls, just so I could reassure myself that I actually was there, that I hadn't fooled myself into thinking a hallucination was reality.

But, just like the coffee table at my parents' house in Jerome, the wall was firm and solid under my fingertips. I looked back around the apartment, recognition slowly dawning.

I had no idea why I'd come here, but I was standing in Simon's flat above the wine tasting room.

Holy shit.

I sent a panicked look around the space, then let out a relieved breath when I realized I was alone. Of course Simon wouldn't be here—it was late Saturday afternoon, and he'd told me he worked weekends so he'd have time to attend classes during the week. No doubt he was some-where under my feet right now.

My hands were shaking, and I fought to still them by grasping the strap of my purse, which—thank the Goddess—was still safely slung over my shoulder. I looked down and saw that I didn't seem to have come to any harm. My feet were still encased in their dark brown boots, and I still had on my green leather jacket.

All right. Now that it had happened a second time, I didn't see how I could possibly deny that somehow I had acquired the gift of teleportation. I must have scared the living daylights out of Cat, disappearing like that right in front of her nose, because of course she had no way of knowing that I'd suddenly had random magical talents start showing up out of nowhere.

Well, I'd been able to blink myself out of my parents' house and back to the casita here in Santa Fe, although that had seemed more like an acci-dent than anything else. I knew I needed to do the same thing now, or risk running into Simon. Why I'd come here, I had no idea, but I'd puzzle that one out later, when I was safely back in my temporary home.

I visualized the casita, the bright accent colors, the dark beamed ceiling. Closing my eyes, I willed myself there, pictured myself calmly sitting on the living room couch.

And…nothing happened.

Goddammit.

My pulse began to race, but I told myself that I needed to focus, couldn't give in to panic. I'd done this before, so there was no reason to think I couldn't do it again.

Once more I shut my eyes, then imagined the casita and me sitting in it.

I didn't move a damn inch. My feet might as well have been nailed to the floor for all the good my visualizing had done me.

All right. Clearly, my magic was failing me now, just as it had failed me all the previous years of my life. I'd have to get out of here the old-fashioned way. Good thing I had plenty of practice.

I went to the door and put my hand on the knob, turned it slowly. All seemed clear on the small landing outside, so I closed the door behind me and willed the lock to engage, then began to tiptoe down the stairs that would lead me to the building's rear exit.

The cramped foyer was only a few steps away

when Simon came around the corner, then stopped dead, staring at me incredulously.

"Miranda? What are you doing here?"

Damn. It seemed that the universe was conspiring against me. Since there was no way I could cover up my presence, I managed to smile and say, "Oh, I wanted to come by and talk. I would have called, but I dropped my phone and it's dead."

None of this sounded very coherent to me, and apparently Simon had the same opinion, since a frown was pulling at his brows. "Why didn't you come by the tasting room? I'm pretty sure I told you I worked on Saturdays."

"Oh, I know," I said quickly. "I realized that after I knocked. I guess I just wasn't thinking. But then I figured you probably wouldn't want me bugging you on a Saturday afternoon when it has to be busy, so I thought I'd just go home and try again later."

"Hmm." His expression was still dubious, but then he shrugged and said, "It's not too bad, but it has been steady. I was just going up to my apartment to get a power cord for the tablet we use for our sound system—it just died on me. And hey," he added, "I'm off in forty-five minutes. Why don't you go up to my place and hang out, and I'll come get you when I'm done?"

"I don't think—" I began, but he cut me off.

"It's fine. I don't mind. And you said you wanted to talk, didn't you?"

That had been a lie, something I'd made up to try to explain why he'd found me almost on his doorstep. However, I realized right then that I did want to talk to someone. I couldn't tell Simon about my magical problems, of course, but I still thought it might help to have sympathetic ear while I unburdened myself about some of my other issues. Looking at the situation logically, I knew it probably wasn't such a great idea to talk to a guy who was interested in me about my man troubles. Problem was, I didn't have anyone else in Santa Fe that I could talk to. At least I'd already told Simon that I was going to patch things up with Rafe, so I had to hope his expectations for a romantic future with me wouldn't be too high.

"Yes," I said. "But I don't want to intrude. It's Saturday night—maybe you already have plans."

He grinned. "Yeah, a date with my oenology textbook. You're not intruding. Really."

At that point, I decided to stop protesting. He'd invited me, after all. And I needed a refuge, someplace to hole up for a while and figure out what the heck was going on with me.

I offered him a smile. "Okay."

He led me back upstairs, then got his keys out of his pocket and unlocked the door. We went inside, and he took a side tour into the kitchen, saying, "You want a glass of water or something?"

Water sounded great. My mouth felt dry, although I didn't know whether its current parched state was from nerves or some strange reaction to this latest round of teleportation. "Water is fine."

He got a glass from the cupboard, filled it from a pitcher inside the fridge, and handed it to me, then went into the living room, where he started hunting around in the drawers of the low painted cabinet that he used as a television stand. "Got it," he said, pulling out a black power cord, presumably the one he needed for the tasting room's tablet computer. "I wish I could hang around, but I need to get back downstairs. I'll be up in about an hour, since I have to do a few things after we're officially closed. The remote for the TV is on the coffee table."

"Thanks," I replied, hoping it wouldn't feel too weird to be here with him gone. Since I'd already accepted his invitation to stay, there wasn't much I could do about it, though.

After shooting me a quick smile, he let himself out. Right then, I wished I wore a watch, but I'd always just used my phone to check the time. Glancing into the kitchen, I was able to see the digital readout on the refrigerator door, which told me it was currently 5:12 p.m. and that the temperature in the apartment was seventy degrees.

Okay, I could do this.

I went to the couch and sat down, then retrieved the remote from the coffee table. It was the hour when the local news was on, and that seemed mindless enough to keep me occupied for the next forty-five minutes. As tempting as it might have been to look around the place, that would have been extremely rude. Simon had trusted me enough to leave me here in his apartment alone, and the last thing I wanted was to abuse that trust.

Instead, I sat on the couch and watched the inevitable stories about fatal car accidents and house fires and local officials under investigation, and wondered if I was crazy for staying here. Rafe and Cat must be frantic over me disappearing again. Damn—I should've asked Simon if I could borrow his phone and let Cat know I was okay. No, wait, that wouldn't have worked; I didn't have her number memorized yet.

Anyway, while I couldn't help experiencing some guilt over Cat's current state of mind, I wasn't sure whether I felt the same way toward Rafe. He'd hid quite a few secrets of his own from me, after all. Maybe the oversight was simply because we hadn't had the chance to really sit down and talk, but he could have mentioned those past girlfriends the night before. He'd had the opportunity, and he hadn't taken it.

By the time Simon reappeared at a little past six fifteen, I had drummed up enough righteous indignation over Rafe's omissions that I wasn't too worried about the current state of his brain anymore. Besides, I was fine. I'd hang out with Simon for a bit, then go back to the casita, or maybe over to Rafe's house. Not having a phone was a real pain, since I couldn't contact him first to find out where he might be. Logic told me he probably had gone home, though, because if Genoveva hadn't seen me disappear—and I had no reason to believe she had—then Rafe was probably doing everything in his power to make sure she didn't know that I was gone. I knew I would have done the same thing if I'd been in his position.

"Hungry?" Rafe asked. "There's a good pizza place down the street that delivers."

Pizza sounded great. I'd had a big breakfast with Rafe, but that was going on eight hours earlier by now. "Sure," I replied. "I could go for some pizza."

He got out his phone, then handed it to me. "Here's the menu. I'm open to pretty much anything, except anchovies."

The pizza with Italian ham and mushrooms and spicy oil sounded good to me. "The Bianca?"

"That's my favorite, actually. Good choice." He touched the screen to select the pizza in question, and the app informed us that the food would be delivered in fifteen minutes. After setting the phone down, Simon headed into the kitchen, only to reappear with a bottle of wine and a couple of glasses.

Doubt crept in. Was it really a good idea to sit here and drink wine with someone who wasn't my fiancé? I tried to tell myself it really wasn't a big deal; I'd just nurse one glass, or at most a glass and a half, and that should be all right, especially since I'd be having food with my wine this time.

Simon was silent as he poured the wine, filling each glass about halfway. After offering one to me, he asked, "Are you going to tell me about it?"

"About it what?" I sipped the wine, a merlot from the tasting room downstairs. He probably got an employee discount or something.

"Well, I figure something big must be going on, or you wouldn't have shown up on my doorstep like this." He took a swallow of wine, but his gaze was still focused on me, dark, intent.

A strange little thrill traced its way down my spine. Once again I found myself wondering how I would have reacted to Simon if I hadn't known I was intended for Rafe. Despite their similar coloring, their looks were very different from one another. Both attractive, yes, but....

And what did it matter, anyway? I wasn't free to make my own choices. Only a few hours ago, I'd been thrilled at the thought of marrying Rafe. A few women in his past shouldn't have changed that feeling. When you looked at the situation logically, it was ridiculous for me to have expected him to have stayed celibate, waited to be with me. Would I have demanded celibacy from a man who hadn't been promised to me, someone I'd met casually?

Of course not.

Problem was, I didn't feel like being logical. I'd denied myself, and it bothered me more than I could say that Rafe hadn't done the same thing. About all I could do was hope I'd get over it eventually…and that I wouldn't bump into any of his old girlfriends when I was roaming around Santa Fe.

"I'm getting married tomorrow," I said, my tone flat.

Simon's face didn't exactly fall, but instead went blank. "Oh."

Not exactly the most encouraging of responses, but since I'd embarked on this discussion, I had no choice but to continue. "Yesterday after dinner I went and talked to him, and we worked things out. Or at least, I thought we did."

A certain confusion entered Simon's eyes. "But you didn't?"

"It's more like…he wasn't honest with me. Not completely."

"Then you shouldn't marry him," Simon said without hesitation.

"You make it sound so easy."

"Well, it should be." Simon drank some of his merlot, then set down the glass. "This is the twenty-first century, Miranda. What're they going to do, lock you in a tower or something?"

"I—"

A knock came at the door then, and Simon got up to answer it. He took the pizza from the delivery guy, thanked him, and shut the door. This all happened so fast, I didn't have a chance to offer to pay for the food, although I belatedly realized that Simon's payment info was probably stored in the app and it had all been handled automatically anyway.

He brought the pizza box over to the coffee table and set it down. "I'll go get some plates."

I waited while he went in the kitchen, although I did have another sip of wine to fortify myself. He returned with the aforementioned plates, bright Fiesta ware, and a couple of paper towels for napkins.

The next minute was a silent one, as we both took our plates and got some pizza, then ate quietly. Then Simon set down his half-eaten piece of pizza and shot me a quizzical look. "You didn't answer my question."

"What, about being locked in a tower?"

He nodded.

How was I supposed to answer that? If there was anyone in Santa Fe who had a tower for locking people up, it would be Genoveva Castillo. Unfortunately, I couldn't mention any names, or say anything that might hint at the witchy nature of the Castillo and McAllister families. "It's complicated."

That lackluster response earned me an arched eyebrow. "Everything's complicated. It's got to be more than that."

Of course it was, but I had to watch what I said. "Can I ask you a question?"

"Sure," he replied, then took a bite of pizza. "I can't guarantee I'll answer it, though."

He wore a lopsided smile, so I guessed he was teasing me, at least a little bit. I pulled in a breath and said, "How would you feel if you'd known since you were little that you were supposed to marry someone, and you made sure never to get in a relationship or get close to anyone because you knew you were going to end up with this one person anyway…and then you learned that the person you were promised to hadn't done the same thing, had sort of proactively cheated on you?"

"Is that what happened?" Simon asked. "This guy you're supposed to be with had other girl-friends?"

I nodded, not trusting myself to speak. It seemed like a good time to have another swallow of wine, to focus on the framed poster on the opposite wall, one that advertised a local wine festival at a place called Los Golondrinas.

An awkward silence fell. I could tell he was thinking over what I had said, but at the same time, it seemed as though his opinion on the matter might not be the same as mine, since he didn't quite look at me, appeared focused on snagging another piece of pizza for himself.

"I'm not sure I would call it 'cheating,'" Simons said at last, once he'd finished doctoring his pizza with some of the parmesan cheese that had come with it in little packets. "It's not like you were together at the time."

"But it's not fair!" I burst out.

He shot me a curious look. "What's 'fair'?" he asked.

Well, he had me there. It would be nice to think that life was fair, but I'd learned that lesson long ago, despite my mostly trouble-free child-hood. If the world was truly fair, I would have inherited the magical gifts I was supposed to possess, would have been able to marry whomever I liked. All right, maybe my sister Emily had felt the same way, since as *prima*-in-waiting, she'd had to endure the consort search, had to marry the person she bonded with, but since that person turned out to be a smoking-hot distant Wilcox cousin, it wasn't as though she'd suffered very much.

"I don't know," I said. "I just know that this whole thing is making me feel like crap."

"I'm sorry."

Looking at him, at the sober expression on his lean features, I thought Simon truly was sorry for me, for whatever that was worth. Unfortunately, his pity wasn't going to change anything about my situation. "Thanks," I said.

"For what?"

"For listening to me babble. I probably shouldn't have dumped any of this on you, but you're the only person I know in Santa Fe who isn't—" I had to stop myself, because I'd almost said, *Who isn't a Castillo.* "Who isn't part of my fiancé's family. His sister is super nice, but I still don't think she'd take my side against her brother."

"Probably not," Simon remarked. "A lot of these old families in Santa Fe are pretty tight."

I tilted my head at him. "How did you know they were an old family?"

"Oh, well—I just figured if they were doing something as old-fashioned as arranging marriages, then they had to be one of the old families. Otherwise, that kind of thing sort of went out at least a hundred years ago."

That made sense. I wondered how many families were like that here in Santa Fe, able to trace their lineage back hundreds of years, long before New Mexico was a state, back to the time the Spaniards had come, bringing God and guns. "What about your family?" I asked.

"My family?" Simon repeated, looking taken aback.

"Yes, your family. Have they been here for hundreds of years?" I grinned, and took a bite of pizza. "You know, you've never even told me your last name."

"I didn't?" He shrugged and went on, "It's Gutierrez. And no, we haven't been here for hundreds of years. My family came up from Mexico in the early 1900s, I think. To some of the really old families, we're still considered upstarts. But whatever. It's not where you come from that's important, but what you make of yourself."

I thought of him riding the train to Albuquerque so he wouldn't miss any classes while his car was in the shop, of how he appeared to take every weekend to work in order to support himself. Hustle, I thought, the kind of initiative I'd never seemed to show. Why would I? My parents had made sure I had just about anything I wanted…except real magical powers. That was a gift beyond even their control.

And Simon was right. It didn't matter who your family was, or where you'd come from. The important thing was what you did for yourself. Right now, it seemed as though I was failing that test, big-time.

"Look," he went on. "I don't pretend to know everything that's going on with you and this guy you're supposed to marry. And maybe I shouldn't be saying this at all, maybe it's not my place…but if you have any doubts—any at all—then you shouldn't marry him. I don't care what kind of arrangement your two families have made. You shouldn't jump into something you're not sure about."

It all sounded so easy when he said it. In a perfect world, maybe I should have been able to go to Rafe and tell him that we needed to delay the wedding, needed to take our time with each other. To be fair, some of this was my fault, since the other evening I'd been absolutely sure that we were meant to be together. His kisses had affected me so much that I hadn't been thinking straight, had thought that surely we were destined to be together.

I wished my mother had warned me about that kind of thing. Maybe she hadn't thought I would have such a physical reaction to the man who was my betrothed. Or maybe because her only real experience with the opposite sex was my father, her consort, she hadn't thought she could provide any useful advice on the subject, because the sparks that the consort bond generated were something far beyond simple attraction. Either way, I'd been caught off guard.

"It's not that easy," I said, and Simon gave me a weary smile.

"No, probably not. But you need to stick up for yourself if no one else will." He pushed a pizza crust around on his plate, deliberately not looking at me. "I want you to stick up for yourself."

"Why?"

"Because you deserve it. You deserve to have the life you want. And also—" His eyes met mine, dark, penetrating, sending an odd shiver down my spine. "I like you, Miranda. I want you to dump this guy because…well, you probably know why."

It was my turn to look away. I knew then that I needed to get up and leave, because matters were in enough of a tangle with Rafe without me getting close to someone else. My biggest mistake had been accepting Simon's invitation to stay here at all. For all I knew, he'd taken my acceptance of his offer as encouragement to pursue me, when all I'd wanted was a place to take refuge for a few hours. And yes, try to talk things out, get a handle on what I should do next. That wasn't fair to

Simon, though. I was just using him to work through my problems, and he didn't deserve that kind of treatment. I might not have known all that much about him, but I did know he was a decent person, someone who shouldn't be saddled with my burdens.

I wiped my hands on the paper towel he'd given me, then got up from the couch. "I really should go."

He stood, too. Although not quite as tall as Rafe, he was still tall enough that the top of my head didn't quite reach his chin. "I'm sorry. I shouldn't have said that."

"No, it's okay. It's just—no one knows where I am, and they've got be worried. I need to get back."

One hand lifted, as if he intended to reach out to me, and I tensed. At once his hand dropped back to his side, and he stepped away from me. "If you have to."

I could see the hurt in his face, and I hated myself for causing it. At the same time, I knew I needed to go. Part of me wanted to reach out to him, but I couldn't allow myself to do that, not when the situation with Rafe was still so unsettled.

"Thank you, Simon," I whispered, and grabbed my purse and hurried toward the door. Just as my fingers settled on the knob, he spoke.

"I hope everything works out for you, Miranda. But if it doesn't"—he paused there, and seemed to gather his breath—"if it doesn't, you know where to find me."

I couldn't answer. All I did was nod slightly, and then I forced myself to slide out the door before I did something I regretted.

Or maybe it was too late for that.

14

EXPLANATIONS

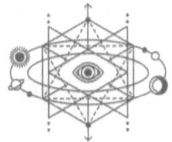

I DIDN'T EVEN TRY TO TELEPORT AWAY FROM Simon's apartment, even though the little foyer that opened onto the alley was completely deserted and I wouldn't have had any witnesses to my sudden disappearance. After the failures I'd suffered recently whenever I'd tried to consciously guide the magical gifts that had inexplicably awoken in me, I didn't want to experience yet another letdown.

Instead, I walked a few doors down to a bar located on the corner, then asked the bartender there if he could call me a Ryde. Luckily, he was accommodating; it was standard practice back where I came from that bars would offer this kind of service, but I hadn't been sure about how they did things in Santa Fe. The self-driving car appeared a few minutes later, and I gave it the address for Rafe's house. That might have been a mistake; I didn't know for sure where he would be, and since I didn't have a phone, I couldn't call. It seemed the most logical place to look for him, though. Besides, I just couldn't face the prospect of going back to the casita and being intercepted by Genoveva. She might not have known about my disappearance, but I didn't want to take the risk.

As the Ryde vehicle pulled up at the curb in front of Rafe's place, I noticed a black Mercedes SUV parked about half a block away. Cat's car. It seemed as though the two of them were lying low together, which made sense. Cat would have gone to her brother for help, and done what she could to avoid her mother and make it seem as if everything was just fine.

I didn't know for sure whether it was a good thing that Cat was there. True, we were friendly with each other, and I might have been able to look on her as an ally, but on the other hand, it was entirely possible that she'd lost patience with me after this latest episode. If that turned out to be the case, then I could all too easily imagine brother and sister joining forces to condemn me for yet another disappearance. True, this one had been entirely involuntary, but I didn't know whether I'd be able to convince them of that fact.

Whatever happened, I needed to get this over

with. There were things I needed to say to Rafe in private, but I had to hope Cat would allow us that privacy once she realized the importance of such a conversation. If not...well, Rafe and I had the prospect of our impending nuptials hanging over both of us. Cat had to understand that the wedding might not happen at all if we weren't able to get things worked out.

I got out of the Ryde and forced in a breath of chilly early evening air, then let it out again. One foot in front of another. That made it a little easier to move down the sidewalk and turn onto the flagstone path leading to Rafe's front door. If I could focus on the small things, I didn't have to think about the big ones.

Like the pleading expression in Simon's eyes as he gazed down at me. The last thing I'd wanted to do was hurt him, but he had to know that we didn't have any chance at a future together.

At least, that's what I needed to tell myself. I needed to believe I would be with Rafe, that somehow all of this would work out. As for my magic, well, I hoped we could get to the bottom of that puzzle as well, once our relationship got sorted out.

Before I could lose my nerve, I leaned over and pressed the button for the doorbell. A simple *ding-dong* sounded within the depths of the house, and I clung to my purse strap, telling myself this would all be okay. Because Cat was here, Rafe couldn't lose his temper too much...could he?

Far sooner than I would have liked, he opened the door. His amber-brown eyes widened in surprise—and, I thought, a trace of relief—just before a frown creased his forehead. "Where the hell—"

"Can I come in?" I asked, forestalling his question. "It's cold out here."

The request seemed to halt any recriminations he'd been about to utter. "Well...sure."

He stepped out of the way, and I went inside the small foyer as he closed the door against the chilly night air. "Cat's here," he said, possibly because he felt he had to say something.

"I know. I saw her car."

He seemed to absorb this piece of information, then led me into the living room. As soon as I came into view, Cat rose from the couch, her expression one of shock.

"Miranda! Are you okay?"

"I'm fine," I said. Whether that statement was actually true, I didn't know for sure. Physically, I was all right. My mental state was an entirely different topic for speculation.

"What happened to you? I saw—I saw you disappear, but that's impossible, isn't it?"

"I guess not," I replied, shoving my cold hands in the pockets of my jacket. The silky fabric that lined them was also cold, but it was better than nothing. "I don't know why any of this is happening —or how—but I did teleport away from the cathedral to another part of downtown." That statement was accurate without giving any real information away, and I hoped it would be enough to tell Cat and Rafe that I had never been in any danger.

"'Any of this'?" Rafe said. His tone fairly dripped with suspicion. "There's more than what just happened at the chapel?"

"I—"

"Miranda, why don't you sit down? You look pale. And Rafe," Cat added, shooting her brother a significant glance, "go get her a glass of water or something. Lord only knows what all this has taken out of her."

Maybe God—or the Goddess—knew, but I certainly didn't. I allowed Cat to guide me over to one of the couches and sit me down. It did feel better to be off my shaky legs, and the obvious kindness of the gesture made me think that maybe she wouldn't give me too much trouble about all this.

Rafe, on the other hand....

He returned to the living room right then and gave me the glass of water he'd been holding. I swallowed some, glad of the cool liquid flowing down my throat.

"Thank you," I said, once I was done drinking. "I know this all looks crazy, but really, I don't understand what's going on any more than you do."

"Was that the first time it happened?" Cat asked as she gave her brother a quelling look. I could tell she wanted to take the lead in asking questions, probably to avoid as much awkwardness as possible.

I'd go along...for a while. At some point, though, those questions would probably veer into territory I only wanted to cover with Rafe.

"Not exactly," I said, and he shot me a narrow-eyed look.

"What do you mean, 'not exactly'?"

"I mean that I had a really short blip last night, when I was alone in the casita. For just a few minutes, I somehow managed to transport myself to my parents' house in Jerome."

"You what?" Rafe demanded, and Cat gave him an exasperated glance.

Ignoring the exchange, I said, "I was only there for a minute. Two, max. I could hear them talking down the hall, and I started moving in that direction. But then I tripped on one of the rugs, and the next thing I knew, I was back in the casita."

"So that time yesterday, and then again today —that's it?" Cat inquired.

"Sort of." Those were the only times I'd teleported, after all. My discussion with ghostly Victoria at Tony's house was something entirely different, although I supposed it could also be classified as a manifestation of powers I hadn't even known I possessed. There hadn't been any incidents with spirits after that first one, however.

Rafe crossed his arms, brow still knitted in a frown. "Sort of?"

Briefly, I described how I had spoken with Victoria's ghost, a magical gift that was my mother's but which had never been mine. As I spoke, Rafe's frown only deepened, while Cat appeared increasingly perplexed.

"Why didn't you tell me?" she asked.

"At the time, I didn't think there was all that much to tell. I mean, while talking to ghosts and spirits is a witchy power, it's also something that civilians have claimed to do from time to time. I suppose I just thought all the energy was coming from Victoria's side of things, so to speak."

Rafe rubbed at the dark stubble on his chin. "You talk to any more ghosts? There are a lot of them here in the downtown area, as Cat knows all too well."

His sister shook her head, looking halfway irritated, but she didn't respond.

All I could do was shrug. "No, I haven't encountered any other ghosts or spirits. I have no idea why Victoria decided to talk to me, but I haven't seen anyone else."

"So where've you been for the past few hours?"

Truth, or lies? He hadn't been too pleased about my meeting up with Simon before, when it had all been an utter coincidence. I doubted Rafe would be happy to hear how my subconscious had somehow decided that Rafe's apartment was the place I needed to go when my weird teleportation talent kicked in. My brain apparently decided it was better to tell a white lie, because I said, "I ended up in a big building that I realized was the Museum of Art. Luckily, no one was in the gallery when I appeared. I thought it might be better if I hung out there for a while, cooled off a bit, and—"

His eyes narrowed at that comment, but he didn't respond. Had Cat told him what she and I were talking about when I went poof? I couldn't tell for sure, but it seemed that way, judging by his current reticence, the sudden tightness of his jaw and mouth.

"—and then the museum was closing, so I left and walked back down to San Francisco Street and got something to eat. I was really hungry by then—I guess teleporting uses up a lot of energy or something. But then I realized you all must be really worried about me, and so I got a Ryde and came over here. I figured you were probably trying to stay away from Genoveva so she wouldn't find out what had happened."

"That's exactly it," Rafe said, his voice grim. "Not so easy when she wanted all of us to go out to dinner tonight, but I told her you and I wanted to have a romantic meal alone, and she seemed to buy it."

"I'm sorry," I told him. And I was. Sorry that I kept seeming to mess things up just when it appeared as though we'd gotten our differences worked out, sorry that I had to lie to him. My instincts told me it was better that he didn't know I'd been with Simon. Of course nothing had happened, but I didn't know whether Rafe would believe that our encounter had been entirely innocent. "And I'm sorry about these weird magical flare-ups. I don't know what's causing them—I've never had any magic talents appear before this. You have to believe that."

"Of course we do," Cat said quickly, as though she wasn't quite sure whether her brother would respond the same way. "We know your parents told our mother you didn't have any magical gifts. Why would they have any reason to lie about that?"

Well, one could postulate that they might have told such a lie to keep me out of this arranged marriage, but that wasn't the case. As far as they knew, I was entirely without magic. As I had been, up until the day before yesterday. "No reason at all," I said.

"Maybe it's something in the air here," Rafe remarked, and I couldn't quite tell whether or not he was joking.

"Maybe," I allowed. "After all, when you're dealing with magic, all bets are off, right?"

"Something like that." His gaze shifted to Cat. "Well, it looks like Miranda is safe and sound, so you'd better head on back. That way Genoveva can stop texting you every five minutes."

"It's all these bridesmaids I'm dealing with," Cat replied. "They're driving me crazy. I don't know why they need me to hold their hand for every little thing."

"Thank God groomsmen aren't that same way."

"No," she shot back, "because they're texting me, too. Somehow I got designated as assistant wedding coordinator or something."

"It's because Mother trusts you implicitly."

Cat screwed up her nose and gave her brother an "I don't think so" kind of look. "More like she doesn't have anyone else to dump all this on, since Louisa and Malena both have toddlers and are busy enough already. But whatever. I'm just glad it's all's well that ends well over here."

About all I could do was smile in response to that comment. Judging by the tension in Rafe's jaw line, he didn't share his sister's assessment of the situation.

And I had a feeling he was going to let me know all about it once she was safely out of the house.

Somehow, though, I managed to summon a smile as she came over and gave me a quick hug, and said she'd text my parents to let them know I was okay. I hadn't realized they'd known I was missing, but I supposed that Cat or Rafe had probably reached out to them for help.

"Oh, would you?" I said. "This not having a phone thing is a real pain."

She assured me she'd take care of it, then said she'd see me in the morning so she could drive me to my hair and makeup appointments. We hadn't visited either the makeup artist or the hairstylist, which made me think Genoveva also had a very distinct vision for what she wanted, a vision that apparently didn't require my input. Which was fine by me. Right then I was so tired, I really didn't care what she had planned, even if it turned out to be pigtails or cornrows.

After Cat left, an ominous quiet fell on the living room. I picked up my glass of water and took another drink, glad I had something I could do to fill the silence.

"Do you know why you did it?" Rafe asked at last.

"Did what?"

"Teleported away from the cathedral."

"I didn't really *do* anything," I told him. "It just sort of…happened."

He'd been standing off to one side, close to the fireplace, but now he came over to the sofa and sat down next to me. I didn't know for sure whether that was a good thing or not; having him this close tended to both excite me and put me on edge. For better or worse, some hidden quality about his physical presence seemed to have the power to set all my nerve endings on fire.

"Miranda."

That was all he said, but it was enough. From his tone, I could tell that Cat had informed him what the two of us had been talking about back at the cathedral, and it wasn't trading our favorite chocolate chip cookie recipes.

I swallowed. "All right…I was upset."

"Because Cat told you about my girlfriends?"

Plural. Not one, but several. Or maybe it had been more than several. For all I knew, Rafe could be the biggest man-whore in Santa Fe. Did I want to know the truth? I didn't think I could answer that question honestly.

"Yes, she told me," I said in a very small voice. "I guess it just came as something of a shock."

"Because you never had any boyfriends back in Arizona."

"Exactly that."

He reached over and took my hand. "I didn't know about that. It's not like your parents talked to my mother very much. I had no idea what was going on with you, what was happening in your life."

I tried to ignore the warmth of his skin, the strength of the fingers that were now entwined with mine. All they did was distract me, and I needed to be able to focus. "Would it have made a difference?"

No reply right away. His gaze traveled to the hearth, where suddenly the wood that was laid there blazed up into a bright fire. Nice trick. Of course all witches and warlocks could call the fire to them—even I could manage such a thing—but not all of them could do it while seated across the room like this. I had to have my finger actually touching the wick of a candle or the kindling in a fireplace to create a spark, but clearly Rafe was far more powerful than I.

I wondered what it looked like when he shifted into animal form, and whether he'd ever allow me to witness such a transformation.

Then he spoke. "I honestly don't know if it would have made a difference."

Anger flared in me, and I tried to pull my

hand away from his, but his fingers clamped down on mine, preventing me from doing so.

"Listen, Miranda," he said, his voice low, urgent, "I'm only telling you the truth. Would you rather hear a pleasant lie?"

Guilt quickly swallowed my irritation, because of course I'd lied to him just a few moments earlier. "I don't know," I muttered.

"I think you do. Anyway, you have to understand how angry I was with my mother for putting me in this situation. She could have reached out to your parents and told them that they no longer had any obligation to the Castillo clan, that the bargain my grandmother had made died with her. But my mother wouldn't do that. She claimed it was because breaking the bargain would have been an insult to her mother's memory, but I think it was also because she's just that stubborn." He paused, fingers clenched on mine, as if he was trying to communicate his intentions with that pressure of skin against skin. "So yeah, I dated a lot of civilians, mostly to spite her. I liked them all…some of them a lot. I knew those relationships would never go anywhere, though. If you're angry with me for not staying pure, well, there isn't much I can do about that, except to say those women are part of my past. You're my future, Miranda. If I'd known how strong and smart and beautiful you were, maybe I wouldn't have bothered with dating civilian women. Maybe I would've saved myself for you. I can't change what I did, so all I can do in this moment is make sure you're happy here and now."

These words were spoken so earnestly, his expression so sincere as he gazed into my eyes, that I thought I might start sobbing then and there. Somehow I managed to hold back the tears, since I really didn't know how he would react if I completely lost it.

How could I hold those past relationships against him? I could understand all too well his anger toward Genoveva, because I'd felt that same anger myself, although probably not as intensely. My parents could only uphold their end of the bargain; they'd never had the power to break it.

"It's all right," I said at last, once I was sure my voice wouldn't shake too badly and I wasn't in any danger of bursting into tears. "I was being unreasonable."

"I don't know about unreasonable. Feelings are just...feelings. It's how we act on them that's important."

And now he was being all too reasonable. Guilt roiled within me. How could I keep secret where I'd been earlier this evening, after he'd just been so open and heartfelt with me? If we were going to make this work, we had to be honest with one another. Voice hesitant, I said, "Rafe, I —there's something I need to tell you."

I could feel his body tense, but he sounded calm enough as he responded. "What is it?"

"I—I didn't teleport to the museum. I was in Simon's apartment."

Dead silence. About the only thing I found reassuring right then was that Rafe didn't try to pull his hand from mine. Maybe he'd simply forgotten he was touching me.

"You mean you went straight there?"

I nodded miserably. "Yes. At first, I didn't even know where I was. Then I realized that I'd materialized at his place. I couldn't figure out why, but I knew I needed to get out of there. I was just going down the stairs when I bumped into him."

Rafe's eyes glinted in the firelight, but he didn't look precisely angry. Quite possibly he was furious, and the strange, blank expression he currently wore was his attempt to hide his reaction to my revelation. "You spent all that time with him?"

"Well, not exactly. He could tell I was upset, but he had an hour left on his shift. I stayed in his apartment and watched TV until he was off work. He came up, we talked, had some pizza. That was it."

"What did you talk about?" Still in that cool, controlled voice, the one that somehow frightened me more than any outward raging. I didn't have enough experience with men to know whether this sort of reaction was normal or not. My father rarely got angry, and when he did, he let you know exactly why he was pissed off at you. I'd never had to play guessing games with him.

"I talked about my situation, about how I didn't know what I should do. Not in any specifics," I added hastily, since I could see Rafe's brows start to draw together in a fearsome frown. "I just needed a friend to talk to. And it did help, Rafe. I knew I needed to come back and be with you."

"And I suppose Simon was very understanding about all this."

"Yes, he was." I paused for a moment, not sure whether I should say anything else. But the lies I'd told earlier still weighed on me, and I knew I needed to tell him everything I could, no matter how awful it might sound. "I mean, he was disappointed. He—he likes me, I guess. But nothing happened. You have to believe that."

Now Rafe did let go of my hand. He pushed himself up from the couch and went over to the hearth, where he took the poker from the set of fireplace tools there and began prodding at the fire. I got the distinct impression he wished he was stabbing Simon with that poker rather than the logs.

Should I go to him? I sat on the couch, staring at the stiff set of his shoulders, and wished I had more experience in these sorts of situations. That way, I might know what to do.

Gathering my resolve, I said softly, "If I'm willing to forgive you all those girlfriends, then you need to let this thing with Simon go. Like I said, nothing happened. Not a friendly hug, not a touch on the hand, not a kiss. Nothing. I left because I wanted to be here with you. Otherwise…."

"Otherwise?"

"I would have stayed there. I would have let him kiss me. But I don't want Simon to kiss me." Now I stood up and went to stand next to Rafe by the fireplace. I reached out and touched his free hand, trailed my fingers over his skin. "I want you to kiss me, Rafe."

For the longest moment, he didn't move, didn't respond. Then, very deliberately, he put the poker back in its stand, turned, and cupped my face in his hands. His mouth came down on mine, urgent, my mouth opening to his so he could taste me. One hand moved from my cheek to my hair, tangling in it, making sure I couldn't get away.

Not that I wanted to. I might have blamed the sensation on standing so close to the fire, but I knew the heat that trembled all through me now had everything to do with Rafe, with the way I couldn't help but react to him. I understood that something of the roughness of this kiss was his way of laying claim to me, of making sure I knew that I was his. An instinctual, atavistic reaction, one I might have resented in anyone else, but now only made me want him that much more.

It was going to be a long wait until our wedding night, even though it was only twenty-four hours away.

At last he let go of me. I staggered back a pace, trying to catch my breath. He remained where he was, although he put one hand up against the hearth of sculpted plaster, as if he needed it to help steady himself.

"Wow," I said at last.

He smiled then, a quick, wolfish grin that reminded me of his inborn talent, the ability to take on an animal's shape. "I guess I got a little carried away."

"It's all right," I said. "Well, more than all right, but you know what I mean."

At once he moved away from the fireplace, and came over and took both my hands in his. "I never used to be the jealous type."

"There's nothing to be jealous about," I protested. "Like I told you, nothing happened."

"Oh, I got that part. I believe you." He bent and touched his lips to my forehead, and even that chaste kiss sent need leaping through me all over again. "It's just the mere thought that someone else would want you, and that the 'someone else' in question is someone right here in Santa Fe…that's what's giving me the most trouble. Someone pining for you back in Arizona is one thing, but…."

"'Want' is kind of a strong word," I said. "All he said was that he likes me."

"Guy code for 'I want you,'" Rafe returned. "Trust me."

I supposed he should know, since he had so much more experience with love and desire than I did. And it really wasn't worth arguing over. I couldn't help but feel sorry for Simon, although I told myself that he'd meet someone else soon enough. He'd probably found himself attracted to me because I was new and different. Anyone as kind and smart and attractive as Simon wouldn't stay single for very long.

"All right," I said. "But it's immaterial, because I'm here with you. There's nothing to be jealous about."

"And you won't see him again?"

That question made me pause. "I can't say that," I said carefully. "Because we're friendly with one another, and frankly, Rafe, you don't have the right to tell me who I can and can't see. I don't have any other friends here."

He began to frown, but then his expression

cleared. "You're right, of course. I shouldn't be acting like something out of a Dickens novel, threatening to lock you up if you don't do as I say. Just—" The words stopped there, as if he wasn't sure how he should phrase what he'd intended to say next.

"Just what?" I asked.

"If you're going to see him, just please let me know. I won't ask to go with you, I won't press you about the details. I guess all I'm asking is that you don't lie to me about it."

The anger had gone from his expression, and now all I saw was worry. I went to him and laid my head on his chest, put my arms around him. "Of course I'll tell you. Anyway, it won't be anytime soon, because you're going to be whisking me away to a romantic week in Taos, right?"

"Right," he said. His lips brushed against my hair. "You'll be far too occupied to even think about Simon."

I grinned up at Rafe. "Is that a promise?"

"Oh, yes," he replied. "Yes, it is."

15

CONFRONTATIONS

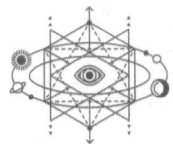

Rafe

IT WAS DIFFICULT SAYING GOODBYE TO Miranda, to stand quietly and let her go inside the casita and shut the door. Crazy how it seemed that each time he kissed her, his body craved more of her, needed all of her, needed to make her his in the most physical way possible. He didn't want to let her out of his sight, wanted her to stay the night at his place. But he knew they would be together forever after tomorrow afternoon, and he told himself that he could wait these last few hours, no matter how difficult the separation might feel at the moment.

As he was walking back to his Jeep, his phone buzzed in his pocket. His first reaction was to ignore the call, but he knew that wasn't a very good idea, not with the wedding so close at hand. The friends and cousins who'd signed on to be his groomsmen were pretty self-sufficient, true, and yet there was still the possibility of some last-minute snafu.

When Rafe saw his mother's number on the phone's display, he had to suppress a mental groan. He should have listened to his gut and let the call roll over to voicemail. However, now that he knew who was calling, he realized he'd have to pick up.

"Yes?" he said, digging in his jeans pocket for the Wrangler's keys.

"Can I speak to you for a moment, please?"

Busted. He'd hoped he would be able to quietly drop Miranda off at the casita and then slip away before his mother even realized he was on the property, but clearly that had been a vain hope. "Sure," he said, wondering as he replied what she was going to grill him about now. Had Cat let slip something about what happened with Miranda this afternoon? Or had Genoveva witnessed Miranda's disappearance after all, despite Cat's assurances that their mother had had her back turned when it happened, and therefore couldn't have seen anything?

Several times during his adolescence, Rafe had wondered whether his mother had eyes in the back of her head. If she really had seen anything in the cathedral, it would just prove his teenage hypothesis.

Mouth set, he turned away from his car and let himself back in through the gate that led into the gardens. A moment on the winding gravel path that traced its way through frost-yellowed grass, and then he was climbing the steps which led him to the veranda and the side door into the kitchen.

It was unoccupied. He went down the hall and peeked into his mother's study, assuming she would be there, but it was empty as well.

Rafe frowned. After dinner, Genoveva tended to retreat to her study, usually to check her emails and phone calls, or possibly to read if no clan business intruded. By now it was past eight o'clock, and so she should have already finished her evening meal. Usually it was just her and Cat, since Rafe's father Eduardo was often kept late at one of his restaurants—by design, as far as Rafe could tell—and sometimes Genoveva dined alone, if Cat had plans for the evening.

He heard the sound of voices coming from the front of the house, and realized his mother must be in the living room. And it wasn't Cat he heard with her, but his father. That was unusual. Rafe grimaced, praying that this was all just a little pre-wedding family gathering and not the grilling he feared.

Cat was nowhere in evidence. Out with the bridesmaids? Maybe; it was the one pretext she could have used to stay away from Genoveva, the one plausible excuse that would have allowed her to avoid any rebukes about not being home the evening before the wedding.

As soon as he entered the living room, Genoveva asked, "How was your dinner with Miranda?"

Rafe had been prepared for this, and so he found it easy enough to reply, "Very good. We went to Andiamo."

It was the sort of intimate place one might take a fiancée for dinner, but because it wasn't one of his father's restaurants, Rafe knew he could safely lie about being there.

Genoveva's mouth thinned. Although she knew competition was necessary, she still was not overly happy to hear about any of the family patronizing an establishment that didn't belong to them. However, her voice was more pleasant than Rafe had anticipated as she said, "I'm glad to hear it. Your father and I were just going over the schedule for the day."

"Ah," Rafe replied. "Well, if you've made any changes, you need to make sure you let me know. I'd hate to show up for photos even ten minutes late."

That comment, with its underlying trace of

sarcasm, elicited a frown, and Eduardo said, his tone mild enough, "I don't think anything's been changed. We just wanted to make sure everything goes smoothly."

Which it should, since Rafe's father's particular talent involved removing any obstacles that might interfere with a preferred outcome. It wasn't exactly the same as having good luck, or otherwise Eduardo could have added a good deal of money to the clan's coffers via some judicious lottery playing, or trying his hand at blackjack in one of the area's numerous tribal casinos. No, it was more that everything tended to work out for him, from the refit of the house's radiant in-floor heating system, which came in under budget and ahead of schedule, to the fourth restaurant in his local culinary empire basically dropping into his palm like a ripe fruit when the previous owner decided he'd had enough of Santa Fe and headed west to Los Angeles. While this talent was focused on Eduardo, those around him did tend to reap the benefits, as a sort of collateral beneficence.

"Well, you don't need to worry about anything on my or Miranda's part," Rafe said. While baiting his mother had become something of a pastime lately, he knew better than to be difficult on this one topic. She was already strung to the breaking point because of having to get this grand event coordinated with only forty-eight hours to plan, and any teasing would not be looked on kindly. "She's going to go to bed early and get plenty of rest, and I plan to do the same."

"Good," Genoveva said. Her eyes were narrowed slightly, as though she was attempting to find something in his remark that she could find fault with, and failing. "Cat is going to fetch her at nine, so we can have a big breakfast here at the house. I'd invite you, but of course you're not supposed to see your bride before the ceremony."

A foolish superstition, but Rafe didn't argue. While he would have endured his mother's company that early in the morning in order to give Miranda some moral support, he knew she'd have Cat at her side, and so, he hoped, she should be able to survive the experience relatively unscathed.

"It's all right," he said, his tone off-hand. "Tony and the rest of the guys are going to meet me for breakfast at Tia Sophia's."

"Good," Genoveva responded. "That way, you can keep an eye on them. I don't entirely trust Tony to show up sober."

Rafe had to suppress a grin. In general, Tony was fairly responsible, despite his off-hand manner, but he'd gone out for a highly alcoholic brunch right before his older brother's wedding, and no one—especially Genoveva—had ever forgotten it.

"I think he'll be fine, but okay."

"Make sure you're at the cathedral no later than three-thirty," she went on, apparently ignoring his comment. "You can change there, since I'm having all the men's suits brought to the dressing room rather than sending them all over town to everyone's houses."

"Three-thirty seems a little early," he protested. "I thought the service wasn't until five. Do you really think it's going to take me an hour and a half to put on a set of tails?"

"It's better to be early than late," she returned. "Bring your laptop if you need something to occupy yourself."

No, thanks. The last thing he needed was his computer getting lost amid the general hubbub, especially since he'd have to rely on Cat or one of his groomsmen to keep track of it. The plan was for him and Miranda to get on the road for Taos immediately following the reception, even though they wouldn't reach their destination until close to midnight. Still, he preferred a late arrival to spending the night here in Santa Fe. That seemed too anticlimactic. Besides, he wanted to make sure he was far enough away that his mother couldn't meddle in his first night with Miranda.

"I'll figure something out," he said.

"Good." Genoveva turned toward Rafe's father. "And you have the rental car all arranged?"

"Yes. It'll be waiting at your house, Rafe."

"My Jeep will do just fine—"

"You are not driving your new bride up to Taos in that rattletrap," his mother said. "The limo will take you home, and then you can pick up the rental car for your drive north."

He bristled but said nothing. For years Genoveva had done her best to get him to give up the Wrangler, saying it was an eyesore and not something the *prima's* son should be driving. He'd ignored her, since she really couldn't compel him to get rid of the Jeep. Now, though, he thought he could see her side of the argument. Miranda was beautiful and passionate and pure. She deserved to go away on her honeymoon in style. And when they got back to Santa Fe, he'd have to buy a car for her. The Wrangler suited him just fine, but Miranda should have something better. Maybe that steel-gray Mercedes convertible he'd seen at the dealership when they went to buy Cat her SUV.

Anyway, all that could be decided later. For now, he just wanted the wedding and reception to be over with so he could have more from his fiancée than mere kisses.

"Okay," he said. "Anything else?"

His parents looked at one another. Then his father spoke. "No, I think that should cover it. We know this day has been a long time coming. We want it to be as perfect as possible. Your mother says that Miranda is an admirable young woman, and from the little I've seen of her, I have to agree. Take care of her, and treat her well."

"I will," Rafe replied, somewhat wounded that his father could believe he would ever mistreat the woman he was supposed to marry. Then again, his past behavior might have led his parents to harbor their own doubts. Not that he would hurt Miranda physically, but that he might inflict a more subtle kind of wound, one of emotional neglect, solely because he had been forced into this.

That wouldn't happen, though. He knew he'd been very lucky to have Miranda turn out to be so close to his ideal. They still needed to get to know one another, but at least he could tell they were physically compatible.

He wanted to laugh at himself for that thought. Physically compatible? More like horny as hell. He'd never before kissed someone who could arouse him so quickly. And better not to think about the way Miranda affected him, because all he'd accomplish was to get hot and bothered, and consummation was still a day away.

"Three-thirty," his mother warned him as he rose from the couch. "And no later."

"I'll be early," Rafe said, which was only the truth. He had a project he could work on if he needed to find some way to fill the time before the wedding, but he doubted he'd be able to concentrate. Might as well show up to the cathedral early and hope that by doing so he could get the time to the ceremony to pass more quickly...and also mollify his mother.

Genoveva only raised an eyebrow at that reply, but she also got up from where she'd been sitting and came over and gave him a desultory hug. An even more awkward hug from his father—they'd never been a demonstrative family—and then Rafe was making his goodbyes and escaping through the front door.

It did feel like an escape. All things considered, though, his parents had been remarkably mellow. Maybe Genoveva had finally decided to let up a bit because the goal was so near in sight. Less than the span of a day, and he would be safely married to Miranda McAllister.

As Rafe backed out of the driveway and began to head for home, he found himself frowning, though. His mother might think all the loose ends were being neatly tied up, but he knew better. There was the issue of Miranda's strange outbreaks of magical talent, for one thing. So far she hadn't done anything that would endanger herself or anyone else, but there was always the possibility that she might, not consciously, but because her powers got out of hand. They'd just have to keep an eye on things, see what happened. It did seem as if this last episode had occurred because of extreme stress, so maybe if they did their best to make sure she didn't get upset, her magical outbursts wouldn't even be an issue.

If necessary, he supposed they could go to his mother for help, but he'd prefer to avoid that. Maybe Miranda's father would get lucky and find something in his research that would allow her to take control of her abilities. Now that Rafe had Angela's number, he could speak with Miranda's parents as needed, and Genoveva would never have to know.

Far more troubling than the question of Miranda's magical powers, though, was this Simon character. Of all the problems Rafe had imagined he might have to deal with, being engaged to a woman he'd never met, the last thing he'd thought he would have to face was having a rival right here on his home turf. Miranda could claim that nothing had happened with Simon, and Rafe was inclined to believe her, even though at first she'd lied and tried to hide their latest meeting. But her stubborn insistence that she should be able to remain friends with the guy—that rubbed Rafe the wrong way. He wasn't the kind of man who needed—or wanted—to keep his significant other all to himself. With time, he hoped Miranda would have her own circle of friends among the

Castillos, and among the town's civilians as well, if she met people she got along with. However, it was one thing to have a circle of girlfriends, and quite another to want to be friendly with a guy who clearly had wanted more from her than mere friendship.

The farther he drove, the more irritated Rafe became. By the time he pulled up to his garage, he realized the last thing he wanted to do was meekly go inside the house and pretend everything was fine, that Miranda's relationship with Simon was no big deal. She wanted to act like it was, but Rafe had a hard time believing that. When she'd teleported out of the chapel in a panicked rage, her destination hadn't been his house or the casita where she'd been staying. No, she'd gone straight to Simon's place. Why would her mind have sent her there, unless it had subconsciously believed that his apartment was her safest refuge in Santa Fe?

That settled it. Rafe put the Jeep in reverse and backed out of the driveway, then headed into downtown, circling the Plaza so he could end up going the proper direction on San Francisco Street. Once he'd pulled up to the curb in front of the wine tasting room where Simon worked and turned off the engine, Rafe sat there for a moment, listening to his heart beat, trying to tell himself that this was crazy. He was getting married tomorrow, and yet he was here in front of the apartment where his rival lived.

His rival. That sounded so…Victorian. But Rafe knew he had to warn Simon away. The situation with Miranda was new and easily compromised. The last thing he wanted was to have some other guy hanging around, possibly making her think of all the opportunities she might have had, if only her parents hadn't agreed to this arranged marriage.

Mouth grim, Rafe climbed out of the Jeep, straightened his jacket, and went over to the sidewalk and looked up. The wine tasting room was closed at this hour, even on a Saturday night, but he noted the lights in the apartment above. It appeared that Simon was at home.

Perhaps that sign of occupancy should have been enough to tell Rafe he should go back to his place. Once he went upstairs and knocked on Simon's door, he knew he'd be past the point of no return.

No, that wasn't precisely true. Rafe was pretty sure he'd passed that point as soon as he got out of the car. There was only one thing he could do now.

He cut down the alley, then turned to his right. A few cars were parked here, each in a spot that proclaimed it was residents-only parking and that violators would be towed. In between two of the parking spaces was a concrete walkway that led up to a door, presumably the tenants' entrance.

The door was locked, but of course that didn't matter to a warlock. Rafe put his hand on the handle and pushed it down, swinging the door inward. Here was a small foyer, with a set of stairs off to the right.

He climbed those stairs, each step seeming to echo in his head with a resounding *thump*. However, he kept doggedly on, telling himself he was doing this for him and Miranda. They needed to be able to concentrate on one another, and their fragile new relationship, without having to deal with interference from an outsider.

The stairs ended in a small landing with just one door. Rafe stood there for a moment, trying to gather himself. His heart was pounding, but from nerves, not because of the steps he'd just climbed.

Then he raised his hand and knocked.

No one answered right away. In fact, the silence that followed his knocks was so profound, he wondered if he'd been mistaken, if Simon had gone out for the evening and had left the lights on because he didn't want to come back to a dark apartment.

But then the door opened, and a man—young man, really, probably five years younger than Rafe

—stared out at him with piercing dark eyes. Something about those eyes awoke a deep, atavistic fear in him, reaching all the way down to the magical gift that allowed him to turn into a wolf or a coyote or a mountain lion. The animal side of him recognized an enemy, making all his muscles tense, adrenaline shooting through his veins.

The stranger gave him a confused smile. "Can I help you?"

"Are you Simon?"

"Um…yeah. And you are?"

"I'm Miranda's fiancé," Rafe replied, not bothering to give his actual name. Better that this guy didn't have any idea of who he was. The adrenaline still surged and seethed along his veins, but he held himself still, not wanting to make a move that might put Simon on his guard.

"Oh." Simon glanced past Rafe, although it was clear enough that no one else stood on the landing with him. "You'd better come inside, then."

Every instinct in Rafe's body was telling him not to, that it was safer to stay out on the landing, and yet he found himself nodding. In the next moment, he had stepped past Simon and stood in the apartment, which looked fairly neat and clean for a guy in his early twenties living on his own. The television was paused, apparently in the middle of some sci-fi show—the screen held a frozen image of two spaceships firing at each other.

Simon moved past him, picked up the remote, and turned off the TV. After setting down the remote, he crossed his arms and fixed Rafe with another of those black stares. His eyes were extremely dark, so dark it was hard to detect the pupils at all. "I suppose you've come here to warn me away from Miranda."

Rafe shoved his hands in his pockets. "Yes."

"Why?"

That question only made him frown. "What do you mean, why? I'd think it was pretty obvious. We're getting married tomorrow, and I don't need some other guy hanging around, mooning after her."

Simon's mouth twisted into a wry smile. "Did she say I was going to hang around and moon after her?"

"No, but she didn't have to. From what I could tell, you like her…a lot. But she's going to be my wife, and you need to stay away."

That lopsided smile didn't fade. "Why so threatened? She needed a friend, so I've been a friend to her, nothing more."

"But you want there to be more, don't you?"

Simon's eyes glinted then, like the cut jet stones in a brooch Genoveva had inherited from her mother Isabel. Voice clear and cold, he said, "Oh, yes. I actually want there to be much, much more. You don't have any idea of the treasure that's dropped into your hands, do you?"

"I—" Rafe began, but it was as though his tongue had stuck to the roof of his mouth. He couldn't get out another syllable, even if he wanted to. Likewise, his entire body felt frozen, his feet glued to the floor. What the hell was going on?

"That's why I made friends with Miranda," Simon continued, his tone friendly, reasonable, as if nothing strange at all was going on. "She has the potential to be so much more than what she is now. All she needs is someone to give her guidance, to show her how to tap into the gifts that have slept within her all these years. And I'll be the one to do that for her."

With every ounce of will he possessed, Rafe struggled against the force that seemed to keep him from speaking, from moving. Nothing happened. It was like those times when he was younger and had awoken from night terrors, his entire body trapped, immobile, beneath the heavy covers.

"Keep trying," Simon said with a chuckle. "I'm afraid you're not strong enough to break free. However, you can still be useful to me. I'm going to let you go after this, Rafe. I'll let you go, and you won't remember a thing. I need you to do a favor for me, though. You see, I need Miranda to come to me of her own free will. She needs to choose me, and walk away from you. That means you need to hurt her so terribly that she has no choice but to run to me. Do you think you can do that?"

Rafe wished he could shake his head. He wanted to tell Simon he would do no such thing. Actually, what he really wanted was to have the use of his hands so he could wrap them around the other man's throat. Never before had he wanted to kill anyone, but now a red, murderous rage rose up in him, making him wish he could see Simon's blood spilled on the floor.

"Oh, don't try to fight it. I can tell you're angry. I need you to forget about that, Rafe. What reason do you have to be angry?"

As suddenly as it had come, the wave of anger dissipated. He stood there, blank and empty, waiting to be told what to do.

Simon smiled. "That's better. It's really simple, Rafe. You're going to tell Miranda you don't love her, that you don't want her. You're going to do this at the worst possible time. Can you think when that might be?"

An image formed in Rafe's mind of Miranda standing before him in her wedding gown. "Yes," he said, his tongue feeling thick and clumsy, as though he'd just been given a shot of novocaine.

"Good. Now you're going to go home and forget that you ever came here. You're going to get ready for your wedding, and no one is going to think there's anything strange about your behavior. Understood?"

Deep within, some tiny part of Rafe's soul, the part that could still think and feel for itself, cried out in rage, trying to get the rest of his body and brain to wake up. But it wasn't enough. He still stood there, half in a stupor, and quietly listened to Simon's calm, insinuating voice before replying, "Yes."

"All right, then. You can let yourself out, Rafe."

He didn't respond, only turned on his heel and let himself out the door, then walked slowly down the stairs. Still in that same haze, he went to his Jeep and climbed in. The vehicle might as well have been self-driving for as little thought as he put into the journey home. However, he reached the house safely, parked the Wrangler in the garage, and went inside.

And when he awoke the next morning, he remembered nothing after going to see his parents.

16

BETRAYALS

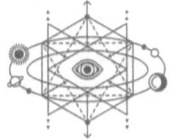

Miranda

I HONESTLY HADN'T BEEN ABLE TO FIGURE OUT what could possibly fill the entire day up to the wedding ceremony, but Cat and Genoveva soon put that question to rest. First, of course, was breakfast at the house, not just with Cat and her mother, but my bridesmaids as well, all six of them. One was Ylena, and another Susanna, and I thought there was a Maria, but after that I lost track. They were all Castillos, of course, cousins of varying degrees, and they seemed friendly and chatty enough. Which was just as well, because that way I could listen to them talk and not have to contribute too much to the conversation. I was more nervous than I'd thought I would be, the butterflies in my stomach interfering with the French toast and bacon I was trying to consume.

Why I was so nervous, I really didn't know. All right, I was about to get married to someone I'd known for a grand total of two days, but I wasn't sure if that was the whole problem. Rafe wasn't a monster, but a handsome, smart guy. We'd already proven that a certain sexual chemistry existed between us. I wouldn't have to pretend I was attracted to him, and although I didn't have much experience when it came to kissing or other forms of intimacy, I could tell from the way I reacted to his embraces that our marriage wouldn't be a cold one...far from it.

No, I was much more worried that my magic might choose an extremely inopportune time to make itself known. So far, the morning had been uneventful, but I still had most of the day to get through, not to mention the ceremony itself. Although nothing had happened to upset me like Cat's revelations about Rafe's former girlfriends, it was still exhausting to realize that after breakfast, we'd all go to the nail salon together, and after that to the hairstylist—apparently we were shutting down a whole salon for those appointments—and then finally to the makeup artist's studio. Considering how big the wedding party was, I wondered whether anyone else in Santa Fe would be able to squeeze in to get their own hair and nails done.

As we were sitting in the pedicure chairs at the nail salon, Cat leaned over to me and whispered, "Are you doing okay?"

"I suppose so," I murmured. Luckily, the other girls were involved in their own conversations and didn't seem to be paying any particular attention to us. Genoveva must have made her own separate arrangements for hair and nails and makeup, because she'd disappeared after breakfast, saying that she needed to be in touch with the florist. I couldn't help but be relieved, since I knew the day would be a lot more survivable without her around. "This all doesn't feel real, I guess."

Cat gave a sympathetic nod. "I can understand that, with everything happening so quickly."

"And also—" I began, then stopped. It was so hard to know what might be safe to talk about. This business with my emergent powers was one thing, but something else bothered me even more. "I hate that I have to do this without my family. I mean, I know that you're my family now, too, but it's not quite the same thing."

"I know. And believe me, Rafe and I had so many arguments with our mother about it, but she just wouldn't budge. I told her it was cruel to deprive you of your family. But…." The words trailed off, and Cat shook her head.

Any chance of her saying more on the subject was gone after that, because our manicurists showed up and started working on our feet and nails. I supposed we could have continued to talk about our families and simply left out any mention of their witchy powers, but even leaving aside that important component, the topic felt way too personal. Instead, we sat there quietly— or rather, I was quiet as Cat talked about the menu for that night's dinner, and the band her father had hired. It did sound as if he'd planned a good party for Rafe and me—and our three hundred guests—and so I tried to smile and be grateful.

A pair of limousines had brought us here after breakfast, and they came and whisked us away to the hair salon at the appointed hour. Even then Cat and I didn't have a chance to talk, since we shared the back of the limo with Susanna and Maria, both of whom kept trying to convince her that they shouldn't have to wear updos, and that everyone would look better with their hair down.

"My mother wants you to wear your hair up," she said flatly, and that seemed to be the end of the discussion. Even the ebullient Castillo cousins apparently didn't want to face off against their formidable *prima*.

At the hair salon, things got a little more relaxed, since the salon owner brought out bottles of sparkling wine from Gruet, a New Mexico winery that specialized in the bubbly stuff. Even I could feel some of the tension leave my neck and shoulders as I sipped at my brut rosé and listened to the stylist, Alberto, wax rhapsodic about my hair.

"So long and thick!" he exclaimed, running a brush through the waist-length locks and letting them fall back down over my shoulders. "Long, loose waves, I think, with the front pinned back."

"Oh, so *she* gets to wear her hair down?" complained Susana from two chairs over.

"Yes, because *she* is the bride," Cat said. "Take a pill."

"I don't know about a pill," Susana returned, "but I'll definitely have more champagne."

She grinned while one of the salon assistants poured her a fresh glass. I watched as she drank, wondering how much of the bubbly stuff she'd consumed already. The last thing I needed was a bunch of tipsy bridesmaids. Then again, if she tripped on her gown or otherwise made a fool of herself somehow, it was Genoveva she'd have to answer to, not me. I didn't need this day to be perfect; I just needed to survive it somehow.

Then it was off to get shampooed and blow-dried, and to sit there as Alberto wound my hair around an impossibly thick curling iron and let the resulting long, loose curls flow down over my shoulders. Good thing Cat had warned me about wearing a button-up shirt; I could only imagine the damage that might result if I had to pull a top up over my head to change into my wedding dress later that afternoon.

The stylist next to me was curling Cat's hair as well, but more tightly than mine, the resulting spirals then pinned up in a complicated arrangement at the back of her head. Since she usually wore it down long and straight, the result made her look quite different, showed off her high cheekbones and almond-shaped dark eyes. Something about her appearance made me think of Rafe, the resemblance between the two of them stronger now, although his eyes were lighter than hers, a warm amber-brown that I'd never seen before I met him.

I wondered what he was doing while I was getting primped within an inch of my life. Drinking with his groomsmen? Maybe, although I doubted he would risk his mother's wrath by getting wasted right before the ceremony. Right then, I hated the stupid tradition that kept the bride and groom apart the day of the wedding. I wanted him there with me, needed the reassurance of his presence. Yes, we'd patched everything up the night before, but I still would have felt better if I could have seen him smile at me, or give a little eye roll at all these elaborate preparations.

After we were done at the hair salon, Susanna announced that she wanted to ride in the limo with the other girls, and took Maria with her. This arrangement suited me just fine, since it gave me a chance to talk to Cat alone—although not for too long, since the makeup artist's studio was only about five minutes away from the salon.

She seemed to understand the limited space of time in which we had to talk, because she said right away, "This thing with your family—I kept arguing with my mother about it—you know, kept hoping she would see reason. But she was like a goddamn mule." Her lips pressed together, and she paused to stare out the tinted window, to look at the people who were looking at us, trying to see who might be inside the limo. This was probably the closest I would ever get to feeling like a movie star, and it did make me feel quite grand, despite my underlying worries. Cat added, "I think it has something to do with her mother. My grandmother, you know."

I wasn't sure if I did know. I tilted my head at her, urging her to go on.

"Well, she didn't talk about it much, but I always got the impression that she was angry at your parents for taking her mother away, for the way she'd died on their watch, so to speak. Lord only knows that my grandmother Isabel wouldn't have done anything she didn't want to, but I think my mother still resented losing her years before she should have. And so one way she could get back at your parents was to deprive them of seeing you get married."

"That's...awfully petty," I responded, trying to wrap my mind around the concept of someone who could harbor a grudge that deep across more than two decades. When they'd gone to her for assistance, my parents couldn't have had any idea that, by helping them, Isabel would lose her life. It had been a great tragedy, according to them, and they'd paid their proper respects. Or at least, they'd tried to; even back then, Genoveva hadn't wanted much to do with them.

"That's my mother," Cat said, and sighed. She reached up with one hand as though she wanted to push it through her hair, then stopped when she realized that doing so would only destroy the careful updo the stylist had just created. "She and Rafe fought a lot more than she and I did, but she's always been the type of person who remembers every single thing you've done wrong...and won't let you forget it, either."

"I'm sorry," I said. All I could do was think of my own free-spirited, laughing mother, who was quick to forgive with a "that's all right, honey," and who had never given me a worse punishment than being confined to my room for an afternoon. Having someone like Genoveva for a mother must have been exhausting.

Cat shrugged. "I'm kind of over it. But I still

hate that she wouldn't let you have at least your parents here, even if she wouldn't allow your whole family to come."

I hated it, too. Unfortunately, there wasn't a damn thing I could do about it. Except…. "They can't be here," I said slowly. "But maybe you can get a couple of pictures of me after I'm in my gown, and we can send them when your mother is looking somewhere else. At least they'd get to see what I looked like on my wedding day."

"Oh, that's a great idea!" Cat exclaimed. "I should have thought of it myself. What's their number?"

I gave it to her, and she entered the information in her phone.

"Great," she said. "I'll try to get a bunch. I know my mother planned to send them a disc of images from the professional photographer, but in a way this is better, because they'll feel like they got to see a little of what was going on during the preparations and not the ceremony itself."

Not quite trusting myself to speak, I nodded. If I thought too much about my parents, about how much I missed them, I knew I'd start to tear up. At least my makeup hadn't been done yet, but I also didn't want to have reddened eyes and a puffy nose when we appeared at our next destination.

They had a team waiting for us there, too,

three makeup artists and a couple of assistants who stood by like nurses in an operating room, ready to hand over the correct brush or eyeshadow palette at a moment's notice. One of the makeup artists, a severe-looking woman named Aline, worked on me exclusively, while the other two split their time amongst the rest of the bridal party.

No exclamations about the length of my lashes or the shape of my mouth here, that was for sure. Aline worked calmly and efficiently, without speaking at all. I sat as still as I could, my gaze fixed on the street outside the plate-glass windows that fronted the salon. There wasn't as much foot traffic here, since we were on the outskirts of downtown, blocks away from the Plaza. Cars drifted by, moving slowly, the people inside hidden by tinted windows.

Right then, I wished Aline was a chatterbox, because that way I could have focused on what she was saying instead of being left to my own thoughts. As the minutes and hours ticked inexorably away, dragging me toward my future, I could feel tension knotting within me, all my worries coming to the fore. It was one thing to reassure myself that everything would be fine, that Rafe and I had come to an understanding and everything after today would be sparkles and unicorns, but I didn't know that for sure. He had his own demons to battle, and while I thought I understood some of the animosity he displayed toward his mother, it still made me uncomfortable. The last thing I wanted was to get caught between them somehow.

And sooner or later we would have to figure out what in the world was going on with my powers, if you could even call them that. If I were lucky, there might be someone here in the Castillo clan who could shed some light on my situation, or possibly there were some family archives which would reveal that such things weren't entirely outside the pale. After all, the family was a very old one, much older than my own. The McAllisters had always been kind of haphazard about their record-keeping, and the Wilcoxes weren't much better. The Castillos could be sitting on a treasure trove of magical knowledge.

But at last Aline was done, and a stranger stared back at me from the mirror. Or rather, if I looked hard enough, I could see something of myself in that glamorous woman with the enormous green eyes and the glossy wine-colored lips, but it took an effort. It wasn't even that the makeup was terribly obvious, only that Aline had known how to use the tools and tricks of her trade to bring out contours in my face I hadn't known existed.

"Wow," Cat said, walking over to the chair

where I sat. She, too, looked extremely chic, with her big dark eyes now even bigger, thanks to some meticulously applied false eyelashes and smoky liner. "You are *stunning.*"

"Thanks," I replied, since I wasn't sure how else I should respond. No one had ever called me stunning before. Oh, sure, people had commented on what a beautiful family my parents had, and I'd been told I was a pretty girl…but it was a big leap from "pretty" to "stunning." "I hope Rafe will think so."

"If he doesn't, he's either blind or an idiot," she said. "But it's almost three o'clock now, so we need to get going. Everyone else is done."

I thanked Aline and let Cat lead me back out to the limousine. It appeared that Genoveva must have handled all the financial arrangements for these appointments up front, because money was never mentioned. Just as well; I wasn't sure I wanted to stop and add up what all the nails and hair and makeup for seven of us must have cost, especially with the sort of star treatment we'd received.

As the limo drew closer to the cathedral, I could feel my heart rate accelerate, and I made myself breathe deeply to offset those fluttery heartbeats as best I could. I clutched the armrest and pretended to listen as Cat talked about all the Castillos who'd been married in Loretto Chapel, including her two older sisters, but my thoughts were elsewhere, wondering what Rafe was up to, whether he was already somewhere within the huge gray stone building. No, surely it wouldn't take him as long to get dressed as I would. He was probably at home, maybe finishing his packing for our trip to Taos. I'd already packed my own bags, and Cat had dropped them off for me at his place earlier that day. I'd fed Loki before I left to have my own breakfast, and I'd told Cat to look after him—if she could find him, that is. As soon as I'd opened the door to head out for breakfast, the cat bolted before I could even blink. Well, he'd apparently fended for himself before I showed up, so I had to hope he'd be able to do the same if he decided to stay away permanently.

At any rate, everything had been set up so Rafe and I could make a quick getaway, and I was fine with that. I thought that once we were away from Santa Fe and alone together, we'd have a better chance to get to know each other. We could just be Miranda and Rafe, rather than a McAllister and a Castillo. Or, I supposed, a Wilcox and a Castillo, although I'd gotten the impression from Genoveva that she seemed to give my McAllister blood more weight, as if she didn't want to acknowledge that a man could be the head of a clan the way my father was. Anyway, I hoped our time in Taos would be a way to really seal our relationship, to prove that we should be together, even though we'd had no control over the situation that had brought us together.

Cat and the rest of my bridesmaids hurried me up into a side entrance. I was glad they knew where they were going, because the cathedral seemed vast to me, and otherwise I would have had no idea how to find the dressing rooms. There were several, as it turned out, two for my bridesmaids and one for me. Genoveva waited there, coldly stylish in a gray silk shantung suit, her hair up in a twist, antique white gold and sapphire drops hanging from her ears.

"Come along," she said. "No time to waste."

I wanted to raise an eyebrow at that comment, since we still had more than two hours to go until the ceremony. However, I didn't quite have the courage to confront her over her false urgency, and so I only nodded and headed for the antique screen that had been set up to one side of the room. Behind that screen was a rolling wardrobe rack where my wedding gown hung, still swathed in the protective bag from the dress shop. Below it were the matching shoes, and on a chair was a small bag with the necessary undergarments, right down to the pale blue garter required to fulfill the requirements of the old rhyme—"something old, something new, something borrowed, something blue."

Well, something new was my dress, but I didn't know about "old" or "borrowed." However, Genoveva had thought of that as well, because after I lifted the lacy bustier and lace-topped stockings out of the bag, I found a small white box underneath. Inside the box was a plain card that said *For Miranda,* and within was a beautiful antique set of jewelry, white gold accented with diamonds and small rosy pearls. They matched my dress perfectly, and again I wondered if Genoveva had decided on the gown in advance and had purposely guided me to choose it.

Even if she had, I couldn't argue with the effect. I had to step out from behind the screen to get help with the row of satin-covered buttons down the back, and at once she came over to me, fingers deftly working the fastenings. I supposed she must have done much the same thing for her daughters, but once again I held back, not quite sure of the reception I would get if I asked that simple question.

Instead, I stood quietly until the dress was fastened all the way. A few tugs, and everything was lying where it should be.

"You look amazing," Cat said, appearing from nowhere. Or rather, she'd been next door getting dressed, and popped in once she was done. One hand was hidden among the folds of her blush-colored gown, and I guessed she was hiding her phone there, so she could take some pictures once her mother was safely out of the way.

"Yes, the gown was a lucky find," Genoveva remarked, carefully adjusting my hair so it fell gracefully over my shoulders. It felt strange to have her standing so close, to catch the faintest trace of Chanel No. 5 coming from her hair or her clothing, but I made myself stay still. I didn't want to flinch or do anything that might show her how uncomfortable I was with even this impersonal intimacy. To my relief, she stepped away after a moment, saying, "I think we will wait on the veil until we're a little closer to the ceremony."

I nodded.

Then Cat said, "Mom, can you go take a look at Maria's dress? She keeps claiming it's not exactly the same color as everyone else's, but I think it's just the funky lighting in these dressing rooms. But I know she'd believe you over me."

Genoveva's mouth twitched in annoyance. "Very well, I'll go take a look. I'm sure it must be the lighting. It had better be the lighting, because if the dress shop somehow sent us a gown from the wrong dye lot...." Muttering to herself, she left the room and closed the door behind her.

"Thank God," Cat said, pulling the phone out from the folds of her skirt. "That was the best story we could come up with."

"Maria's in on it, too?" I asked, smiling despite

the nervous butterflies that kept fluttering around in my stomach. Or maybe that was just the remains of my breakfast getting compressed by the heavily boned bustier I had on under my gown.

"Of course," Cat replied. "The last thing we wanted was my mother asking questions and the other girls not knowing what she was talking about. They also think it stinks that your parents couldn't be here, so they wanted to help. Now smile," she added, lifting her phone to take a picture.

Forcing a smile was more difficult than I'd thought it would be. But somehow I pasted one on, hoping it would look halfway convincing.

"Oh, that was terrible." Cat lowered the phone and gave me a direct look. "You need to look like you're slightly happy about all this and not like you're getting dragged to the gallows."

"I am happy," I protested. "But I'm also nervous."

"I know," she said. "Just don't think about the wedding itself. Think about getting out of here, going to Taos with Rafe. It sounded like you were looking forward to that."

Oh, I was. Away from Santa Fe, to a resort where Rafe would make love to me. That all sounded delicious.

I smiled.

"Perfect," Cat said, pressing the button on her

phone's camera several times. "That was much better. I'll get these sent off to your parents right now."

My smile faded as I watched her play with the phone a bit more, making sure my parents would receive those precious bits of data, the ones that would show I was happy and ready to face my future, even if they couldn't be there to watch. Was I happy? I honestly didn't know. I thought I might be, very soon...or at least three or four hours from now, after I'd survived the ceremony and the reception, and Rafe and I were on the fabled high road to Taos.

"I've told the bishop over and over that he needs to get the warm LED lights for these rooms," Genoveva said as she opened the door and let herself back in. Cat quickly tucked the phone away behind her. "This bluish light is terrible for the complexion, and even worse for matching colors. Maria's dress is fine, as you tried to point out to her. But now that little drama is over, thank God."

She went to a large box that was sitting on one of the dressing room's side tables, lifted the lid, and pulled out my veil and tiara. "Cat, if you would help me."

Cat went over and took the tiara from her, and then Genoveva came to me, veil in hands. Since she was taller than I, I didn't have to bend to allow her to set it on my head. Even though I'd tried it on before, it felt strange to have that gossamer fabric settle over my shoulders, flow down my bare arms. Quietly, Cat came up and placed the tiara on my head, taking care to get it straight and also not disturb all the hard work of the hairstylist.

"There," Genoveva said, inspecting her daughter's handiwork as she moved around me, making sure to get a full 360 degrees so she didn't miss any possible bad angles. "I think that is going to do very well. It's four-thirty—I need to go check and make sure the doors are opened, since the guests will be arriving soon." She began to head toward the door, then paused and sent me a severe look. "Don't even think about sitting down in that dress."

"I won't," I promised, glad that I had chosen shoes with relatively low heels.

"If you need water, there's a pitcher on the table, and some glasses. Cat, make sure she uses a straw."

After delivering that final command, the *prima* once more sailed out of the room and shut the door behind her.

At once Cat lifted her phone to take a few pictures of me in all my veiled glory. To my surprise, once she was done, she handed the phone over to me.

"My mother will be busy for at least ten minutes. Go ahead, call them."

A fierce gratitude rushed through me at her words. I wished I could lean over and give her a hug, this soon-to-be sister of mine, but I knew I might crumple something and invoke Genoveva's wrath. Instead, I gave Cat a tremulous smile and pushed the button to connect the call.

I was worried that it might ring and ring and go to voicemail, but apparently my parents were on standby after receiving the first batch of photos from Cat. The call was answered after the first ring. "Is this Cat?" my mother's voice asked.

Hearing her, I wanted to break down in tears right then and there. Fiercely commanding myself to remember my mascara, I said, "No, Mom. It's Miranda."

I didn't think I'd ever heard anyone sound so relieved. "Oh, thank the Goddess. Yes, Cat texted me to let me know you were all right, but after what Rafe told us about you disappearing—"

"I'm fine," I cut in quickly. "It was just…well, I don't know what's going on, exactly, but we'll figure it out one way or another. I just wanted to let you know I was okay, and that everything is going well. I'll be walking down the aisle in about twenty minutes."

My voice wavered a little on that last word, but I don't think my mother noticed…or possibly she wanted to make me think she hadn't noticed. "I wish we could be there."

"I wish it, too, Mom," I replied. "But you got the pictures?"

"Yes, we did. They're beautiful. You're beautiful. We're very proud of you."

Damn, she was making it very hard for me not to cry. I pulled in a breath and told myself I didn't dare have raccoon eyes at my own wedding. It was just...after so many years of seeing myself as a failure, as someone who'd let down my clan by being utterly without powers, I didn't quite know how to respond when my mother said that she and my father were proud of me.

"I—I'm glad. And I don't want you to worry about me. Rafe is...Rafe is wonderful. I think we're going to be very happy together."

"I'm glad to hear that, darling." A pause, and then she said, "Your father would like to talk to you."

Unfortunately, I never got to hear what he had to say. The doorknob began to turn, and Cat took the phone from me, said quickly, "Sorry, we really need to go," and ended the call.

I wanted to be angry with her for interrupting before I had a chance to talk to my father, but I knew she was only trying to protect me. I blinked, and turned toward Genoveva as she entered the room. "Are we ready?"

"Yes, I think it's time for everyone to get lined up," she replied, her gaze moving from me to her daughter as her eyes narrowed slightly, as if she could tell we'd been up to something but couldn't precisely guess what.

"I'll just go and corral everyone," Cat said, her voice somewhat breathless, and slipped from the room, phone hidden somewhere in her skirt.

"This way," Genoveva said, still looking somewhat suspicious.

I didn't trust myself to speak as I followed her out of the dressing room and down a long corridor. From behind me, I could hear hushed laughter and whispers as my bridesmaids hurried to catch up with us.

At the end of the hallway waited Rafe's groomsmen, his cousin Tony among them. One dark eyebrow lifted as he took in my bridal splendor, and his lips pursed, as though he intended to let loose a whistle. However, the man standing next to him stuck an elbow in his ribs, and Tony subsided.

The exchange made my mouth curve in a smile. Still smiling, I stood and watched as Cat went to stand next to her cousin, and the rest of the bridesmaids and groomsmen fell in line. Belatedly, I realized I had no one to walk me down the aisle.

But then Rafe's father appeared, dashing and

handsome in his black tailcoat, and offered me his arm. "I hope you'll allow me to stand in?" he said.

"I'd be honored," I replied, looping my arms through his. Yes, Eduardo wasn't my father, but at least I'd have a father figure to accompany me to the altar.

From within the chapel, the organ boomed, playing the first chords of the wedding march. Cat and Tony disappeared into the foyer, followed by the bridesmaids and groomsmen. Then it was my turn.

"Come along, my dear," Eduardo murmured to me. "Just keep your eyes ahead, and look for Rafe. You'll do fine."

With that he guided me through the foyer, and out into Loretto Chapel, which was quite transformed from the last time I'd been here. Blush-tipped roses and white lilies decorated the altar and the pews, and every single one of those pews was packed with people. Were they all Castillos? They must be. I quailed at the thought of having to meet all of them and get to know their names, but then I told myself I needed to heed Eduardo's advice and keep my eyes forward, stay in the moment.

Look for Rafe.

There he was, standing at the altar, so handsome in his tails, his dark hair carefully slicked back, that my breath caught. Somehow, though, I managed to keep moving, my chin up. These people might all be Castillos, but I was a McAllister and a Wilcox. Where I came from, that counted for a lot.

We came to the altar, and Eduardo guided me to the lower step where Rafe waited, then let go of my arm so he could go take his seat in the first pew next to his wife. I turned toward Rafe, whose eyes looked odd to me, strangely opaque and glittering, nearly black rather than the warm brown I knew they actually were.

It must have been a trick of the light which made him appear that way, almost a stranger. We'd reached the blue hour of dusk, which lent an oddly luminous glow to the stained glass windows, blending with the dim illumination from the enormous wrought-iron chandeliers overhead. The vast, shadowy spaces of the chapel looked odd, not quite substantial, although that could also have had something to do with the banks of taper candles that flickered to either side of us, adding to the aura of mystery.

The priest opened his mouth to speak, but Rafe said, quite loudly, "No."

I stared at him, a strange, sick feeling starting somewhere in my stomach. "No…what, Rafe?" I asked in a murmur.

He barely glanced in my direction. Instead, he turned away from me, away from the startled priest, and called out to the watching ranks of Castillos, "I am not going to marry this woman. I don't love her. I don't want her."

No. The word reverberated in my brain, an echo of the same negation Rafe had just uttered a few seconds earlier. This couldn't be happening. How could he be saying these things, when just yesterday he'd kissed me and said everything was going to be okay, that he wanted this?

Both Genoveva and Eduardo hastily stood as the rest of the audience looked on in horror. "Rafe!" Genoveva's voice was a sharp whisper. "Stop this at once!"

"No, I won't," he replied, his tone oddly flat, almost dead. Then he turned toward me. "I mean it, Miranda. You were stupid to think I would ever go through with this."

I saw his mouth moving, but it was as though the words couldn't quite penetrate my brain. My heart thudded, heavy as lead in my chest, heavy as the enormous bells far above us that tolled the hour. This wasn't happening.

Everyone was staring at me. Suddenly, I couldn't breathe. The air caught in my throat, choking me.

I had to get out of there.

The cathedral dissolved around me, and I was gone.

17

RECRIMINATIONS

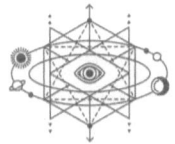

Rafe

THE WORDS SOUNDED HORRIBLY DISTANT, distorted, as if they were coming from very far away, traveling down transmission lines that had been torn and battered by summer's fierce monsoon storms.

"What the hell were you thinking?"

He blinked, realized he was surrounded by his family, his mother and father and Cat, and his two older sisters as well, both of whom were scowling so fiercely, he wasn't sure whether the lines in the middle of their brows would ever smooth out again. "What—what happened?"

"What do you mean, what happened?" Genoveva demanded. Her hands were planted on her hips, and her dark eyes were fairly shooting fire. It was possible that Rafe had seen her this angry before, but he really couldn't remember when. Her tone sharpened, became sarcastic. "What, are you trying to tell us that you don't remember how you insulted your fiancée and disgraced all of us in front of the entire clan, upset her so badly that she somehow managed to vanish right in front of everyone?"

Rafe put a hand to his head. It ached, felt as heavy as if he'd just gone on a drinking spree with Tony and some of his party-animal cousins. He honestly couldn't remember much of anything since he'd left the house this afternoon. A vague recollection of driving to the cathedral and parking around back in the small lot that was reserved for those who had particular business there, but after that...?

Looking around, he saw that he was in a smallish room, a plain rectangle that contained some chairs and a few long tables placed up against the thick adobe walls. It felt crowded in there with his entire immediate family glaring at him, although he thought that had more to do with their palpable anger than the actual square footage of the space.

"No," he said, "I don't remember anything." The vague thought surfaced that he was supposed to be getting married sometime today, and he glanced around again, a strange uneasiness filling him. "Where's Miranda?"

His mother's mouth tightened. Cat, hands on her hips, wrinkling the pale pink satin gown she wore, stared back at him and snapped, "Well, that's a really good question, isn't it? After your little performance out there, she disappeared. Poof —right into thin air. No one knows where she went."

Rafe put a hand to his head. Cloudy, indistinct images were bubbling up into his brain—the cathedral packed with every Castillo clan member who would fit, staring into a mirror and fiddling with the black silk bow tie he wore as Tony laughed at his first clumsy attempt…Miranda's wide green eyes staring up at him in horror.

He could see the despair in every inch of her beautiful face, but he couldn't remember why she'd looked that way, or what he'd said to her.

"Wait a minute," his oldest sister Louisa said. She'd been hanging back behind the others, but now she pushed her way past her parents and came to stand next to Rafe. Putting a gentle hand on his arm, she went very still for a moment. Her talent was detecting where magic had been used, and because she was the *prima*-in-waiting and very strong, quite often she was also able to identify who had used that magic and what its purpose might have been. Still frowning, she said, "I think someone cast a spell on him."

"What?" Genoveva stepped forward and lifted a hand in front of Rafe's face, as though feeling the air currents that moved around him. Her talent wasn't quite the same as Louisa's, but because she was *prima,* she could do almost the same thing, although not with quite as much precision. Her brows drew together as she moved her hand back and forth. "I'm sensing something, too. Something…dark."

Well, he was glad they were able to get a sense of what had happened, but Rafe still didn't know what was going on, didn't know who could have cast a spell on him, or why. "I don't feel anything," he said, his tone rough with frustration.

"Of course you don't," Louisa replied calmly. Her two children were nowhere in evidence; her husband Adam must have kept them with him someplace else in the cathedral complex. "You're the subject of the spell—it's necessary that you not be able to feel a thing."

Anger coursed through him. Who the hell would have the guts to cast a spell on the *prima's* son? And for what purpose?

Those questions needed to be pushed aside for now, however. The important thing was finding Miranda. Rafe still didn't know precisely what he'd said to her, but clearly it had been bad. Very bad.

"We need to go look for Miranda," he said.

Cat's expression shifted from frustrated anger to worry, while both his mother and Louisa didn't appear terribly concerned about Miranda's fate. Possibly at the moment they cared more about who had cast a spell on him, and why.

His father, though...he seemed worried as well, dark eyes shadowed with doubt. "You say that, Rafe, but how exactly are we supposed to locate her? Cat told us that the normal methods of tracking someone down don't seem to work when Miranda does her disappearing trick. Marco can't help us, she doesn't have a phone, and we don't know how far she's actually able to travel. She could be anywhere."

Rafe opened his mouth to protest, then shut it again when he realized his father was only telling the truth. There really wasn't much they could do, except hope that Miranda would overcome her hurt and return to them.

And why would she do that? he asked himself. *If I were in her shoes, I wouldn't come back here.*

He still didn't know what he'd said to her. He wasn't sure he wanted to know.

The one thing he did know was that there didn't seem to be much point in hanging around the cathedral. Miranda wouldn't return here, even if she had remained somewhere in the vicinity.

His gaze moved to Cat. Of everyone, she

seemed the most sympathetic. In his mother's face, he'd seen a flash of impatient anger when Louisa claimed he was the victim of some dark spell, as if Genoveva thought he should have been able to deflect such an attack. Anger stirred within him, too, but for both his mother and whoever had made him a target. His talent was a strong one; he wouldn't deny that fact. However, his gift didn't lie in defensive magic. To think he'd have the ability to avoid being affected by this kind of attack didn't make a lot of sense. When you got right down to it, most witches and warlocks didn't even cast spells in the way that civilians thought they did. Everyone in the witch world had a special talent they could use almost as easily as they breathed, and didn't stray much beyond that. Spells existed, true, written down in grimoires that were kept in secret cupboards and handed down from generation to generation. The casting of such spells was generally frowned upon, though, and was only the province of the strongest and most experienced witches and warlocks in a clan, not something the rank and file would use.

Gaze focused on his sister, Rafe said, "I need to get out of here. Cat, would you drive me home?"

Her lips parted, as though she was about to reply, but Genoveva cut in before she could speak.

"I don't think it's a good idea for you to be alone if someone truly has attacked you with a dark spell."

"I won't be alone," he said. "Cat will be with me."

"Right," Cat put in, coming to his rescue. "He might as well be at home. We're not going to solve this mystery by hanging around here. And Mom, Dad, you should probably get over to the restaurant and handle all that. I'll take care of Rafe."

He wasn't exactly sure what Cat meant by "all that," but if it gave her the opportunity to spirit him away, he was all for it.

Eduardo nodded, although his expression was still troubled. "Cat's right, Genoveva. We need to get over there and try to address this mess as best we can."

It was clear that she wanted to argue. To Rafe's relief, though, she appeared to relent and said, "All right. We'll regroup and see what we can do next. For now, we need to keep this to ourselves. With any luck, we'll be able to locate Miranda quickly, and there won't be any need to tell her parents that this has happened again."

Rafe wanted to wince at that "again." The last time Miranda had disappeared, it had been his fault. From the sound of things, it was his fault now, too, although he still didn't know exactly what had happened.

"Come on, Rafe," Cat said, coming toward

him and looping her arm through his. "Let's get you home."

No one stopped them as Cat pulled him out of the room and led him down the hallway outside, all the way to the back of the building, where a door opened onto the parking lot. In the dull orange glow of the sodium vapor lights off the street, he could see his Wrangler off to one side, as well as his father's Mercedes S-Class. No sign of Cat's SUV, but then he vaguely recalled that she must have been brought here in a limo.

He got in the passenger seat, while Cat went around to the driver's side and buckled her seat belt. A touch of her finger to the ignition and the Jeep started right up, even though his car keys and wallet and everything else had to still be inside the building somewhere, along with the clothes he'd changed out of to get into this tailcoat and tuxedo pants.

"My stuff—" he began.

"It's all right," Cat said. "Tony texted me to say he would drop everything off at the house for you."

That was a relief. A minor one, but right now, Rafe would take what he could get.

He nodded, and Cat guided the vehicle out onto Cathedral Way, then turned left on Paseo de Peralta so she could head to the neighborhood northeast of downtown where his house was located. It was strange to see her so dressed up, elegant enough for a Hollywood party, maneuvering his battered old Jeep through Santa Fe's traffic.

"Cat—what happened back there?"

She sent him a quick sideways glance before returning her attention to the dark streets ahead of them. "You really don't remember?"

"No. That is, I got a few flashes, but it's not enough to put together the entire story."

Her mouth tightened, and she didn't reply for a moment. "Let's wait 'til we get back to your place."

He wanted to protest but realized it probably was better to discuss all this while sitting down. Jaw tight, he watched the familiar streets pass by outside, remained silent as Cat turned down onto his street and then into the driveway. Still quiet, he got out after she turned off the engine, and waited for her to climb out of the driver's seat and come to meet him.

No need of house keys for a warlock—he laid his hand on the front door and it opened before them, revealing a dark foyer and even darker hallway beyond. At once he touched the switch just inside the door, turning on the recessed lights overhead.

Rafe didn't go to the living room, but continued to the kitchen, to the cabinet where he kept his tequila and whiskey and scotch. He hesitated for a second, then pulled out the bottle of Avión silver and two shot glasses.

Cat stopped a few feet away from him and gave the bottle of tequila an askance look. "You really think that's going to help anything?"

"No," he replied. "But it might not hurt, either."

A small sigh escaped her lips. "You may be right. Pour one for me, too."

He filled both shot glasses and handed one to her. Lifting his, he said, "*Salut.*"

She swallowed about half hers, while he knocked back his entire shot and poured another. That earned him another dubious glance, but Cat didn't say anything.

"All right," Rafe said after he took a healthy swallow. The tequila sang along his jangled nerves, soothing, blunting the edges of his worry and his confusion. "Now, tell me what happened."

One freshly manicured finger tapped against the side of the shot glass, which was emblazoned with the logo of the Buffalo Thunder resort, about twenty miles north of where they currently stood. "All I can do is tell you what I saw. I'm still not sure exactly what happened."

"Whatever."

She pulled in a breath and drained the rest of the tequila he'd poured for her. Without speaking, she held it out so he could pour her another. Which he did, although not quite as full as the last time.

"You'd have to ask Tony or one of your other groomsmen whether you were acting weird before the ceremony," Cat said. "I honestly don't know, because I didn't get a chance to see you. But once Miranda came up to at the altar, you looked at her like you'd never seen her before, then stood there and announced to everyone watching that you didn't love her, that you weren't going to marry her."

His sister might as well have thrown the contents of the bottle of tequila in his face. He blinked, and reached with one hand to grasp the edge of the counter to steady himself. "I *what?*"

"You rejected her in the worst way possible, in front of hundreds of people," Cat said, her tone flat. "Do I need to say it any plainer than that?"

"No, I guess not." With a shaking hand, he raised the shot glass to his lips and drank the remaining tequila it held. No wonder Miranda had blinked herself away. Could he have come up with a worse way to demean her, disrespect her?

And the horrible thing was, he really didn't remember any of it. Or maybe that was a good thing. If those memories ever did come back to him, he wasn't sure whether he could face them.

Cat said, "But if it was a spell...then I guess it

wasn't really you talking. The question is, who was it?"

"I don't know," Rafe replied. The tequila was doing its work, smoothing the edges of his worry and frustration, but underneath all that, he could still feel a raw, roiling anger. Who the hell would have wanted to interfere in his marriage to Miranda? His parents wanted it—and therefore, so did the Castillo clan by extension—and as far as he could tell, Miranda's parents were resigned to the situation. If they hadn't wanted their daughter to marry him, then they could have made things a whole lot simpler by refusing to put her on the train in the first place.

His sister went over the sink and rinsed out her shot glass, signaling that she didn't want any more to drink. After wiping her hands on the towel that hung from the refrigerator door, she said, "Are you sure? Anyone who's said something strange to you over the past few days, anyone you might have encountered who would have a vested interest in making sure this marriage didn't happen?"

"Who would that be?" he said wearily. Once again he reached for the bottle of Avión silver and poured himself a shot. Cat's right brow lifted in disapproval, but she didn't say anything. Probably because she knew he wouldn't listen to her, and also because if he had to get drunk, he might as well do it safely at home. "You think anyone in our clan is crazy enough to do something like this? Hell, I don't even know of anyone who has the ability to plant that kind of suggestion in someone's head."

"Neither do I," Cat admitted. She reached up to run a hand through her hair, bumped into the elaborate updo some hairstylist had concocted for her, and then said, "Oh, fuck it," as she began to pull out hairpins and set them on the countertop. Once her hair was lying loose on her shoulders, she gave a sigh of relief. "That's better. Those goddamn things were giving me a headache. Anyway, no, I don't know of anyone with that kind of skill in the Castillos, but that doesn't mean it couldn't have been someone from Arizona. A Wilcox or a McAllister, or maybe someone from the de la Paz clan. There's so much about Miranda we don't really know. It sounds like she really did her best to keep herself pure for you, for lack of a better term, but for all we know, maybe she had a secret admirer, someone who wanted to sabotage your wedding."

That sounded plausible, although you'd think if there was a warlock in any of the Arizona clans with that kind of an obsession with Miranda, someone should have noticed. Then again, he'd never been there. He didn't know any of those people, didn't know what they were capable of.

Cat's suggestion made more sense than anything else he'd come up with so far.

When he lifted his shot glass to take another drink, though, Rafe couldn't help feeling as though he was missing something important, something right under his nose. Maybe that was just a part of the spell wearing off, although of course he couldn't be sure.

"I don't know," he said wearily. "It's something we can ask Miranda's parents when we talk to them, I suppose." He paused then, and sent his sister a considering look. "*If* we talk to them, I mean. Do you think Genoveva was serious about keeping this whole thing on the down-low?"

"I'm not sure. It's been a little crazy." She fiddled with the hairpins on the counter, pushing them around with one finger, watching as they made odd, angular patterns against the tile. "I mean, Miranda disappeared, and everyone was sort of in shock, and then Mom and Louisa and Malena got up from their seats and hustled you away from the altar. Dad was apologizing, telling everyone to go ahead over to the restaurant if they wanted to, since there was a ton of food waiting for them." Cat paused and shook her head. "I have no idea if anyone even took him up on the offer, but I hope so. At least then that food won't go to waste."

"Sorry about that."

Her shoulders lifted. "If this really was a spell, then it's nothing you should have to apologize about. But if that turns out to be true...." The words trailed off, and for the first time, Rafe saw actual fear in his sister's face.

"If it's true," he prompted, and she bit her lip.

"If it's true, then we need to find out who it was...and what in the world they wanted with Miranda."

18

REVELATIONS

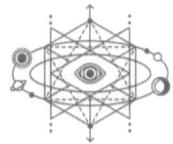

Miranda

I STOOD ON A LANDING, A DOOR WITH chipped dark brown paint directly in front of me. My chest heaved as though I had just run a foot race, although I knew I hadn't come here under my own power.

Well, not under foot power, anyway.

Every part of me shook, and I couldn't seem to draw a deep enough breath to get the air all the way down in my lungs, down where it might help to still my body's trembling, or send the oxygen my blood needed to keep my standing upright.

I placed one hand on the wall, felt the cool plaster beneath my fingers. The lighting here wasn't very good, just a simple wrought iron fixture a few feet away from the door in front of me, but I knew where I was. I supposed I should have realized I would come here, to this place that had become my only refuge.

Simon's apartment.

Around five-thirty on a Sunday afternoon. Would he be here, or would he have gone to spend some time with friends and family? For all I knew, he might be downstairs in the wine tasting room, since I didn't have any idea how late it stayed open on Sundays. However, I knew I didn't dare go down and check, not looking like the quintessential runaway bride in my long silk gown and veil and ridiculous tiara.

What in the world would he think once he saw me like this?

Not that he had to see me, of course. I could just tiptoe down the stairs and call a Ryde—

Well, no, I really couldn't do that. I didn't have a phone. I didn't have a wallet or I.D. or money or anything. And because this stupid power of mine seemed to enjoy toying with me and then disappearing again, I couldn't just snap my fingers and send myself back to the casita, or even all the way home, to the comfort of my familiar room in the Flagstaff house, or the family room in the big Victorian in Jerome where we'd all spent so many hours together.

I probably could have walked back to the Castillo compound, but I wasn't quite ready to face the ignominy of trudging through Santa Fe's busiest part of town while wearing a goddamn wedding dress. The same for going to Rafe's house, although I thought I'd rather walk naked down Cerrillos Avenue than ever have to face him again.

When I looked at it that way, it didn't seem as if I had much of a choice.

I drew in a breath, followed by another. *You can do this,* I told myself, although, judging by the way I stood there on the landing and didn't make any move to knock on Simon's door, it seemed that maybe I wasn't so sure I actually could do this after all.

Gritting my teeth, I reached out and knocked. There. I'd done what I could. The universe would have to meet me at least partway.

The door opened, and Simon stood there in a T-shirt and jeans. Socks, no shoes. I wasn't even sure why I registered that particular detail, except that it kept me from having to look him in the face.

However, even though we weren't meeting eye to eye, there was no avoiding the expression of shock and surprise that passed over his features. "Miranda? What the—?"

"Can—can I come in, please?"

"Um—sure. Of course." He stepped out of the way so I could move past him, and I walked into the apartment with as much dignity as I could muster, my heavy skirt and accompanying petticoat clutched in one hand to give me a little more freedom of movement.

The TV was on—a football game. Simon hurried over to the coffee table and picked up the remote, then shut off the television. There was a half-drunk beer on the table as well, and the rind from a piece of pizza. In an odd haze, I realized it was one of the leftovers from the pizza we'd shared the day before.

"Sorry about that," he said, and I waved a hand.

"Oh, it's okay. I did kind of just…show up."

"Yeah." He eyed my wedding gown. "Do you want to talk about it?"

I really didn't. Then I would have to revisit the agony of hearing Rafe say those terrible words, of having to look into his dark eyes and see a complete stranger there.

However, since appearing on someone's doorstep while wearing a wedding dress complete with veil and tiara was the sort of thing that generally begged for an explanation, I knew I'd have to say something. "It's all—" I broke off, and paused to remove the tiara and veil. I set them down on the arm of the couch. "That's a little better. At least now I feel like I can think."

"Do you want a beer?"

I really didn't like beer very much, but right then a beer sounded like a great idea. "Sure."

Simon went into the kitchen and reached into the refrigerator, bringing out another bottle of Cumbres Ale. He popped the top. "Glass?"

"No, in the bottle is fine."

He returned and handed me the beer but didn't sit down, instead remained standing on the other side of the coffee table, almost as if he didn't want to risk getting too close to me.

That seemed to be the theme for the day.

I raised the bottle of beer to my lips and took a sip, trying not to wince at the bitter flavor. It was better than nothing, after all, and I needed to do something to try to blunt the edges of the hateful words that kept echoing in my mind.

I am not going to marry this woman. I don't love her. I don't want her.

Simon crossed his arms, watching me with worried eyes. "So the wedding didn't happen?"

"No." I swallowed some beer, barely wincing this time. That was better.

"What happened?"

"He—" I couldn't quite force the words out, even though I knew I had to. "He called it off. Of course, it might have been better if he'd done that before I was standing there right at the frigging altar, but better late than never, I guess."

"Jesus." Simon passed a hand through his hair.

"I'm so sorry, Miranda. But any guy who would do that kind of thing doesn't deserve you."

I tipped more beer into my mouth. "I don't really need the pity pep talk, Simon."

His eyes narrowed. "It's not pity, and it's not a pep talk. I mean, you're beautiful and you're smart and strong. If this jerk can't appreciate you, then he really doesn't deserve you. You can do better."

"Oh?" I asked. "Do better with whom? You?"

"Maybe. Yeah."

I stared up at him. "You're serious?"

He didn't reply, but instead came over and sat down on the couch next to me. For one frightening second, I thought he was going to lean in and kiss me, and I didn't know how the hell I was going to deal with that. However, he didn't kiss me, but instead reached over and took the hand that wasn't holding the beer bottle. His fingers were warm and strong, thinner and longer than Rafe's.

I wanted to shake my head to rid itself of that thought. I didn't need to be thinking about Rafe. He had brutally dumped me in the worst way possible. He could go straight to hell.

"I am serious," Simon said. "But you've just been through a horrible experience. I'm not going to push you. I only want you to know that you have someone who wants to be there for you."

His touch shouldn't have reassured me. I

should have pulled my hand away. I didn't, though, because I liked the sensation of his fingers brushing against mine. Maybe it was only because I needed that human touch, needed to know I wasn't alone in the howling wilderness that my life seemed to have become.

"After all," he continued. "You must have felt that way, too, or you wouldn't be here. Why come to my apartment, and not back to where you're staying, or even to the train station, if you wanted to be away from this guy, away from Santa Fe?"

"I—I don't know," I replied, the words barely a murmur. And the truth was, I really didn't know. I only knew that something kept drawing me back to Simon. Jerk that he was, even Rafe had recognized that fact. He hadn't been happy at all when I'd expressed my wish to keep Simon as a friend.

How that apparent jealousy was supposed to line up with his unceremonious dumping of me in front of three hundred witnesses, I wasn't sure. Then again, I didn't know why I should expect consistency from someone who acted as if he was falling in love with me one day and then threw me out of his life the next. As far as I was concerned, that kind of behavior indicated some serious mental issues.

Simon's fingers tightened on mine. Not in a bad way, but more as though he wanted to emphasize what he was saying. I knew if I'd tried to pull away, he would have let me.

"You're here," he said. "You came here, to me. That has to mean something."

"As I pointed out the other day, you're the only person I know in Santa Fe who isn't a—who isn't part of the family I'm trying to avoid." I didn't say this in a snarky way, only to remind him of a fact he might have forgotten.

"I know that. Still." He paused, then gently let go of my hand. "Miranda, I know there's a reason why you were drawn here. And—and I need to tell you something."

"Tell me what?" I asked, praying he wasn't going to take this moment to inform me of his undying love. While such words might have been balm to my wounded ego and aching heart, I didn't want to go there. Not now, not soon after what Rafe had done to me.

Not so soon after he'd kissed me.

"I might not have been entirely truthful with you," Simon said.

Oh, wonderful. Was it too much to ask of the universe to have a man in my life who didn't lie to me, who didn't make me think one thing in one moment and another in the next? I pulled in a breath, bracing myself for whatever revelation was yet to come. "About what?"

"This," he said quietly.

He didn't move, or do anything I could see. But I felt it then, felt the little tingle at the back of my neck that told me I was in the presence of a warlock, someone of witch-kind.

I stared at him, my heart thudding heavily in my chest. "You're a warlock?"

Those dark eyes caught mine and held. I didn't think I could have looked away even if I wanted to. "Yes."

"But…how? You didn't feel like a warlock." I realized how that sounded as soon as the words left my mouth. Fighting to hold back an embarrassed flush, I added, "I mean, I always get a tingle when I meet someone of witch-kind for the first time, but I didn't get that from you."

"I hid it," he said simply.

"'Hid it'?" I repeated. "How?"

"It's one of my talents."

"One? How many do you have?"

"A few."

I stared at him in consternation. It wasn't normal for a witch or warlock to have more than one or two inborn gifts, along with the minor talents for opening locks and lighting fires that we all possessed. I'd heard whispers that my late uncle had been able to command all sorts of magic, but it wasn't the sort of thing my parents wanted to talk about, since he'd delved into fields of study that had been forbidden for centuries and had lost his life because of it.

"Why would you hide that from me?" I whispered. "Especially since you had to have known I was a witch, if a pretty crappy one."

"You're not a crappy witch." He reached out and took my hand again, twining his fingers with mine. I almost fancied I could feel that tingle again, although I couldn't be completely certain. "An unusual one, sure. Anyway, I wasn't hiding my nature from you—I was hiding it from the Castillos."

"So you're not a Castillo?" He didn't really look like any of the Castillos I'd met so far, but that didn't mean much. In a family as large as theirs, and one that covered so much territory, there was bound to be a lot of variation.

"No."

"Where are you from, then?"

"From Tucson."

Which meant he was a de la Paz. I'd never heard anyone mention his name, but again, that didn't surprise me. The de la Pazes were a big clan, with branches in the Phoenix area and down in Tucson and through most of the southern part of Arizona, all the way down to the Mexico border. I'd met some of them, but only the ones who had a direct connection to the McAllisters, like Ali and Matthew, my cousin Caitlin's children. She was married to a de la Paz warlock and lived in Tucson. But there were hundreds, if not thousands, of de la Pazes whose names I didn't even know.

"What are you doing in Santa Fe?" I asked, genuinely curious. It took a lot of balls to come uninvited to another clan's territory, even if you possessed a talent like Simon's, one that would conceal you from other witches and warlocks.

"Following you," he replied, still with his eyes locked with mine.

I swallowed against the sudden dryness in my throat. "Following me?" It took a lot of effort to hold back the nervous giggle I felt rising in me, or to keep myself from pulling my hands away. "Why?"

"I knew there was more to you than meets the eye, Miranda McAllister. I didn't think it was possible that someone whose parents were so powerful would have no magical talents of her own. And I thought that if I came here, maybe I could help you."

"Help me how?"

His fingers tightened on mine. "Like I said, I have a lot of gifts. I suppose I thought that I might be able to share them with you."

"It doesn't work that way," I protested. Very gently, I pulled my hand from his. To my relief, he let go, although he remained sitting where he was, still with those night-dark eyes boring into mine.

"That you know of," he replied. "When I heard about you, heard you were a *nunca*—"

I flinched, even though I didn't want to. Too many years of hearing that hated word, although it was never said directly to my face.

Either Simon didn't notice my reaction, or he decided it was better not to call attention to it. He went on, "My clan has records that go way, way back. Long before we were even settled in Arizona, back when we still lived in Sonora. I found some accounts that made me think I might be able to help you."

I did my best to ignore the stirring of hope within me. While I couldn't dispute my waking powers, the way they'd seemed to come to life only after I met Simon, I still wasn't sure he could do very much to help me control them. So he'd read a few stories about people like me. He was still just a kid, probably my own age. He couldn't have any real experience with this sort of thing.

"If you thought that, why didn't you go to my parents and tell them? I'm sure they would have listened to you."

"By the time I'd found out anything useful, it was too close to your twenty-first birthday. I knew you'd be coming to Santa Fe, because you were promised to Rafael Castillo." Simon paused there, his mouth thinning in dislike. Clearly, he didn't have much love for Rafe.

Well, that was one thing we had in common.

"Which was why you decided to follow me."

"Exactly. I thought I could still try to help. I came without asking for permission—I knew I wouldn't get it, not from Zoe Sandoval, my clan's *prima*, or from the Castillos." His tone turned pleading. "But I'm asking for permission from you, Miranda. Please let me help you."

I swallowed. My throat was dry, but I didn't want to reach for my half-drunk beer. "What would this 'help' entail?"

"I'd train you. We can leave this place, go someplace quiet where you can learn without interruption."

Did I like the sound of that? I wasn't sure. It sounded like a ploy to get me alone, away from anyone who could help me. Then again, I wasn't even sure the Castillos would want to help. They had to have sided with Rafe, even though his actions in the cathedral had been beyond the pale.

"Back to Arizona?" I asked.

"No," Simon replied at once. "Too much risk of running into someone who knows you, or who knows me. It's better to stay in New Mexico. Once you've learned to really work with your powers, then you can decide where you want to go."

I fell silent. So many questions ran through my head, I didn't know which one to ask first. However, I had to ask something. "Why didn't my parents try to help me?"

"They couldn't have known. I don't think anyone even in the de la Paz clan really knows about this sort of thing—I was looking in some really old, obscure records." He glanced toward the window, where I glimpsed the full moon, white and ghostly, then looked back at me. "I guess it depends on what you want from your life, Miranda. Do you want to always feel like an outcast, an outlier in a community of outliers? Or do you want me to help you claim your powers, become the witch you were meant to be?"

Once again I was quiet. I thought of that cold, strange glitter in Rafe's eyes as he stared down at me, as though I was some insect who'd had the temerity to crawl across his shoe. I thought of Cat's friendly smile, and Genoveva's haughty air of disapproval. How much did I really owe these people? I'd come here in good faith, to fulfill the bargain my parents had made before I was even born, and as far as I could tell, they'd thrown that good faith in my face.

And while I loved my mother and father, and knew they'd done their best to raise me without bias, to treat me just like another member of the clan, it had hurt them to see their own daughter without powers, when she should have been one of the strongest in the clan. I wanted to make them proud, make them happy that I finally could be equal to my brother and sister in terms of the talents I could control.

When I thought of it that way....

I pulled in a breath, then reached out and took Simon's hand.

"Tell me what I have to do."

~

The Witches of Canyon Road series continues with *Darker Paths*.

Sympathetic Magic

Protector

Spellbound

A Cleopatra Hill Christmas

Impractical Magic

Strange Magic

The Arrangement

Defender

Bad Blood

Deep Magic

Darktide

Books 1-3 and Books 4-6 of this series are also available in two separate omnibus editions at special boxed set prices. Chronicles of Cleopatra Hill includes the series' two "back in time" novellas, *Bad Blood* and *The Arrangement*.

THE DJINN WARS*

(Paranormal Romance)

Chosen

Taken

Fallen

Broken

Forsaken

Forbidden

Awoken

Illuminated

The first three books of this series are also available in an omnibus edition at a special low price!

THE WATCHERS TRILOGY*

(Paranormal Romance)

Falling Dark

Dead of Night

Rising Dawn

THE SEDONA FILES*

(Paranormal Romance)

Bad Vibrations

Desert Hearts

Angel Fire

Star Crossed

Falling Angels

Enemy Mine

The first three books of this series are also available in an omnibus edition at a special low price!

TALES OF THE LATTER KINGDOMS*

(Fantasy Romance)

All Fall Down

Dragon Rose

Binding Spell

Ashes of Roses

One Thousand Nights

Threads of Gold

The Wolf of Harrow Hall

Moon Dance

The Song of the Thrush

Books 1-3 and Books 4-6 of this series are also available in two separate omnibus editions at special boxed set prices.

THE GAIAN CONSORTIUM SERIES*

(Science Fiction Romance)

Blood Will Tell

Breath of Life

The Gaia Gambit

The Mandala Maneuver

The Titan Trap

The Zhore Deception

* Indicates a completed series

ABOUT THE AUTHOR

Christine Pope has been writing stories ever since she commandeered her family's Smith-Corona typewriter back in the sixth grade. Her work includes paranormal romance, fantasy romance, and science fiction/space opera romance. She fell under the Land of Enchantment's spell while researching her Djinn Wars series and now makes her home in Santa Fe, New Mexico.

Christine Pope on the Web:
www.christinepope.com

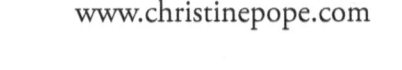 facebook.com/ChristinePopeAuthor

 twitter.com/ChristineJPope

 pinterest.com/ChristineJPope